Acclaim for the authors of
Dreaming of a Western Christmas

LYNNA BANNING

'Banning pens another delightful…heartwarming read.'

—*RT Book Reviews* on
Smoke River Bride

KELLY BOYCE

'Boyce captures the spirit of the American West.'

—*RT Book Reviews* on
Salvation in the Sheriff's Kiss

CAROL ARENS

'One exhilarating read… Take a deep breath and enjoy!'

—*RT Book Reviews* on
Rebel with a Cause

D0652829

Lynna Banning combines her lifelong love of history and literature in a satisfying career as a writer. Born in Oregon, she graduated from Scripps College and embarked on a career as an editor and technical writer, and later as a high school English teacher. She enjoys hearing from her readers. You may write to her directly at PO Box 324, Felton, CA 95018, USA, email her at carowoolston@att.net or visit Lynna's website at lynnabanning.net.

A life-long Nova Scotian, **Kelly Boyce** lives near the Atlantic Ocean with her husband (who is likely wondering what he got himself into by marrying a writer) and a golden retriever who is convinced he is the king of the castle. A long-time history buff, Kelly loves writing in a variety of time periods, creating damaged characters and giving them a second chance at life and love.

Carol Arens delights in tossing fictional characters into hot water, watching them steam, and then giving them a happily-ever-after. When she's not writing she enjoys spending time with her family, beach camping or lounging about a mountain cabin. At home, she enjoys playing with her grandchildren and gardening. During rare spare moments you will find her snuggled up with a good book. Carol enjoys hearing from readers at carolarens@yahoo.com or on Facebook.

DREAMING OF
A WESTERN
CHRISTMAS

Lynna Banning,
Kelly Boyce,
Carol Arens

Published in Great Britain 2015
by Mills & Boon, an imprint of Harlequin (UK) Limited,
Eton House, 18-24 Paradise Road, Richmond, Surrey, TW9 1SR

DREAMING OF A WESTERN CHRISTMAS

© 2015 Harlequin Books S.A.

ISBN: 978-0-263-24812-8

The publisher acknowledges the copyright holders of the
individual works as follows:

HIS CHRISTMAS BELLE © The Woolston Family Trust 2015
THE COWBOY OF CHRISTMAS PAST © Kelly Boyce 2015
SNOWBOUND WITH THE COWBOY © Carol Arens 2015

Printed and bound in Spain
by CPI, Barcelona

CONTENTS

HIS CHRISTMAS BELLE

Lynna Banning

Author Note

I always think of Christmas as a time of hope—a time for recognising and accepting our differences and reaching out to our fellow human beings. It was no different on the frontier of the Old West, when people from so many different backgrounds came together and learned to appreciate each other.

For my niece, Leslie Yarnes Sugai,
and my great-niece, Lauryn Akimi Sugai

Look for Lynna Banning's
Smoke River Family
Coming November 2015

Chapter One

Smoke? Smoke was the last thing he wanted to see. The very last thing. The puff of black dust rose higher, and Brand's heart sank. What now? A Sioux raid on a wagon train? A pine tree struck by lightning exploding into flames and starting a fire?

He reined in the black gelding and sat studying the sky. Hell's bells, another puff of smoke. Dead west. Not the direction he was riding this morning. Not the direction he wanted on any crisp December morning, not after the telegram about Marcy.

Back in Oregon his sister had loaded her pockets with rocks and waded into Lake Coulter. What Brand didn't know was why. Why would his sweet, beautiful little sister take her own life? Maybe he'd never know why. But he sure as hell didn't want to head west, back to Oregon. Made his gut shrivel just to think about it.

Another puff of smoke climbed into the cloudless blue sky and he groaned aloud. What the...? Those were smoke signals! And he knew exactly where they were coming from.

He leaned out of the saddle to spit onto the hard brown earth of eastern Idaho and reined the black around.

* * *

Fort Hall looked just as run-down and dingy as it had a year ago. He rode in past the bored-looking sentry and headed straight for the sutler's squat stucco building. As he tied up his mount, two disheveled cavalry soldiers clumped down the wooden steps. One snapped a salute.

"Major."

Brand gritted his teeth. He'd mustered out a year ago and now served as Colonel Clarke's scout, but every so often someone forgot he no longer needed to salute him. He tramped up the rickety board steps, his rowels chinging in the hot, still air, and pushed through the open door.

"Jase?"

A bearded older man with intelligent blue eyes looked up from the cash register. "'Bout time," he growled. "I hoped you might see my smoke. Somebody said you'd been spotted hereabouts. Where ya come from?"

"Oregon. What's up?"

Jase grinned, revealing a jaw full of yellow teeth. "Seen my signal, huh? Didn't think ya'd ferget how we done it in the old days, but ya never know, do ya? You might be gone back east. Or dead. Or—"

"Well, I'm not. I'm goin' to that cabin I got in Montana for Christmas. So why the signal?"

"Got a problem," the older man said. "Big problem." He tipped his graying head toward the back room.

Brand studied the curtained doorway. "Yeah? What kind of problem?"

"You'll see. Whynt'cha go on back?"

"Jase, I can't help wondering why this isn't Colonel Clarke's concern and not mine."

"You'll see, Brand. C'mon, I'll show ya."

Brand followed his old friend through the dusty curtain and stopped short. A young woman made an attempt to straighten up on the rush chair Jase had provided, then gave up and hunched over her belly, her arms clasped across her waist.

Jase laid one leathery hand on her shoulder. "Miz Cumberland, ma'am?"

She jerked up as if somebody'd just shot an arrow into her spine, but she said nothing.

"She sick?"

"Don't think so, Brand. She's damned scared is what she is. Kinda like battle-tired, I guess you'd say."

Brand studied her. No apron. Faded blue dress. Shoes that hadn't been walked in that much. Not sunburned. That was odd. Nobody, especially not women out here in the West, escaped the punishing rays of the sun.

He looked closer. Her skin appeared pale and as smooth as cream. Even the hands clasped tight across her middle were white and soft-looking. No red knuckles, and no telltale freckles. Looked as though she'd never washed a plate in her life. A hothouse rose if there ever was one.

He stepped back and spoke to Jase, keeping his voice low. "How'd you get mixed up with her?"

Jase sighed and went a little pink. "Jes' lucky, I guess."

"She alone?"

"She is now. Fella drivin' her wagon out from Independence got killed. Shot through the heart. She drove the wagon to the fort with him in it."

"Husband?"

"Don't reckon so. Kept callin' him Mr. Monroe," Jase said. "She ain't said more'n two words since she got here. Wagon was pretty well burned up. Burial detail took the body."

Brand leveled a long look at the man he'd slogged through the war with. "So why'd you signal me? Nothing I can do to bring this Monroe back, and you say the wagon's destroyed."

"Yeah." Jase scraped the toe of one boot back and forth across the plank floor. "Thought you might be willin' to—"

"No."

"Ah, hell, Brand, she's all alone. Said she's on her way to Oregon to get married. You bein' a tracker an' a damn good guide, I thought mebbe—"

"Double no." The last place on earth he ever wanted to see again was Oregon.

But just then the woman looked up. Damned eyes were like two pools of emerald-green water. Shiny. As if she was gonna cry. Or already was.

Ah, hell. He squatted in front of her. "Miss Cumberland? My name's Brandon Wyler."

"How do you do, Mr. Wyler." Her voice sounded scratchy.

"I'll make this short, ma'am. You got two choices. One is to head back where you came from. Two is to stay here at Fort Hall until a detail goes east. The colonel's got guest quarters, and maybe Jase here could use some help in his store."

She studied him, working even white teeth over

her lower lip. "I wish to go on to Oregon. My fiancé is expecting me."

"I can't help you, ma'am."

"Oh, but—" She sent Jase a desperate look. "Mr. Brownell said you might—"

"Yeah, well, Mr. Brownell didn't check with me first. I'm not goin' to Oregon this late in the season. Besides, I'm heading in the opposite direction."

Jase bumped his arm. "No ya ain't, Brand. Colonel said he's sendin' you to Fort Klamath."

"Colonel didn't check with me, either," Brand growled.

"I have money, Mr. Wyler."

"So have I, Miss Cumberland. Don't need yours."

"But…"

"Sorry."

Jase edged toward the curtained doorway and signaled Brand to follow. "Ya might wanna check with the colonel, Brand."

Brand's heart sank right down to his boot tops. "You know somethin' I don't, Jase?"

"At ease, Major Wyler."

Brand rolled onto the balls of his feet and stared at the photograph behind Colonel Clarke's bald head. His wife, maybe.

The colonel tented his stubby fingers under his chin. "We wouldn't want to leave a lady in distress, now, would we? That's not the army way."

"Colonel, I don't think—"

"This is the army, Brand. You're not paid to think. Now, you've got your orders."

"Well, hell, Colonel, I'm not in the army. Not anymore."

"Prove it."

"Now, wait a damn minute…"

"That's an order, Major," he snapped. "Dismissed."

Chapter Two

"Yeah, she's waitin' for ya, Brand. Ain't too happy, but she's waitin'."

Brand glanced at the slim figure pacing determinedly back and forth in front of the sutler's canned goods display. Small as they were, her leather shoes made sharp staccato sounds on the wood floor, and her white hands were clenched at her sides. Looked as if she was as mad as hell.

Well, so was he. Every bone in his tired body was shouting *don't do this*. But the colonel had other ideas. His only hope was to get her to change her mind about going to Oregon.

"Jase, lay out some flannel shirts about her size and some jeans and a boy-sized pair of boots." While the older man selected the items and piled them up on the counter, Brand approached his charge.

"Miss Cumberland?"

She stopped pacing and spun to face him. Her face had lost that dazed look she'd had an hour ago. Now her green eyes flashed with anger.

"Yes? What is it, Mr. Wyler?"

"I'm taking you to Oregon, like you wanted."

"Oh? Have you hired a carriage?"

He laughed out loud. "A carriage! Ma'am, you're

smack in the middle of Indian country. We don't have roads out here, just rough trails. If we're lucky."

"Perhaps a wagon, then?" She eyed the growing stack of clothing Jase was collecting and raised one eyebrow.

"Look over there on the counter, ma'am. See those boys' duds? That's what you'll be wearing."

"Surely you are joking?"

Brand clenched his jaw. So, Miss Fancy Drawers wanted to ride in style and wear dresses and corsets, did she? Tough luck. So what if her eyes still looked kinda funny—made his chest go tight—he still didn't want to do this.

"We'll be traveling on horseback."

Her mouth sagged open and then snapped shut. "Horseback! You mean I will be riding on a horse?"

"That's what *horseback* means." His voice sounded exasperated, even to him. "You ever been on a horse?"

"No, I have not. Where I come from, ladies do not—"

"Well, they do out here, Miss Cumberland. So if you're in such a lather to get to Oregon, you might as well get used to the idea."

She just stared at him with that hurt look in her eyes. Then she stared at the pile of shirts and jeans Jase had loaded up on the counter. "I do not think…"

"Take it or leave it," he said. "Or you could go back east, like I said."

She bit her lower lip, considering the matter, and Brand tried not to think about how lush her mouth was.

"Very well," she said at last. She stuck out her hand. "I agree. We have a bargain, Mr. Wyler."

Without thinking he gripped her hand and shook it. Never in his life had he shaken hands with a woman. He'd waltzed with them, flirted with them, kissed them, made love to them. But shaken their hand? This one was so proper she squeaked.

But her hand felt small and warm and womanly in his. Maybe not squeaky, just stiff and overproper.

"Ya wanna try on them boots, miss?" Jase said from behind the counter.

"Boots! I have proper shoes, thank you."

"Boots," Brand snapped. "Winter's just around the corner and on the trail you'll want all the warmth you can get. Might hold those other duds up to you, see if they fit."

Again she stared at him, her eyes even wider and greener than before. Kinda slow in the brain department; you'd think she'd see the clothes and put two and two together.

She dropped her gaze and very tentatively fingered the shirt on top of the stack, a red plaid. Jase shook it out and held it up to her frame. "Too big," he muttered. He snaked it and two others out of the pile and replaced them. The jeans looked about right.

She disappeared behind the door curtain with the boots. Jase grinned at him and added a wool poncho, a wide-brimmed black hat and a leather belt to the stack.

"You got her between a rock an' a creek, Brand. Don't think she'll be too happy till she's broke in them boots."

Serves her right, Brand thought. She'd maneuvered him into this—he could maneuver right back.

She stomped back through the curtain, slapped the boots on top of the pile and propped her hands at her waist. "What else?" she demanded.

He turned to Jase. "Ammunition. Coffee. Bacon. Jerky. Couple cans of beans and tomatoes. And a blanket." He'd borrow a saddle for the mare she'd be riding, along with saddlebags and an extra canteen. Didn't figure they'd go five miles before she caved in.

"Put it on my tab, will you, Jase? Better yet, send the bill to Colonel Clarke." Yeah, he liked that idea.

"I prefer to pay my own bills," Miss Cumberland said, her tone frosty. "I have adequate funds on my person."

Brand studied her, wondering where she'd stashed it. "Best keep that fact under your hat, miss."

"But—"

"And," he couldn't resist adding, "start learning to take orders. Here's your first one—take these clothes over to the colonel's quarters and pack 'em up in the saddlebag I'm gonna bring over. Colonel's wife will help. Be ready at dawn."

Her eyes rounded. "You like giving orders, do you not?"

"Got any objections?"

"I most certainly do. It is rude and officious behavior."

Brand studied her flushed cheeks. Good. He'd made her good and mad. Maybe she'd give up this whole insane idea.

"Well, like I said, ma'am, take it or leave it. You ride to Oregon on my terms, or you don't ride at all."

The look she sent him could bake biscuits.

First thing the next morning, he gobbled Jase's overfried eggs and bacon, outfitted his gelding and a sure-footed mare he'd picked out with bedrolls and his saddlebag, and strode over to Colonel Clarke's quarters to collect Miss Suzannah Cumberland.

She was waiting on the front porch, and he had to look twice to be sure it was really her. The red plaid shirt was filled out in all the right places, and the jeans clung to her saucy little butt like they'd been washed and shrunk on her body.

He looked at her hard and his mouth went dry. She looked crisp and clean and brand-new. And damn pretty. She'd caught her shiny wheat-colored hair at her neck with a red ribbon, and the wide-brimmed black hat he'd picked out rode jauntily on the top of her head.

He swallowed and led both horses up to the porch. "Here's your mount. Name's Lady."

She nodded. Brand picked up her saddlebag and slung it behind the saddle, then waited.

She didn't move.

"Come on, Miss Cumberland. We're wasting daylight."

"I—I did not expect the horse to be so large," she said. The quaver in her voice made Brand's gut tense. *Oh, for cryin' out loud.*

"All horses are 'large.'"

"Yes, I see." Still she didn't move.

"You want to change your mind?" he prompted.

"N-no. I will adjust."

Adjust! Riding a horse took a lot more than "adjusting." What she needed to do was get on the damn horse.

Slowly she descended the wide porch steps and edged over to where he stood holding her mare's bridle. "How do I…I mean, is there a method for mounting?"

"Yep. Put your left foot in this stirrup and grab onto the saddle horn, that little knob in front of the saddle."

She did as instructed, and he laid one hand on her behind to boost her up. It was so warm and plump under his palm he broke out in a sweat.

She peered down at him. "It is quite far to the ground. Farther than I thought."

"Hold on to your reins and for God's sake don't kick the horse." He mounted the black, leaned over and lifted the reins out of her white-knuckled grip. "Relax. I'm going to lead your horse till you get used to ridin'." He touched his boot heels to the gelding's sides and moved forward. The gray mare stepped after him, and Miss Cumberland let out a screech.

"It's moving!"

"Damn right," he said dryly. "Horses do this all the time. Just hang on."

He walked both mounts past the goggle-eyed sentry and out the gate while she clung to the saddle horn with both hands and made little moany sounds. God, four hundred miles of this was going to be pure hell.

After a couple of miles he pulled up and laid the gray's reins in her hands. The gloves Jase had picked out for her were so large the ends of her fingers were floppy. He didn't want to think about those soft lily-white hands getting sweaty inside the leather.

He didn't want to think about her at all. Either she'd get used to the rigors of the trail or she wouldn't. Wouldn't be his fault if she suffered. This wasn't his idea, and it sure wasn't his choice.

Suzannah detested this man. He was blunt and overbearing and ungracious as only a Yankee could be. A Yankee with no social graces. If it weren't for her beloved John's letter, written in haste before a campaign, she would turn tail and run back to Mama and the plantation she loved.

Her back ached. Her derriere had gone numb hours ago, and the need to relieve herself was beginning to feel overpowering. Did this man never rest? How much longer could she stay in the saddle without begging him to stop? She caught her lower lip between her teeth. How humiliating it would be to beg!

But…humiliating or not, in a short time she would be reduced to doing just that. A very short time. She could scarcely imagine begging a Yankee for anything. Papa would turn in his grave.

The man—Brandon, he'd said his name was—had led her horse for an hour this morning, but then he'd stopped, grunted something and handed the reins to her. From then on she was on her own. He had not spared her so much as a single glance of those hard gray eyes. No approval of her desperate efforts at controlling this huge gray beast. Not a word of encouragement.

She eyed his lean, blue-shirted frame moving easily on the shiny black horse in front of her. Not once had he looked over his shoulder to see if she was still plodding along behind him. Odious man! Her beloved John would never, never treat a lady this way. Never.

She was concentrating so hard on the dust-swirled trail ahead of her she failed to see his raised arm and the signal to stop until she almost blundered into him.

"Water ahead," he said. "Gotta rest the horses."

"The horses! What about the riders?"

"Water's for them, too." He spoke the words while gazing ahead to a single spindly-looking tree, more dirty gray than green. Never once did he look at her. Fury battled with desperation as she tried to estimate how long it would take to reach the shade. And personal relief. Too long.

"Could we not move a bit faster?" she called.

He didn't answer, just kicked his mount into a trot. She touched her boot heels to the horse's sides as he did, and it jolted forward. With a cry she hurtled up level with him and would have passed him had he not leaned sideways out of the saddle and grabbed her reins.

"Whoa, girl. Whoa." He then proceeded to walk both animals toward the tree as if he had all the time in the world. Well, *she* didn't.

He pulled up by a stream tumbling over large flat rocks, and Suzannah gritted her teeth. The sound of running water triggered something in her body, and without thinking she swung her leg over the saddle horn and dropped to the ground.

Her legs buckled. She grabbed onto the dangling stirrup and suddenly there he was behind her, one hand gripping her leather belt.

"I have to—"

"Yeah, I'm sure you do. Over there." He laid his hand on her back and shoved her toward the tree.

There was no privacy at all. The tree trunk looked no wider than a sleeve press, and the sparse branches would not screen a four-year-old child.

"I trust you will turn your back, Mr. Wyler?"

"We'll take turns. You first."

It was so much easier for a man, she fumed. Just unbutton and… She, on the other hand, would have to shimmy her jeans down over her hips, then lower her underdrawers and squat practically in plain sight.

She perched on her haunches with her bare bottom exposed and watched to be sure he didn't peek. While she did her business, he brought their horses to the stream and bent to fill his canteen. He did keep his back to her, for which she thanked the Lord who created men and women.

His voice startled her. "You finished?"

"Y-yes."

"Come on over here, then. Fill up your canteen."

She tried to stand, but her legs shook so they wouldn't support her weight. She kept squatting near the ground and wondered how she could pull up her drawers and jeans without standing up. She hadn't been this embarrassed since she fell in the mud hole under the cypress tree back home when she was nine.

Think! She needed some way to pull herself upright, but… A low-hanging branch would do, but the tree's foliage started several feet over her head. The tree trunk, that was it. She reached for it with both hands and managed to scrabble her fingers against the bark.

"Miss Cumberland?"

"Oh, leave me alone!" she cried. Inch by inch her fingers clawed their way up the trunk until she was halfway vertical. When her belt was once again cinched in the waist of her jeans she wanted to weep with relief.

"Ma'am? You all right?"

"I am perfectly all right, thank you."

"Kinda stiff, I'd guess."

She opened her mouth to lambaste him, but then heard the unmistakable sound of a stream of urine hitting the ground. Why, he wouldn't dare!

But he did. He stood in plain sight with his back to her. She turned away with a huff and after a minute he called that it was time to mount up.

"I am coming, Mr. Wyler." She took two steps toward the horses and realized she could scarcely move, much less mount her horse.

He met her halfway, took one look at her crabbed walk and snorted. "You sure as hell are no horsewoman."

"And you sure as hell are no gentleman!" she blurted out. *Oh, my! Mama would wash my mouth out with soap for that.*

"You got that right." Then he chuckled and gave her a thorough once-over. "You look half-dead."

She did not deign to answer such an uncouth remark. Instead she lifted her chin and tried to edge past him.

"Guess I should have stopped sooner," he said.

"You were paying no attention whatever to me, Mr. Wyler."

"Not true," he replied. "Maybe not the fancy kind of attention you're used to, but attention nevertheless."

Before she could draw breath, he scooped her up into his arms and plopped her into the saddle.

"Ow!" It slipped out before she could catch herself.

"Sore, huh?"

She didn't trust her voice, so she sat up as straight as she possibly could and nodded in what she hoped was a regal gesture.

"Well, damn," he said under his breath. "I plumb forgot how green you are."

He slung both canteens behind his cantle and swung up into the saddle. "Five more miles," he said. "Think you can make it?"

She nodded again, but he wasn't looking. He walked his mount close to hers, caught up her reins and laid them in her lap. "Try to keep up."

She ached to slap him. She wanted to ask how long it would take to travel five more miles, but he spoke before she could form the question.

"About another hour and a half."

She stifled a moan. In addition to being the most insufferable male she had ever encountered, he could read her mind, too.

Chapter Three

Brand surreptitiously glanced back at her whenever the trail had a twist in it. She was working hard to stay upright in the saddle, but he could see she wouldn't last much longer. Good. Maybe she'd think better of her crazy plan and turn tail back to Fort Hall.

But he had to admit that even though she drooped lower and lower over the saddle horn, he didn't hear a whimper out of her. She might be hurting, but she sure had sand. He'd known women who'd be bawlin' and beggin' by this time.

An hour passed, and still the woman on the mare behind him made no sound. Aw, hell. She'd been through a lot, and he knew she was hurting; maybe he should cut her some slack.

Up ahead he spotted a copse of cottonwoods and a clear, rushing stream. End of the trail for today. He dismounted, looped the reins over a willow branch and walked back to the mare and its rider.

Her eyes were closed, her face sweaty and dust-streaked under the brim of her hat. She'd need help standing up.

He moved the toe of her boot out of the stirrup, reached up and settled his hands at her waist. With one smooth motion he lifted her down and moved toward the creek.

"Miss Cumberland, I'm gonna set you down in the cold water. Be good for your sore muscles."

"Mmm…" she groaned.

He went down on one knee to lower her body into a wide part of the creek. The water was ice-cold and she jerked when it soaked up her jeans.

"This will help," he muttered. "Just sit quiet. I'll come get you out in a while."

She nodded without opening her eyes. He left her lolling in the deep pool and went to tend the horses and roll out the bedrolls. Supper would be canned beans and coffee, and if she didn't like it, that was tough. There weren't any silver spoons on the trail.

He built a fire, boiled up some coffee and pried open the tin of beans. Then he tramped back to the creek and lifted a dripping Suzannah Cumberland into his arms. Even wet and shivering, she felt damn womanly. He settled her beside the fire and folded her hands around a tin mug of coffee. "Hope you don't take milk or sugar."

She made no answer. Brand lifted the beans off the warming rock and jammed in the spoon. "Guess we'll have to share. Only packed one spoon."

He sneaked a look at her face and bit his tongue. Her eyes were closed. She was beyond caring about spoons or beans or anything else. As he watched, moisture seeped out from under her eyelids and smudged her dirty cheeks.

He dug the spoon into their supper and lifted it to her lips. "Open your mouth."

Obediently she parted her lips and he shoveled in

a spoonful, devoured a bit himself, then fed her another. Alternating between her and himself, he soon scraped the bottom of the can. He held the mug of coffee to her mouth, but she shook her head.

When her body began to tilt to one side, he knew she was finished. Quickly he grabbed a blanket, wrapped it around her and tipped her backward until she lay next to the fire. Her clothes were almost dry.

He cleaned up the camp, fed the horses and dropped another thick branch onto the fire, then stretched out on his bedroll. He laid his rifle next to him and stuffed his Colt under the saddle he used as a pillow. For a long time he lay unmoving, listening to her breathing even out.

What the hell had he gotten himself into? Nursemaiding a spoiled Southern belle across a rugged, dry land so she could meet up with her intended. Poor bastard.

An owl tu-whooed in the pine tree and Suzannah stirred uneasily. It flapped two branches closer and called again.

"Whazzat?" she muttered sleepily.

Before he could answer, she had dropped off again. Then a coyote barked, quite close to their camp, and she jolted to a half-sitting position. "What was that?"

"Coyote," he said. Carefully he pressed her shoulder and after a moment she lay back down.

"Do they bite?"

"Bite?"

"You know, do they attack people?"

"Only if they're…" He was going to say *rabid*, but thought better of it. "Cornered," he substituted.

"Why on earth would anyone want to corner a coyote?"

He chose not to answer, and in a few minutes he knew she'd fallen asleep again. She sure was an odd woman. It was obvious she was more at home in a fancy front parlor than the harsh, wind-scoured land of eastern Idaho. Sure was crazy what some women would do for love.

He sucked in a breath as pain slammed into his heart. His sister was dead because she had loved someone, or thought she did. Her last letter burned in his shirt pocket. *He no longer wants me, Brand. I can't live without him.*

Jack Walters was his name. He'd seduced her, then abandoned her at the altar. If he ever laid eyes on the man, he'd kill him.

Chapter Four

❧❧❧

Suzannah had scarcely opened her eyes, and maybe would not have had she not smelled coffee and frying bacon.

"I take it you're from the South?" Mr. Wyler's voice intruded into her before-breakfast thoughts. That was an impertinent way to start a conversation, especially so early in the morning with the sunlight just peeking through the tree branches.

"I was born in South Carolina," she said, her voice drowsy with sleep. "My family had a plantation before the war. Afterward…" Well, she would not go into *afterward*, with Yankees overrunning the place. They had left the house untouched, but the fields were burned and the trees cut down for firewood. She struggled up on one elbow.

"That how you met this man at Fort Klamath you're travelin' to meet up with?"

"That," she said in her best lofty voice, "is none of your business."

He merely shrugged and forked over a slice of bacon. "Suit yourself."

"Well, it isn't," she pursued. Then she found herself explaining about John. "I actually met him at a ball my father gave for some Yankee officers who had been kind to us after the war. He proposed, and shortly afterward he had to report back to duty."

She pawed away the wool blanket she was wrapped up in and tried to sit upright. Lord in heaven, every muscle in her aching body screamed in protest. At the groan she tried to suppress he sent her a sharp look.

"Hurt some?"

"It hurts a great deal," she corrected. "I feel as if I have picked cotton for a week."

"Bet you never picked cotton or anything else for an hour in your whole life. Here." He handed her a mug of coffee. "Don't make it with chicory, like you rebs do. Don't grow chicory much out here in the West."

She took a tentative sip and wrinkled her nose. A vile brew, worse than Hattie's on one of her uncooperative days.

"That bad, huh?"

"Oh, no, it's just that…" Oh, why should she prevaricate with this man? "It is a little strong, yes."

"Good. It'll keep you awake for the next ten hours."

She gasped. Ten hours? On horseback? She couldn't. She simply couldn't.

He handed her a tin plate with crisp bacon slices and two misshapen biscuits. She looked around for a fork and met his amused gray eyes.

"Fingers," he said in a dry voice. "Or, if you want to feel cultured, you can crook your pinkie." He said nothing more, just gulped down three audible swallows of coffee and reached for a biscuit. The underside was scorched, she noted, but she did wonder how he had managed to make biscuits in the first place.

"Baked on a hot rock," he said as if she had spoken the question aloud. "Indians do it."

"Indians make biscuits?"

"Nope. They make bread out of acorn meal. Same thing."

Oh, no, it wasn't. No Indian culinary creation would ever cross her lips. He munched up seven slices of the crisp bacon and scooped another biscuit off the flat rock near the fire.

"Mr. Wyler, where is your home?"

"Don't have one. I was born in Pennsylvania, but…"

"You moved out west," she supplied.

"Not exactly. I ran away from home when I was about nine because my pa was drunk most of the time and my momma died. Got to Missouri and holed up till I was old enough to join the army. I was fifteen."

"I am surprised they accepted a boy that young."

"Lied about my age." He tossed the dregs of his coffee on the fire. "You finished?"

"Am I finished what?" she shot. "Questioning? Or eating?"

He laughed at that. She noticed his teeth, white and straight against his tanned skin. Also he had a dimple, of all things. So he wasn't always so grim—he must smile occasionally if he had worked up a dimple.

She gobbled the last of her bacon and one biscuit and managed another swallow of his awful coffee. Then she tried to stand up. A thousand swords

poked at her defenseless muscles, and she almost—
almost—let herself scream.

He stood and reached out his hand, but she waved
it away. "I am not helpless."

"Like hell." He stepped in, caught the leather belt
around her waist and hauled her to her feet. "Want
me to walk you over behind a bush?"

"Certainly not." She took a step and her knees
buckled.

Brand didn't say a word, just marched her over
to a huckleberry bush. He thought about unbuttoning her jeans for her, but gave up the idea when she
glared at him and shooed him away.

While she was occupied he packed up the camp,
saddled the horses and stowed her bedroll and saddlebag. "Ready to ride?" he asked when she reappeared.

"Of course not. I have not yet washed my face."

He gestured toward the rippling creek. "There's
the stream."

She stood for a long moment eyeing the water,
and he could hear the wheels turning in her head.
Finally she lifted her slim shoulders in a shrug and
shook her head. She'd braided her hair while she'd
been behind the bush. Good move. He handed over
her wide-brimmed hat.

"Which way are we goin'? West? Or back to Fort
Hall?"

"West," she said through her teeth. "I am not a
quitter."

"Never said you were. Just givin' you a choice."

"I choose to go on."

Brand nodded, manhandled her over to the horse,

grabbed her around the waist and lifted her into the saddle. Sure didn't weigh much.

With a sharp intake of breath, she clutched the saddle horn and leaned over it. Guess it hurt her to straighten up all the way. He kinda felt sorry for her since he didn't plan to slow the pace today. Or any other day. Served her right, getting herself involved with a man she hardly knew.

Today, Suzannah decided, was even worse than yesterday. After ten minutes on horseback, her body rebelled; after six hours in the saddle she suspected she would not survive this journey. Why, *why* had John not accepted her father's offer? Surely being part owner of a plantation was an honorable calling? Had he done so, she would now be safe and comfortable at home and John would be joining her in South Carolina for Christmas, not the other way around.

She forced herself to forget her fiancé for the moment and concentrate on riding the huge animal beneath her. Despite its size, she rather liked her horse. It didn't talk back. Did not bark out orders. And it certainly did not disapprove of the fact that she was from the South. She detected disapproval in every comment Mr. Wyler made, when he deigned to make any at all. Which was annoyingly rare.

She wasn't used to being ignored. She was used to being catered to, taken care of by faithful servants who had loved her from the moment of her birth. Hattie would commiserate with her over this disastrous turn of events. Imagine, her hired driver being murdered and then finding herself thrust upon this uncivilized ruffian of a Yankee army officer. A major, Colonel Clarke had said.

Only the Union Army would promote such a man. Her father's regiment would not have stood for it. Of course Papa's regiment had been shelled into oblivion, but even so there must be honorable men in the Union Army—just look at her John!

Before the sun had climbed halfway to noon, her shirt was sticky with perspiration and droplets of moisture rolled off her neck and dribbled down between her breasts. Even her head felt hot. She snaked off her hat and used it to fan her damp face until Major Wyler shouted at her.

"Put that damn hat back on! You want to die of sunstroke?"

"At the moment, Major, that does not seem like such a bad idea. Besides, it's December. The sun doesn't burn in winter."

"It does at this altitude. Put your hat on."

All morning he just kept clopping along ahead of her. She began to watch the way he rode. He had a loose-jointed, relaxed way of sitting on his shiny black mount, and he moved with the animal as if he was part of it.

She was making a supreme effort to keep her spine straight, as Mama had taught her, but it was an effort. Being so proper was earning her a stiff back and a sore derriere.

She was beginning to realize how different things were out here in this godforsaken country. Burning sun. Few trees. Scrawny bushes. And some kind of screechy birds that seemed to be following them.

And only the occasional creek. Already her canteen was practically empty, and surely the horses must be thirsty? She studied the baked earth as she passed over it. All at once Mr. Wyler was there beside her.

"Another hour and we'll stop to water the horses."

He was still worried about the horses, not the people? All she could manage was a nod. Her throat felt so dry and dust-clogged she doubted she could utter a word.

"Here." He shoved a red bandanna into her hand. "Dust's getting bad. Tie this over your nose and mouth."

She did as he directed, but still he did not ride on ahead.

"Better yet, stay beside me."

Again she nodded, and he fell in next to her. But he did not talk. Men out here were definitely not good conversationalists.

The wind picked up. Her eyes teared as flecks of dirt scratched under her lids. She dribbled the last of the water from her canteen into her cupped palm and tried to splash it into her eye sockets. He watched her for a few minutes, then ostentatiously wet his own bandanna, a blue one, with his canteen and wiped his eyes with it.

Oh.

"Don't use too much water," he ordered. "The stream up ahead might be dried up."

Her spirits plummeted. "What will we do then?"

"Rest the horses and ride on."

"When do we stop for lunch?"

He shot her a hard look. "When I say so."

Goodness, he was gruff! She would bet the contents of her piggy bank he had never been...

"Are you married, Mr. Wyler?"

"Nope."

"Were you ever married?"

"Nope."

Why was she not surprised? He was the most unsociable male she had ever had the bad luck to encounter.

"The next question most folks ask is why not?"

She felt his gaze on her and she stiffened. "I see."

"No, you don't."

"Very well, I will ask. Why are you not married?" *And if you say it is none of my business I will scream good and loud.*

"Never met a woman I couldn't live without."

She stifled a laugh. She would wager there had been legions of them. "Possibly the candidates felt the same," she retorted.

His laugh startled a chattering squirrel on a pine branch.

"Possibly," he allowed.

Suddenly he drew up and pulled a long shiny rifle from the leather scabbard at his side. "Rein in," he murmured. "And don't move."

Her heart kicked hard against her rib cage. "What is it?"

"Hush up!"

Well!

He aimed the rifle at something off to the left and waited so long she thought he was just pretending. Then he squeezed the trigger, and a deafening crack sounded next to her ear. Her horse jerked and side-stepped. His did not move a single muscle.

"Supper," he intoned. "Stay here." He slid the gun back into the case and stepped his horse forward.

She pressed her lips together. *Stay here. Go there. Do this. Do that.* The man was impossible. No wonder he wasn't married.

She watched him dismount and bend to pick up something off the ground. When he returned, a limp furry creature hung from one hand. A spot of crimson spread across its neck, and blood dripped from the wound onto the ground.

He shot her a glance and saw her shock, but he only shrugged. "Let's move out."

Chapter Five

Watching Suzannah out of the corner of his eye, Brand knew she was so exhausted she could barely stay in the saddle. The stream should be just over the next hill, but he wondered if she could hold on that long.

"You all right?" he ventured.

Her chin came up. "I am quite all right, thank you."

But she was having trouble keeping her eyes open. Maybe the glare. Or maybe she was holding on with the last of her strength.

He didn't like her much, but he had to admire her guts. Except she wouldn't say "guts." She'd have some fancy-ass term like *courage*. Or maybe *perseverance*. Yeah, she'd like that one. More syllables.

By the time they made camp and he'd fed the horses and wiped them down, she had settled herself beside the stream with her bare feet in the water. Her head drooped onto her bent knees. One thing he'd say about the lady from the Southern plantation, she didn't complain. In fact, she'd hardly said a word since he shot the rabbit.

He dressed it quickly, skewered the cut-up parts on green willow sticks and propped them over the fire. Then he set the coffeepot on a flat rock close to the flames and unrolled their bedrolls.

He eyed the rippling stream. After forty miles of chaparral and up-and-down trails, he was so hot and sweaty it didn't take but two seconds to decide on a bath.

"Gonna walk downstream a ways," he said as he passed behind her hunched-over frame. She didn't move, but a muffled sound came from between her knees.

"Coffee'll be ready pretty quick. Supper, too. You hungry?"

Another sound, maybe a ladylike groan. He took it for a yes.

An hour later she was still sitting with her feet in the creek, but she'd straightened up some. He stopped beside her.

"Blisters?"

"I didn't look. All I know is my feet feel as if I have been dancing a reel on hot coals."

"Dry 'em off. I'll take a look."

"Oh, no, I—"

"Don't argue." He squatted beside her. "Give me your foot."

Suzannah lifted one foot out of the water and instantly he took possession of it, running his warm hands over her instep, her toes. He bent his head and rubbed his thumb along her raw heel.

"Yep, got a blister. Big as a four-bit piece. I'll get some liniment." He picked up her other foot and studied that, as well. "Mighty delicate feet. I'd wager you haven't done much walking. Got two messed-up heels."

He rummaged in his saddlebag and returned with a bottle of brown liquid. The label said Horse Liniment. He crouched next to her, but she shrank away.

"I do not think horse liniment is a proper medicine for a human foot, Mr. Wyler."

"Maybe not, but it's what I've got. And it's needed." He shook the bottle and grasped her foot. "By the way, my name's Brand. Might as well use it since we're, uh, traveling together." He uncorked the liniment and smoothed some over one raw heel, then the other.

"Leave your boots off for a few hours."

A soothing warmth settled over her abraded skin, and she sighed with pleasure.

"Better?"

"Yes. Thank you."

He rose abruptly and tramped over to the fire pit. "Come and get it."

She hobbled the few yards to the fire, smelled the coffee and roasting meat, and tensed her stomach muscles to stop the rumbling. She'd had two desiccated biscuits at noon; now she was so hungry she could eat anything, even a… She swallowed hard. A dead rabbit. She sat near the fire and he handed her an unidentifiable hunk of roasted meat on a stick.

"Careful, it's hot."

"Oh, I do hope so. I do not think I could face a raw piece of rabbit."

"You could if you were hungry enough."

"All my life I have had plenty to eat—until the war, that is. Then we had to scrounge and improvise."

"Yeah? What did you improvise?"

She looked off toward the pinkish-orange sky

where the sun was sinking behind a mountaintop. "Coffee. We made coffee from roasted acorns. We ate all the chickens, even the rooster, and when there were no more eggs, Sam, our overseer, found birds nests with eggs in them. Quail, I think they were. After that, we ate the quail, too."

"You ever wonder whether fighting the war made sense?"

"Yes," she said quietly. "I wondered that every single day for four years."

He sent her an intent look, his speared rabbit piece halfway to his mouth. Unguarded, his eyes changed from hard gray steel to something softer, dry moss, perhaps. She wondered suddenly what he saw in her face.

"You miss your life in the South?"

"Yes, I do. I guess you might say I am…a little homesick."

"You ever wonder why you're chasin' all over hell and gone after a Northerner?"

She could not answer that, at least not truthfully. If John had agreed to move to South Carolina, she would not be here.

He poured two mugs of coffee and set one beside her. "Don't answer that. Whatever the reason, you're here now, and I'm stuck with you."

"And I," she said sharply, "am stuck with you. I do not like you very much, Mr. Wyler. And I am quite sure you do not like me."

They finished their meal in silence so heavy it felt as if the air weighed more than a loaded wagon. After supper she rolled herself up in the wool blanket, rested her head on her saddle, and closed her eyes to shut out the sight of Brand Wyler.

The wind sighed through the trees. She listened for a coyote's call so it wouldn't startle her as it had that first night, but all she heard was the fire popping out an occasional spark. How many days must she endure this man's company? Four hundred miles, the colonel had said. At forty miles per day, that meant ten days on the trail with Mister Gruff and Bossy.

Goodness, it had been two. In eight more days she would be completely undone.

In the morning Brand had to shake her awake. When she poked her head out of the blanket she'd burrowed in he noticed her braid had come undone; her hair curled around her face and straggled down to her shoulders. It was the color of gold and looked as soft as dandelion fluff. Made his hands itch to lace his fingers through it.

She opened her eyes, found him staring at her and popped up like a jack-in-the-box. He jerked his gaze back to the coffeepot. Her voice stopped him cold.

"We will travel another forty miles today, I assume."

"Forty miles? You think we can ride forty miles every day?"

She blinked those unsettling green eyes. "Yes, of course. Why ever not?" She crawled out of her bedroll and stood up. "I calculated it all out last night. Four hundred miles divided by forty is ten. It will take ten days to get to Fort Klamath."

"Like hell it will."

Undaunted, she poured herself some coffee and

stood blowing on it. A good ten minutes dragged by while he considered how to tell her the facts of life on an iffy trail through the mountains. The more he thought about it, the madder he got. This pampered greenhorn thought they could just sashay over to Fort Klamath as though it was an afternoon buggy ride? She sure as hell had a bunch of learning to do.

"Well?" she said. "You have not answered my question, Mr. Wyler. Why can't we reach the fort in ten days?"

"You don't have any idea what you're up against, do you? Hell's bells, lady, you don't have the sense God gave a goose. You have—"

Without thinking, Suzannah dashed her coffee into his face. "A quick temper," she said with satisfaction. The coffee dripped off his chin and soaked his shirt.

Without blinking he began to undo the buttons, then shrugged it off over his head, wadded it up and tossed it at her. "Wash it out," he ordered. He tipped his head toward the creek.

She stared at his bare chest. He was as lean and brown as a hazelnut, with rippling muscles and not an ounce of fat anywhere.

His eyes bored into hers and her anger bubbled up anew.

"I would press it as well," she said in a voice laden with poison, "but I did not pack a sadiron."

"Stop talking and start washing," he ordered. "Go on." He gestured at the creek. "Get to it."

Twenty minutes later she smacked the sodden bundle against his chest and propped her hands at her waist. Without even blinking he unfolded the laundered shirt, shook it out and pulled it on sopping wet.

"It'll dry," he remarked, anticipating her comment. "Might wash your own shirt out as well," he said. "Must be…uh…dirty."

"It is no such thing! How dare you insinuate—"

"I'm not insinuating, I'm smelling."

"Oh."

She could hear him chuckle. How she detested that sound!

"Take it off," he said. "I'll turn my back."

She would *not* undress in front of this man. But he stood in front of her, waiting, and she knew he wasn't going to move until she did what he said. She reached one hand to her top shirt button and hesitated. The look in his eyes grew unsettlingly warm.

"Go on," he said softly. "I know you're wearing underclothes, and I've seen women's duds before."

"Turn around," she said sharply.

He pivoted on one boot heel and propped his hands on his lean hips.

"You are no gentleman, Mr. Wyler," she said to his broad back.

"I don't have to be."

"If you want my cooperation, it would help if you were at least polite."

"Just for the record, Miss Cumberland, out here on the trail all I have to be is prepared for anything, and—" he started a gusty whistle between his teeth "—patient as a damn saint."

She made quick work of rinsing out her shirt and had it buttoned back on before he finished the second verse. "That's a song sung by some of the workers on the plantation," she said uncomfortably.

"So?" One eyebrow quirked. "You never sang 'Oh, Susanna' in school?"

"Certainly not. I had tutors. Besides, I was not allowed to sing except in church."

"Bet you didn't have much fun growing up, didja?"

She opened her mouth, then shut it so fast her teeth clicked. No, she had not had fun. She had played with the young children on the plantation until one day Mama put a stop to it, and from then on she spent all her free time on lessons in deportment and learning how to give a proper tea party.

Until the war. After the war there was no reason for tea parties.

Brand tried not to look too hard at the outline of her breasts where the wet shirt was plastered to her skin. She wasn't much fun, but she sure was pretty.

"Mount up," he barked. "Got a long ride ahead."

When she saluted smartly he laughed out loud. Maybe he was wrong about the fun part.

Chapter Six

By midafternoon they still had not stopped to eat or rest the horses, or do any of the things he had done the previous day. Suzannah was too tired to ask why, and anyway, she thought she knew. Mr. Wyler was trying his darnedest to get her to turn back.

Well, she would not. She would pull up her socks and grit her teeth and keep going just to spite him. And, of course, to reach Fort Klamath and her beloved John. Her arrival would be such a surprise for him, a real Christmas present.

Her fiancé would never, ever treat her in such an inhumane manner. John was a thousand times more gentlemanly than Major Brandon Wyler. Her fiancé might be a Northerner and only a lieutenant in the army, but he was a far, far better man. And not only that—

Suddenly Mr. Wyler halted his horse and raised his hand. Her stomach rumbled in anticipation of a meal at last.

"I hope we are stopping for lunch," she ventured.

He did not answer, just dismounted and walked back past her a good thirty paces, studying the ground. Then he straightened and stood looking off toward the hills, his eyes narrowed. With a shake of his head he strode back to his horse and slipped the rifle out of the leather case.

Oh, she did hope it was another rabbit! She was so hungry she would eat it half-cooked. Or even *not* cooked.

But he did not raise the gun or aim it at anything. He just stood without moving, looking back the way they had come.

Suzannah shifted in her saddle. "What is wrong?" she called.

"Shut up!" he hissed. Still he did not move, and then he slowly raised the rifle, pointed it at something off to their right and sighted down the barrel. The back of her neck began to prickle.

Minutes passed and nothing happened except for the raucous cry of a crow somewhere over her head. She squinted her eyes and peered in the direction the gun barrel was pointed, but she could see nothing but scrubby brush and sparse clumps of trees.

And then she noticed a faint puff of gray dust far off in the distance. It seemed to be moving, and abruptly Mr. Wyler lifted his rifle and walked back to the horses.

"We're being followed."

Her body went cold. "What? Are you sure?"

He pinned her with a look that straightened her spine. "Lady, if I say someone's following us, you can bet your diamond earrings there's a rider on our trail."

"But who is it?"

"Don't know." He swung into the saddle and positioned his horse nose to tail with hers. "Do you know who shot your driver, Mr. Monroe?"

"N-no."

"Hate to ask this, Suzannah, but what did the wound look like?"

"I don't understand."

"Was there more than one shot? Where did the bullet enter? Was the flesh clean or ragged around the—"

The color left her face and Brand broke off.

"He was sitting on the driver's bench," she said unsteadily, "driving the oxen, and I heard a crack and he tipped over to one side and fell off onto the ground. I climbed down and…and there was a lot of blood. I dragged him to the wagon and I…I don't know how I got him inside, but I did."

"You see anybody?"

"No. I was inside the wagon when it happened."

"Did you hear more than one gunshot?"

"Y-yes. Three, perhaps. Why are you asking all these questions?"

"Trying to figure out who killed Monroe. And why. Who knew that you were carrying a large amount of money?"

"Mr. Monroe did. I paid him in cash, in advance."

"In private? Did anyone see the transaction?"

"I don't think so. It took place at the bank in Independence."

Brand nodded. "Pretty public place, the bank in Independence."

"Could it have been Indians?"

"Indians would have whooped and hollered and probably taken the man's scalp. And you."

"Me!"

He leveled a scathing look at her. "Well, hell, lady,

think about it! A pretty woman way out on the plain. Shouldn't have to paint you a picture."

"Oh. Well." She was quiet for a long moment. "Then who do you think it was?"

"Had to be some lowlife out to steal some money. Probably followed your wagon train all the way from Missouri, hanging back until Monroe got separated from the others."

Brand wondered why whoever it was hadn't closed in on her and just taken what they wanted. Something must have scared them off—Indians, maybe. Now he figured whoever was following them would still be hanging back, trying to catch them unawares. Up ahead was scrubland, then the trail started climbing over rocky ground into the mountains. They didn't have much time.

"Suzannah, think you could get that horse of yours to go a little faster?"

"I suppose so. How much faster?"

"We're going to try to outrun whoever's behind us."

"But—"

"No time for *but*s. Come on." He wheeled his mount and kicked it into a trot, then looked behind him to watch her. When he saw her gig the mare into a canter, he touched the black with his heel and broke into a gallop. He could tell she didn't know how to run a horse full-out, because the mare's hoofbeats flagged, then sped up, then flagged again. By some miracle she managed to keep up.

He prayed she wouldn't lose her nerve. The trail started climbing, then veered into a section of large flat rocks. Her horse's hooves clattered right behind him and he had to smile. She was probably terrified, but the girl was no coward. A kernel of admiration lodged in his brain.

They climbed up a mountainside so steep the horses began to slow and stumble. He shot a glance at Suzannah behind him and smiled again. Her face was white and set, but she wasn't falling behind.

More rocks, and more struggle for the horses, and then the trail suddenly leveled out at the entrance to a cave. Bear den, probably. Or an Indian hideout. Didn't matter. He pulled his gelding to a halt, dropped out of the saddle and waited for Suzannah. When she trotted up, he grabbed for the mare's bridle.

"Whoa, girl. Easy, now."

Suzannah's breathing was coming in hoarse gasps. He waited until she could talk, then signaled her to dismount.

"We'll hole up here," he said.

"What? Where?" She leaned over the saddle horn, panting hard.

"In that cave. Horses, too. Hurry up."

She slid from the saddle like a sack of wheat. He grabbed the reins out of her hand and led both horses to the mouth of the cave.

"Inside," he ordered. "Quick." He laid his free arm across her shoulders to hurry her up. She was shaking so hard she could scarcely make her legs work, but she managed to stumble to the cave entrance.

"It's dark in there!"

"Yeah. Move it!"

She shrank back. "Are…are there wild animals in there?"

He gave her a little shove forward. "Only in the winter."

She took two steps past the opening and froze, her eyes huge with fear. "But it *is* winter."

"Keep moving," he ordered. He maneuvered the two horses under an overhanging rock near the cave.

"Mr. Wyler, I do not think—"

"Right. Don't think. Just do what I say, and do it quick. Get the saddlebags and the bedrolls and stash them inside." He lifted off both saddles and set them just inside the entrance, then grabbed his rifle and a length of rope. Quickly he hobbled the horses, caught his saddlebag as Suzannah lifted it off and dug in the depths for two handfuls of oats.

The cave smelled musty, but it was clean except for wisps of dried grass here and there. Dark as Hades, but safe. When his breathing returned to normal he assessed their refuge.

He assessed Suzannah, too. She'd moved only a few steps past the entrance, and he could see that her body was still shaking. Her breathing was so jerky he thought she might be crying, but a glance at her face told him she wasn't. At least not yet.

He moved forward and laid one hand on her shoulder. "We'll be safe here. Not comfortable, maybe, but alive come morning."

She just stared at him. "And what do we do in the morning?"

He thought her lips were trembling, but in the dimness he couldn't be sure. "In the morning we'll find out who's following us."

"And tonight?" she said in a small voice.

He hesitated. She was plenty scared, but she

wasn't crumpling up into a pile of jitters. "Tonight we count our blessings and give thanks to the god of caves. Then we eat supper and get some sleep."

"Can you build a fire? It is extremely dark in here."

"No fire. Can't risk someone seeing the smoke."

"H-how will we keep warm?"

An inappropriate thought popped into his mind. He squashed it flat before it made a permanent home there and swallowed over the sudden thickness in his throat.

"We'll manage."

For their supper he handed out cold biscuits and slices of jerky, which he pared off with his jackknife.

After her first bite, she wrinkled her nose. "I don't guess I care for jerky."

"Learn to like it." He handed her his canteen. "Let it soften up in your mouth before you try to chew it."

Suzannah knew she should be grateful she was alive and sheltered, at least for the time being, and that her stomach was reasonably full. It was strange how having very little in the way of comforts made her value all the more what she had taken for granted in Charleston. She supposed there was a lesson in that, but she was too exhausted to think what it was.

Brand dropped her saddle at her feet. "Where do you want your bedroll spread out?"

"Oh. I—" Despite the impropriety, she wanted it as close to his as possible.

Oh, my. In the past few days she had done things she had never before dreamed possible. At first she had been frightened at being alone on horseback with a strange man. She was also angry, but she guessed that was based on fear. Now she had the oddest sensation, as if her skin was stretching and stretching into some new and different creature.

He rolled his blanket out on the hard floor of the cave, looked at it for a long moment, then without a word stalked outside and returned with an armload of pine boughs. He spread them out, laid his blanket on top, and arranged her bed in the same way. Right next to his.

She should be outraged at his presumption. But she wasn't. She should be self-conscious about sleeping next to a man to whom she was not married. But she wasn't.

Something was most assuredly happening to her! She thought about it for the next hour as the cave gradually grew dim and then pitch-black and cold. This was like a dream, but rather than being a terrible nightmare, it was almost an exciting adventure.

She smiled up into the dark. "I miss your coffee."

"Yeah." After a long silence he rose and positioned both horses to block the cave entrance, then shoved his saddle to the head of his bed.

"Mr. Wyler? Do you think anyone could find us here?"

"Nope."

Brand drew in a long, slow breath and stretched out on his blanket. God help him, he didn't want to think about what was outside this cave, just what was inside. Suzannah and himself.

One of the horses nickered softly. He could still taste the spicy tang of jerky on his tongue, feel the rustle and crunch of the pine boughs under his body. He propped his head on his folded arms.

He could smell Suzannah's hair, kind of sweet, like violets. He liked the way she smelled, even when her skin was sweaty.

"I miss seeing the stars," she said abruptly.

Brand did not answer.

Sure was quiet up here. He listened hard to the sighing of the wind in the pines. Sometimes the sound made him feel lonely, and sometimes, like now, it made his throat feel so tight it was hard to swallow.

Except for his baby sister, Marcy, he'd never really understood women. He could never grasp how they could be so blind, how they could marry someone because of some kind of romantic dream, giving their life over to someone else just to satisfy an itch.

Maybe that was why he'd never been tempted to get too close to a woman. At least not a respectable woman.

Marcy had only been four years old when he'd lit out. When she turned twelve, he went back for her, to get her away from Pa. She boarded with their aunt Sally in Klamath Falls until she got engaged, and then…

He closed his eyes.

His horse moved restlessly at the mouth of the cave and Suzannah stirred in her sleep. He rolled sideways to look at her, but she was facing away from him, hunched up like a kid. Watching her, something flickered in his chest, something warm and insistent, like the feeling he got when he was hungry or craving a shot of red eye after a long ride.

He guessed he'd been without a woman for too long, otherwise he wouldn't be watching this one so closely. But he *was* watching her. In fact, he'd been acutely aware of her ever since they'd ridden away from Fort Hall.

A small animal of some kind made a skittery noise outside the cave and Suzannah murmured something in her sleep.

"It's okay," he said, keeping his voice low. "Maybe a squirrel." Very carefully he curled his frame around hers, and when she muttered uneasily in her sleep he laid his arm across her waist and pulled her backward, tucking her hip into his groin.

Big mistake. Her warm body made his breath catch and damned if he didn't start to get hard. Then she made things worse by wriggling her curvy little butt tighter against him.

He clenched his jaw. *Don't think about it.* He shut his eyes and concentrated on taking in air as slowly as possible. *And for God's sake, don't move.*

Never should have listened to the wind. All at once he felt more alone than ever before in his life. Somewhere deep inside he understood something he'd never confronted before—being connected to someone, someone he cared about, was damn dangerous. His sister had given her heart to someone she loved and died because of it.

Not for him. He would never hand his heart over to another human being. Never. He might feel lonely at times, but that was a damn sight better than the agony of losing someone.

But God, Suzannah felt good pressed up against him.

He needed to think about something else, anything else.

Who was trailing them? And what would he do when he figured out who it was?

Chapter Seven

Suzannah dragged her tired body into the saddle and gripped the reins in her floppy-fingered leather gloves. Breakfast had been half a dry biscuit and more cold, tough slices of jerky, but no coffee. She realized with a jolt that she had started every morning since she was thirteen years old with at least one cup of coffee, and sometimes two. The absence of the brew this morning had left her headachy and short-tempered.

She wondered if Brand felt the deprivation as keenly as she did. Probably not. Nothing seemed to bother the man riding ahead of her, his wide-brimmed sand-colored hat tipped at a jaunty angle over his dark head, his broad shoulders relaxed. At least he wasn't humming "Oh, Susanna."

But he was setting a bone-jarring pace on the narrow path down the mountain. Only once in the past hour had he glanced back to check on her; she could tumble off the edge of the cliff and he would never know.

"Lean back in the saddle when you're goin' downhill," he called. "Helps the horse keep its balance."

She nodded, but he had already refocused his gaze on the trail ahead. She pressed her lips together and swallowed back the angry words that threatened to tumble out of her mouth.

When the trail leveled out near the bottom, Brand drew rein and waited for her to catch up. "Whoever is following us is ahead of us now," he said. "I've got a plan."

Suzannah blinked. This was the first time he had shared any information about anything with her. Why now? All at once a terrible suspicion crept into her mind.

"We are in danger, aren't we?"

He wouldn't look at her, and that told her more than any words he might come up with.

"Well, are we?" she persisted.

"Yeah, maybe." His lips were unsmiling, his eyes were troubled and he had a strange, set look on his tanned face.

"What is it?" she said. "What is wrong?"

"Need to find out who's following us. That means—" He broke off and spit to one side. "Oh, hell, Suzannah, that might mean putting you in danger."

"How? I mean, what would doing whatever it is you propose require?"

He rolled his lower lip inward over his teeth and heaved out a sigh. "Some hard riding, and then some long waiting. We need to get around in front of them and—"

"I see." She cut him off with a decisive nod.

But she didn't see. For one thing, he hadn't paid the slightest attention to her while she had struggled with long hours in the saddle, thirst, even hunger. Forcing her horse up this mountain as fast as she could ride had not caused him to slow down or even look back at her.

She studied his impassive expression. Unless she was very much mistaken, he was hiding something. Well, she was hiding something, too. Major Brand Wyler was short-spoken to the point of rudeness. He had rough manners—no, he had *bad* manners. But in spite of everything she was beginning to like him.

She liked the way his lips quirked when he was trying not to laugh at her. She liked the calm, steady way he went about things, making coffee in the morning or saddling the horses or even plopping her in the cold creek as he had that first night.

And she trusted him.

"What do you propose?" she repeated. "Tell me."

He looked off across the sunbaked valley stretching before them, his gray eyes narrowed. "I propose we make a wide detour—" he tipped his head to the right "—then cut back to the trail ahead of them and lie in wait."

"Them?"

"You said you heard three shots. More'n likely there's more than one of them."

"What do you think they want?"

"You. The money you're carrying in that cloth belt around your waist. And the rest, the gold that Colonel Clarke insisted I carry in the bottom of my saddlebag."

Her breath caught. "How do you know where I keep my money?"

"Felt it last night when I—"

"When you what?" she demanded.

"When I laid my arm over your middle. You

were moaning some in your sleep. Thought you were scared."

Suzannah stared at him. Was that a touch of color under his tan? It *was*. It surely was. The man was blushing!

Her insides went all squishy. The last thing she would have expected from this taciturn, hard-bitten man was concern for her feelings. She had discovered something about Brand Wyler, something she felt certain he worked hard to keep hidden. The man had a softer side. Wonder of wonders, Major Wyler wasn't all hurry-it-up and don't-ask-questions—the man was actually capable of human feelings.

"And," she said hesitantly, "you were going to protect me, is that it?"

"Still am."

Tears stung under her eyelids. No one had ever said that to her, promised they would protect her, even during the worst of the war years. Not even her fiancé.

"Very well, Brand. Do whatever you think best. I will try hard to keep up."

They rode down into the dry, cold valley and swung a wide arc to the north, pushing the horses hard. Suzannah was as good as her word. She managed to keep up with him, *how* he didn't know, since she was such an inexperienced horsewoman. But with each passing mile his respect for her grew. Sure was a fast learner. Either that or she'd be half-dead by the time he called a halt.

Brand knew exactly where he wanted to be when they cut back to the trail, a rock-strewn flat-topped hill he'd often used for reconnaissance. From the top he could see for miles in any direction, screened from view by a dribble of granite boulders. Clarke's Castle, he called it. And it was still a good twenty miles ahead of them.

They stopped only once to refill the canteens. By the time both winded horses clattered up the mountainside, the wind was chilling the back of his neck and his mouth was so dry he couldn't work up enough moisture to spit.

He rode on, pushing the black straight up the incline. Behind him he could hear Suzannah's harsh breathing. It sounded more like sobbing, but she was hanging on. Warmth bloomed under his breastbone. She was one helluva woman.

Her horse stumbled, and he shot a glance behind him. Her braid had come loose and strands of wheat-colored hair straggled around her face. Under the hat brim her face looked dead white with exhaustion. But damn, she kneed that mare as if she'd been riding up mountains all her life. For a gently bred Southern belle, she sure was surprising.

At the top of his castle lookout, he dismounted and waited for her. When she came into view she was bent over the saddle horn, gasping for air, and his throat closed up tight. He grabbed his canteen, unscrewed the cap and sloshed some water into his palm. Then he kicked her boot out of the stirrup and stood up on the metal bar to reach her.

"Look up," he commanded.

She lifted her head and he slathered his wet hand over her face and around the back of her neck. He thought about the front of her neck, where her shirt gapped open, but decided against it.

"Better?"

She nodded. He held his canteen to her lips and suppressed a smile. No Southern lady ever gulped water like she was doing now. Finally she handed the container back to him and dragged the back of her hand across her mouth. The gesture was so unladylike it made him want to cheer.

He stepped down from the stirrup and reached up for her. With a hoarse sigh she tipped sideways into his arms, and he carried her to the cluster of sheltering boulders on the rim and settled her on the ground with her back against a flat rock. He unsaddled the horses, dropped the saddles and both saddlebags next to her, grabbed a double handful of dry grass, and wiped the animals down. Then he hand-fed them some oats.

Before he could join her, she surprised him.

"Can you see them anywhere?" She was still winded, but she managed to huff out the question.

He grabbed the canteen and moved to the lip of the plateau. Not a sign of a horse or a rider, not even a telltale puff of dust. Thank the Lord for that; at the moment he could use some food. And some rest.

"No sign of anyone," he said. But as he ate the jerky he sliced off, he kept one eye on the valley below them.

Suzannah gobbled down the rounds of jerky as fast as he could pare them off. Last night he'd thought she didn't much like it, but she was sure wolfing it down now. Again he had to smile. Was it possible that if you scratched the surface of an over-refined Southern belle you might find a human being?

He glanced over at her. Not just *any* human being, he amended, but Suzannah Cumberland.

Chapter Eight

Brand watched the sun sink behind the far-off hills, looking like a fat orange balloon too weary to stay aloft. He closed his eyelids for a few moments and opened them to a sky tinged with purple, and then gold and orange.

"Be dark soon," he said. Suzannah nodded tiredly and slid farther down on her bedroll. Pretty soon he'd have to tell her what he'd decided. But not yet. Let her enjoy the sunset.

But she surprised him again. "You're leaving, aren't you?" She sounded resigned but not frightened, and that made him wonder. Maybe she was just too exhausted to care.

"Yeah. I'm seeing smoke below us. Campfire, most likely. Gonna ride down and investigate."

"Now? At night?"

"Yes, now. I'd be seen in daylight."

"How long will you be gone?"

She didn't ask how long she would be all alone up here, and that raised his eyebrows some more. She could sure surprise him.

"Depends on what I find, whether it's someone following us or someone else. Suzannah, you ever fire a pistol?"

She popped up on one elbow. "No. Papa would never let me near any of his firearms."

"Not even during the war, when the Northern army came through?"

"Yankees, you mean," she said, her voice hardening. "No, not even then. Mama and Hattie kept a loaded rifle in the closet under the staircase, so we felt safe enough. And John…"

"That's your intended?"

"Yes. John offered to lend me a revolver when he left, but by then the war was all over."

"Did he teach you how to fire it?"

"No, he didn't. He was there only two days, and then…then he was gone."

Brand bit back a snort. "Two days! You agreed to marry a man after knowing him only two days?"

"Well, yes, I did. I grant you it was a very brief courtship, but…you see, there weren't a great number of eligible men left after the war, and…and Mama never let me forget I was approaching spinsterhood. I guess I let myself get swept off my feet."

"How old is spinsterhood, Suzannah?"

She hesitated. "I will be twenty-four in June."

Annoyance tightened his jaw muscles. Two days! Forty-eight hours and he'd managed to leave with her heart in his pocket? This John must be some fast-talking stud. How had the man swept a woman like Suzannah off her feet in just two days?

He decided he didn't like John Whatever His Name Was one bit. And he was annoyed as hell at her for being swept.

Forget it, Wyler. Her heart and her spinsterhood are none of your concern.

He scrabbled in his saddlebag for his extra revolver. "Suzannah, I'm gonna show you how to shoot this." He laid it on her blanket. "Be careful. It's loaded."

She stared at it, then gazed up at him. "Why?"

"Because I don't want to leave you alone up here without some way to protect yourself."

"Why not take me with you?"

"No. Too dangerous. I don't know who's down there." He scooted over close to her. "Sit up."

She shook off her blanket and sat cross-legged beside him. He lifted the Colt and positioned her hands around the butt.

"Hold it up steady, but don't put your finger on the trigger until you're ready to fire. That's it. Now, sight down the barrel."

The weapon wobbled in her grip. "It's heavy," she said.

Brand blew out a breath. "That's all, 'it's heavy'? Not 'I don't want to do this' or 'Don't go and leave me' or anything a million other women would say in this situation?" He shook his head in disbelief.

"I don't guess I am a million other women, Brand."

"Yeah." He forced his attention back to the weapon in her hands. "Yes, it's heavy. That's why you need both hands. Don't try to do some fancy quick-draw maneuver—you'll shoot yourself in the foot."

"Brand?" She looked into his face, her green eyes widening.

"What?" Now she was gonna cry or beg him not to go.

"When I fire it, will it kick back?"

Whoa. Why the South had lost the war with women like this at home was beyond him. His regard for Suzannah Cumberland flared once again into grudging admiration.

"Yeah, it'll jerk some. Don't let it scare you, just grip it tight." He saw her knuckles whiten as she tightened her grasp on his Colt.

"Brand?"

"Yeah?"

"Thank you."

He just plain didn't know what to say to that. He was so damn proud of her he wanted to pat her shoulder or shake her hand or something. Hell, he wanted to kiss her.

He squashed that thought and got to his feet. "Suzannah, you gonna be all right up here?"

"I will be perfectly all right. Well—" she gave a little laugh "—maybe not 'perfectly,' but all right enough." She laid the Colt down and gingerly shoved it under her saddlebag.

Brand picked up his saddle and moved to the large boulder where he'd picketed the horses. With his back to her he checked his revolver, grabbed the gelding's reins and hauled himself up into the saddle.

Suzannah crawled out of her bedroll and stood watching him, a half resigned, half pensive look on her face. Looking down at her, something began to crack inside his chest. He picked up the reins, then tossed them down and dismounted.

He reached her in two long strides, grasped her shoulders and kissed her. Hard. God forgive him, he wanted to do it again, and for a lot longer, but he forced himself to release her and remounted without looking at her.

He reined the horse away, and when he glanced back she was standing motionless right where he'd left her, the fingers of one hand covering her lips.

The knot in his chest cracked all the way open.

He kissed me! And it was wonderful, heart-thumpingly, stupendously wonderful! No man had ever kissed her like that, not even John.

She watched his horse disappear down the steep hillside and still she did not move. She was trembling all over, and then she was crying, and then… Oh, she simply couldn't think straight.

But why did he do that? Why?

Slowly she walked back to her bedroll, absentmindedly patted the saddlebag where she'd hidden Brand's revolver and stretched out on top of the blanket. In another hour the stars would come out.

She would lie here quietly and wait. And try not to think about what had just happened.

He saw the campfire glow from a long way off and slowed his horse to a walk. When he got close enough, he dismounted, tied the black to a cottonwood tree and started off on foot.

It didn't take long. There were three men. He could take two easy, but three, he didn't know for sure. He drew his revolver, held it down close to his thigh and moved into the circle of firelight.

Chapter Nine

"Gentlemen."

"What the—?" The heavyset man facing Brand across the fire leaped to his feet. "Who the hell are you?"

"Name's Brandon Wyler. And you?"

One of the other men twisted on the log he sat on and surveyed Brand with hard black eyes. His matted hair hung past the open neck of a grimy shirt, and Brand couldn't help noticing his necklace of elk's teeth. The third man, younger than his companions, looked downright skinny and his blond hair hung in greasy-looking strands past his fuzzy chin.

Silence.

He kept his revolver trained on the heavy one. "Talk to me," Brand snapped. "What are you doin' out here in the middle of nowhere?"

"H-hunting," the blond kid answered. He didn't sound too sure. "That—that's right, isn't it, Jim?"

"Shut up, Granger."

"Hunting what?" Brand pursued.

The heavyset man propped his pudgy hands on his hips. "What's it to you, mister?"

"Nothin' much. I'm hunting, too. Didn't want my horse to scare your quarry away." He paused long enough to take a look at the silent third man.

Round-shouldered, dark-skinned, with a drooping black mustache.

"I'm chasin' after a woman," Brand continued. "Following her, actually. Pretty. Blond hair. Came out from Missouri with a wagon train, but I lost track of her after Fort Hall. Colonel there told me she picked up a guide and started south to Texas. That's where I'm headed. You run across her?"

"Nope," Fatso said quickly. "Uh, how come you're tryin' to find her?"

"Money. She's carrying a lot of cash and she owes me for a horse I sold her." He watched the three men look at each other, then at him.

"Texas, huh?" Fatso said.

"Yeah. Hired a guide, like I said. Lost track of them a couple days ago, but I figure I can pick up their trail. Used to live halfway between here and Texas, so I know the trails. Maybe you fellas could use some company?" Brand carefully made a show of putting his gun away.

Again the men exchanged glances, and Brand knew they'd taken the bait. Already the skinny kid was edging toward a saddled pinto at the edge of their camp.

But Fatso pinned Brand with small, hostile eyes that were too close together. "We don't want company, mister. Why don't you just ride on outta here?"

"Sure thing. Maybe I'll see you fellas on the trail."

"Don't look too hard. Like I said, we don't want company."

Brand faked anger. "Hey, I don't want you hornin' in on my quarry. Don't want to share the goods with anybody, know what I mean?"

"Sure do. Now, turn around, mister, and vamoose."

Brand pivoted and headed for his horse. Behind him he heard Fatso's voice. "Granger, Jim, saddle up! We're ridin' out."

Good riddance, he thought. He could hardly wait to get back to Suzannah. But just as he stuffed his boot into the stirrup, he heard the sound of a gun cocking and then the roar of its discharge. A bullet slammed into him. White-hot pain tore through his right shoulder and he sucked in his breath.

"Got 'im," someone shouted. "He won't be botherin' us anymore."

He had to mount, but he couldn't grab the saddle horn and haul himself up by brute strength. He had to get back to the top of Clarke's Castle and Suzannah. He gritted his teeth and reached up again.

Someone is coming. Suzannah listened for a moment, then jolted upright and fished under her saddlebag for the revolver. Lifting it in both hands, she pointed the barrel toward the noise, careful not to touch her finger to the trigger.

What was it, an animal? A wolf? The hair on the back of her neck rose. Could it be a bear? Did bears live on hilltops?

The sound came closer. Her mare shifted nervously, and Suzannah held her breath. Could she aim accurately in the dark? Even if she did, could she kill anything?

A horse! She heard hoofbeats, moving slowly, just beyond the boulders. Very slow hoofbeats, and… Oh, God. She tried to control her shaking hands, slipped off the safety and slid her forefinger over the trigger.

And then she heard something odd, someone whistling through his teeth—"Oh, Susanna."

"Brand?"

"Yeah," came a tired voice.

She was on her feet and running as his head appeared over the rocks. "Brand!"

"Suzannah," he rasped. "For God's sake, put the gun down."

She tossed it onto the ground and kept moving toward him.

"Gotta help me down, Suzannah. My shoulder's hurt." He dropped the reins, brought his leg over the saddle horn and reached down to her with one arm. With a groan he latched on to her extended hands and slid to the ground.

He staggered, and she grabbed him around the waist. "Easy, easy," he panted. "Don't bump my arm."

"Which arm?"

"Right. It's my shoulder, really. Gunshot."

She cried out, then clapped her free hand over her mouth.

"Walk me over to my bedroll, will you?"

Step by halting step she guided him the twenty feet to his blankets, and he dropped to his knees. "Think you could unsaddle my horse?"

After some fumbling she figured out how to loosen the cinch under the animal's belly and dragged off the saddle. She staggered under the weight.

"Make some coffee, will you?" he called.

"I thought you were afraid of smoke being seen."

"Dig a fire pit. Use the shovel tied on my horse. Scoop down about ten inches."

Brand watched his ladylike lady dig what had to be the first hole she'd made in the earth since making mud pies when she was a girl. She followed his instructions, and when the coffee was bubbling over on her scrabbled-together fire, he asked for the final thing he needed.

"Look in my saddlebag for my whiskey flask and some linen for bandages. And the jerky," he added. "All of a sudden I'm damn hungry."

Her relief was so obvious he had to laugh. "You cannot be at death's door if you are hungry," she quipped.

"Coffee 'bout ready?"

"After I tend to your shoulder." She found the bandages and the whiskey and settled beside him. "Lean forward."

She stripped off his bloody shirt while he clenched his jaw. She peered at him. "Do you want some whiskey?"

"No. Save it for…just save it."

"There doesn't seem to be very much blood," she said.

"Bullet must have gone clean through."

"Does it hurt?"

"Like a son of a— Yeah, it hurts."

She twisted her hands together. "What should I do now?"

"Pour the whiskey over it."

She uncorked the flask, clamped her teeth together and dribbled the contents over his bloody shoulder while he hissed in his breath and swore.

"Such language!" she remarked when his fist released her shirt-sleeve.

Brand closed his eyes while she rustled around the camp getting out mugs for the coffee. "Any whiskey left?"

"Yes. But save some for me, please."

For her! Lord save them, the trail to Oregon was corrupting his Southern belle. He heard the coffee dribble out of the pot and, still keeping his eyes closed, he reached for a mug. It was hot and strong and so full of grounds he ended up chewing most of the first mouthful, but he didn't say a word, just gulped down swallow after swallow while she unfolded his pocketknife and did her best to saw off rounds of jerky.

"Open your mouth," she ordered. She laid a piece of the salty-tasting dried meat on his tongue. He chewed it up and swallowed it down. His shoulder throbbed like a son of a gun, but he tried not to think about it. Instead, he closed his eyes and thought about Suzannah while she fed him sips of coffee and more jerky as if she'd done it all her life.

"You know something, Suzannah?"

"I know a great many things, Brand. I was very well educated when I was a girl. Papa had acres of books. What would you like to know?"

"Nothing that's in any book," he growled. "I wanted to say that, fancy education or not, you are one extraordinary woman."

"Oh, I do hope so. I do want to make John a good wife."

He snapped his lids open. "Hand me the whiskey."

But three slugs of the liquor didn't take away the sour taste of John's name on her lips. He listened to her pouring coffee for herself and slicing off more rounds of jerky and wondered why the whiskey wasn't working.

"How do you know you really want to marry this man?" he heard himself say. "You've only known him for two days."

"I just know. John was so dashing and so personable, and attentive and, well, flattering...with such fine manners. I just know."

For some reason her words made him mad. "That's what it takes to get a girl like you, huh? Fancy manners and flattery?"

Her mouth dropped open.

"I have—" He sucked in a breath. "I *had* a younger sister. She fell in love with some damn flashy army officer who was just toying with her. He left her at the altar, and—" he swallowed over the rock in his throat "—she, uh, she drowned herself."

Her face changed. "Oh, Brand, what a terrible thing."

"Yeah, well, I guess that's why I believe in long engagements. Gives a couple of lovers time to get to know each other."

She was silent for a long minute. "You think I am foolish, do you not?"

"I think... Doesn't matter what I think."

"Yes, it does. Tell me."

He began playing with his pocketknife, turning it over and over in his hand and rubbing his thumb over the smooth handle.

"Seems to me like a man and a woman have two choices. They can fall into bed with each other and damn the consequences. Or they can do what men and women do to spend time together—takin' walks by the river and dancin' with each other and goin' on picnics and all those things. Then they can—"

"Fall into bed with each other," she supplied.

His laugh stuttered into the quiet.

"It is the same in the end, is it not?" Her voice told him he should drop the subject, but something inside him wouldn't let it go.

"Might not be the same, no. Might be that if she looked hard enough at a man she'd see something in him that should warn her off."

"And you wish your sister had done just that."

Brand looked past her hunched shoulder into the soft darkness. "Yeah. If she had, she'd be alive today. If I ever meet up with the bastard who destroyed her, I'm going to kill him."

She hesitated. "What good will that do?"

"It'd get him off the face of the earth, for one thing. And it might make me feel better about my sister."

Suzannah said nothing. After a while she refilled his coffee and then her own and sat sipping it slowly. He watched her slim, delicate fingers cradle the tin mug. An army wife? He didn't think so. Even an officer's wife, like the colonel's lady, Violet McLeod got pretty well ground down between sandstorms and Indian skirmishes and God knew what else out here in the West.

"There's precious little to compensate a gently reared woman at an army post," he said carefully.

"There is her husband," Suzannah insisted. "There is always the love of her husband."

What the hell, her mind was made up. She didn't want to see the danger staring her in the face. And anyway, what difference did it make if she wanted to throw her life away out in Oregon? But it ate at him just the same.

Something he said must have whanged into her because she sat looking down at him for a long time, her eyes troubled. Slowly he reached up and touched her shoulder, spread his fingers against her warmth and drew her down to him.

His lips grazed her forehead, moved to her cheek and then hovered a scant inch from her mouth.

"Suzannah," he murmured. "Don't do it, Suzannah. Don't marry him."

Chapter Ten

If she lived to be a hundred, Suzannah would never understand her feelings at this moment. Brand slipped his hand behind her neck and tugged her down until his mouth met hers. His lips were warm and firm and gentle with restraint, but she could feel his wanting. She tasted salt and coffee and hunger, such a deep hunger that her breath stopped.

He made a sound in his throat and wound his fingers into her hair. Colors danced under her closed eyelids, like starbursts, and she felt his heartbeat grow ragged. *What is happening?*

"Brand…"

"Don't talk," he whispered against her lips. He kissed her again, and then again, each time inviting. Enticing. *This is glorious. Unbelievable.*

Surely she was dreaming! His hand cradled her head and his mouth…his mouth was so insistent, so delicious on hers. Was this how a man and a woman felt when…when…?

She pulled away but hung mere inches from his mouth, listening to their breathing. His heart beat against her palm and she wondered if he could feel hers fluttering against his chest.

"I'm not sorry I did that," he said at last.

I am not sorry, either, she sang inside. *Not sorry at all.*

With a wry smile he let his hand fall to his side. "Must be dreamin'," he breathed.

Dreaming, yes, that was it. She had to be dreaming.

"No more whiskey for either one of us," she managed. Then she realized she had not had a single, solitary drop of liquor. Nevertheless, she still felt intoxicated.

And now she understood what the Indians meant by "strong medicine."

Brand woke near dawn to find Suzannah snuggled close to him, her head tucked between his chin and his good shoulder, her small hands folded under her chin. His heartbeat thundered against his ribs and he fought to keep his arm by his side and not wrap it around her sleeping form.

He sure wasn't thinking clearly when it came to this woman. She made him feel more off balance than he could ever remember, and sure as God made green grass and peach trees, he didn't need this complicating his life.

But he drifted off to sleep smelling her hair and remembering the feel of her mouth under his.

In the morning he eased his aching body away from her and packed up everything one-handed, trying to keep his eyes off her sleeping form. He managed to make coffee before she woke up, and when she finally did open her eyes he busied himself with saddling both horses.

She didn't say a word while she downed her mug

of coffee. Wouldn't look at him, either. Guess he'd overstepped last night. Sure would like to overstep again, but they had about six days of riding ahead of them, and at the end he'd have to hand her over to another man. Smart thing would be to keep his hands off her.

She braided up her hair like she always did, settled her hat on her head and pulled it so low he couldn't see much of her face. Then she walked to her mare, stuck her foot in the stirrup and pulled herself up into the saddle. She sat waiting while he slung both saddlebags on their mounts and kicked dirt over the fire.

He moved out in the lead and tried not to think about another week on the trail with her. Looked like it'd be a long, long day today. Quiet, too.

That lasted until the sun told him it was around ten o'clock and, even though they'd ridden side by side for the past three hours, she still hadn't said a word. It was hell trying to figure out a woman, especially this woman. She was delicate and tough, and both smart and dumb; her head was stuck so deep in the sand over this John of hers she'd be ninety before she wised up.

Each time they stopped to rest and water the horses, Brand kept a sharp eye out for a telltale puff of dust behind them. None showed, and he'd seen no sign of another living soul. His shoulder ached, and the longer he rode the stiffer it got. He tried to work his arm back and forth every hour or so and prayed it would heal clean. Last thing she'd need was a guide with a fever and a bum arm.

By late afternoon Suzannah still hadn't spoken a

single word, and he couldn't stand it any longer. He pulled air into his lungs and twisted to look at her.

"Sure wish you'd say something."

"Very well." Her voice reminded him of his mother's primroses, all neat and proper with nary a petal out of place. "Do you think we are still being followed?" she asked.

"Nope. I gulled them into turning south, heading for Texas. Forgot to tell you last night."

"How did you accomplish that?"

"Told 'em a bunch of lies."

"How many were there?"

"Lies? Or men?"

She sniffed. "Men, of course."

"Three."

They rode across a valley and up into some green foothills, following a good-size stream. Dusk started to fall.

Brand unsheathed his rifle. "I'm going hunting. Try to get a rabbit or a grouse. Keep riding and stay on the trail."

She said nothing, and he loped away into the trees. An hour later he caught up to her, a fat rabbit hanging off his saddle horn.

"I did not hear a gunshot," she remarked.

"Used a snare. A shot might be heard."

He picked a campsite sheltered by larch trees where the creek they'd been following widened. Suzannah dismounted, stretched her aching back muscles and studied the stream. She was hot and tired and sticky with perspiration.

"I'm going to take a bath."

"No, you're not."

"Why not? I cannot stop thinking about how good that cool water would feel, and I could wash my hair and rinse out my shirt and—"

"No."

"Brand, be reasonable. No one is following us—you said so yourself."

He tramped up and down beside the stream and finally turned to face her. "I want you where I can see you."

"That," she replied, "would be highly improper."

"Maybe so, but it's also highly safe. Take it or leave it."

"What will you be doing?"

"Setting up camp. Tending the horses. Dressing out that rabbit for supper. I don't want you too far out of sight."

She considered his words, then fixed her gaze on him and considered the man who spoke them. He wasn't exactly honorable; after all, he'd kissed her twice without asking permission. But he was honest, and she trusted him.

"Very well," she agreed at last. She dug a bar of soap wrapped in tinfoil out of her saddlebag and unfolded a clean shirt. Green this time. She was sick of the red plaid and it was beginning to get dirty again. And anyway, if she washed it out and put it back on wet, he would look at her in that same hot way he'd done before. She surmised, somewhat shocked, that a wet shirt plastered to her skin must reveal her nipples.

She found a spot where the creek bank gradually shelved off into the water and was screened by a leafy bush. She turned to see where Brand was.

She could just see the top of his head as he moved around camp, and he was not looking at her. She unbuttoned her shirt and shrugged it off, then realized she had no towel. Well, she would simply have to air-dry.

Submerging her body in the rippling water felt heavenly, even if it was ice-cold! She lolled and rubbed the soap over her skin and lolled some more before she rinsed off the bubbles. Then she unwound her braid and washed her hair. She soused the red plaid shirt up and down in the creek, tossed it over a bush, and waved her arms in the air to dry her skin.

A delicious, stomach-rumbling smell drifted from the camp. Meat! Thank heavens, supper would be not jerky but rabbit. She moved her arms faster.

Working slowly with only one hand, Brand spitted the cut-up rabbit pieces, arranged them over the coals and stood up. A flash of something pale caught his attention and he narrowed his eyes. Jehoshaphat, it was Suzannah. Naked. Her arms outstretched, her face tipped up toward the disappearing sun. Her back was to him.

His mouth went dry. She was so beautiful it made his throat ache. She was one hundred percent female perfection from the flare of her hips to her knobby spine to her slim shoulders. All perfection. Her hair was loose and maybe damp the way it clung to her neck and upper back in little straggly curls.

Turn away, Wyler. Turn around.

He closed his eyes. He couldn't turn around.

When he opened them she was buttoning up a

green shirt and shaking the wet hair out of her eyes. He groaned out loud. Five days to go. Five days of trying not to look at her, smell her. Touch her. Four days of riding side by side during the day and sleeping next to her all night.

And he was plumb out of whiskey.

When she returned to camp he made a decision. "Watch the rabbit, will you? I'm goin' for a swim."

"It's too shallow to swim," she said at his back.

He didn't answer, just walked straight into the cold water and lay down in the creek. Even the icy water didn't cool him off.

He stood up, took off his clothes and lay back down.

"Do you want my bar of soap?" she called.

"No."

"It's scented with lavender."

"Keep it. And stay away from the creek."

When he finally dragged himself back to camp, his boots were squishy and the wet garments he'd wrestled back on dripped water wherever he stood. With a silent curse he dug out a clean shirt and headed back to the creek, washed out his dirty shirt and socks and his drawers, and tossed them over the bush next to Suzannah's red shirt. By the time he returned to camp his nerves were steadier.

Suzannah gave the spitted rabbit another quarter turn and set the coffeepot close to the fire. She'd watched Brand make coffee, and now she knew how to finish off the brew by dumping in a cup of cold water before pouring it. For some reason knowing how to do this buoyed her spirits. Every army wife must know such things, she supposed. Now she was one step closer to being just that, an army wife.

Brand tramped back into camp, his dark hair looking damp and unruly and his jeans soaking wet.

"Did you bathe?"

"Not exactly," he said dryly.

She gazed up at him. "Well, *what*, exactly?"

That made him laugh. The sound sent a shiver up the back of her neck. She liked this man. Even if he lacked the manners to ask permission before kissing her, she liked him.

John had asked permission, but, well, it wasn't the same. Oh, bother! Properly raised women were not supposed to enjoy such intimacies.

But you enjoyed it with Brand, Suzannah. Admit it. You enjoyed it so much it frightened you. You even wanted more.

Hush up! She could not allow herself to think such wayward thoughts. Instead she busied herself rummaging in his saddlebag for the tin plates and the spoon they shared for supper.

Brand squatted next to her at the fire pit and poked a finger at the rabbit. "It's done. You hungry?"

He needn't have asked. She wolfed down two nicely browned pieces and when she looked longingly at a third, he chuckled. "For someone as slim as, um, slim as you are, you sure have a good appetite."

"Riding all day makes me hungry, I guess."

"Got berries for dessert," he remarked.

Her eyebrows went up. "Berries?"

"Wild blackberries. Picked 'em while you were... picked 'em earlier." He'd picked them to occupy his mind and keep his hands busy while she was splashing in the creek. Females didn't realize what the sound of a woman taking a bath did to a man.

Chapter Eleven

Brand popped a handful of fat, juicy berries into his mouth and grinned at Suzannah. "You ever pick blackberries when you were a kid?"

"No, I never have. We, um, had servants who gathered our food for us."

"You ever wonder whether you might have missed a lot, growing up so protected?"

"No, I never wondered that before," she said, her tone thoughtful. "Now I am wondering why I didn't."

"Ever sneak cookies? Climb trees? Run away from home?"

Suzannah wished he wouldn't look at her that way, his gray eyes wide and unbelieving. "No, I never did any of those things. Did you?"

He crammed another palm full of blackberries into his mouth. She ate hers carefully, one by one, and licked her fingers. In a way she envied his gusto.

"Yeah, I did all that, and more. Guess you might say I didn't have your fancy upbringing."

"Where did you grow up, Brand?"

"Before I lit out from home or after?"

She blinked. "Before. Where were you born?"

"Philadelphia. Wrong side of town, though. When I left I ended up in Ohio, and then I joined the Union Army."

"Did you…did you ever fight in South Carolina?"

"Nope. But I fought everywhere else—Vicksburg, Bull Run, Chancellorsville. War is a bloody, awful business. Glad it's over."

She studied his face but saw no bitterness, only resignation. "Yes, the war was truly terrible. After it was over it was worse for the South, so many of our boys killed or wounded. Over half the men of Roseboro never came home."

"And one night your father just up and invited a Yankee officer to a ball at your plantation?"

"Well, yes, he did. Papa said the fighting was over and now we should all try to get along with each other. It wasn't a ball like we had before the war, though, with an orchestra and everything. After the war we tried to keep our spirits up, and we could still dance a Virginia reel."

"Bet he regretted it when you left home to follow your Yankee officer out west."

"Papa never knew. He died in a riding accident only a month after meeting John. Mama pitched a fit, though. It was hard to leave her so soon after Papa's death, but John was so insistent, I…did what he said."

Brand chased the last blackberry around and around on his plate. "I came out west to fight Indians."

"You must have been successful since you were promoted to major."

"Not so much. Like I said, war is pretty awful. After it was over, I scouted for Colonel Clarke for a while."

"And then?"

"Then I got to like some of the Indians better than

my own men, so I mustered out. Doesn't pay to see your enemies as human beings sometimes."

"On the contrary, I think it always pays to do so."

He laughed softly. "You mean 'love your neighbor' kind of thing?"

"Yes, exactly. I am quite sure my John feels the same."

"But you don't know," he said, his voice hard. "Bet you never got around to discussing it."

"Well, no, we never did," she said in a small voice.

"And now you're goin' all the way out to Oregon to marry this man you never discussed anything with." It wasn't a question. It came out sounding like an accusation.

"Yes, I am. I am going to Oregon to marry him, and don't you dare say one more thing about it!"

He tossed the dregs of his coffee into the fire. "Suzannah, I have to tell you I think you're makin' a big mistake."

She clenched her teeth. "You listen to me, Brand Wyler. There is more to a relationship than…well, than kisses."

"Yeah." He looked straight at her, his face set. "But that's a good start. If they're good kisses, that's an important indication of something."

"That is shallow and superficial. Just because something *feels* good doesn't mean it *is* good." Lordy, how straitlaced and prim she sounded.

He did not look away. "What's wrong with feeling good?"

Suzannah swallowed. She wished he would look somewhere else. She knew her cheeks were flushing;

her whole face felt hot. "Nothing is wrong with it, I guess. But that is not how I was raised. I was brought up to expect that a man would have high regard for my person and my breeding and my good name. One false step and a girl could be ruined."

"You mean," he said dryly, keeping his eyes on her face, "that your reputation as a respectable virgin would be compromised."

"Yes, exactly. That is what happened to your sister, was it not?"

"Not exactly. This scoundrel, Jack something, took advantage of Marcy. He promised to marry her, then he never showed up for the wedding. She wrote me about it, said she was devastated."

"Poor girl," Suzannah murmured. "Poor, foolish girl."

"Yeah," he muttered.

"Brand, why are we talking about all this? I know my fiancé is an honorable man. Furthermore, I know exactly what I am doing."

"Like hell you do." He stood up suddenly and paced around the camp with his hands jammed in his back pockets. Finally he stopped in front of her.

"Suzannah, I think you have to know a man, really know him, before you decide to spend your life with him. I think you have to like that man, and I think you have to like that man's kisses…and I think you have to feel like you want more than that."

She jumped to her feet and confronted him, hands on her hips. "Well! I do not care one whit what you think, Brandon Wyler. So let that be an end to it."

Brand stood eye to eye with her. She was good

and mad now, but he didn't care. He wished someone had talked some sense into Marcy; to his dying
day he'd regret that he hadn't been there to do that.
Maybe she wouldn't have paid any attention, kinda
like Suzannah was doing now, digging in her heels
and refusing to listen. Maybe that's why he couldn't
let it alone.

And maybe it's more than that.

He pivoted on one heel and gazed out across the
hills, now glowing purple as the sun sank in the west.
He couldn't figure out how this overprotected slip of
a woman from a South he never wanted to see again
could raise his hackles so fast. She was stubborn and
argumentative and so damn convinced she was right
it set his teeth on edge.

Ah, hell, why should he care?

He didn't, really. Or at least he told himself he
didn't. But he sure couldn't ignore what had happened to him when he'd kissed her. Something inside
his chest swelled up until it hurt, and the next thing
he knew he felt as though he was flying.

"Time to turn in," he barked. Without glancing
at her, he unrolled his blanket, positioned his saddle
at his head and shucked his boots. She marched
around camp for a good quarter of an hour, then
spread her bedroll about as far away from him as
she could get.

Better that way, he acknowledged. He didn't want
to see her curled up in a ball with just the top of her
blond head peeking out, or hear those little sighs
she made in her sleep, or smell the violet scent of
her hair.

Long after the fire burned down to a handful of

faint orange coals, he lay awake calculating not how many days it would take them to reach Fort Klamath, but how many hours.

And every one, one too many.

Chapter Twelve

Shortly after dawn Suzannah felt something hard poke her derriere. She ignored it, and a moment later it poked again.

"Wake up," Brand ordered.

She groaned and snuggled deeper under her blanket.

Something metallic clanked beside her and she inhaled the pungent smell of frying meat. Opening one eyelid, she saw a tin plate loaded with slices of steaming-hot jerky and two fat, fluffy biscuits. Beside it sat a brimming mug of hot coffee.

She propped up on one elbow and leaned over to sniff the meat.

"It's fried," Brand explained from the other side of the fire. "Maybe not as good as bacon, but we don't have any bacon."

She reached for a slice, gobbled it along with one of the biscuits and washed it all down with a swallow of coffee. Despite all his maddening male know-it-all faults, she had to admit Brand made excellent coffee, now that she'd come to like it.

"Get up," he ordered. "Got to get goin' before the sun's up."

Had she ever known a more annoying man? He

was all nag-nag-nag and push-push-push, and she was heartily sick of it.

"Let me alone," she protested.

"Can't. You want to get to Fort Klamath, and I want to—"

He broke off, but she knew what he'd been about to say. He wanted to be rid of her. The feeling was most certainly mutual.

"Suzannah…"

"Oh, very well," she said. "Do stop badgering me, Brand. You're worse than Mama at her most officious moments."

His dark eyebrows went up. "Your momma bossed you around?"

"Well, she tried to. I don't guess I 'bossed' very well."

His laugh surprised her. Brand might be an overbearing bully, but at least he had a nice laugh—rich and rumbly.

She dragged herself upright, stuffed her feet into her boots and noticed that her blisters no longer hurt. Then she slipped three more slices of fried jerky past her lips and devoured another biscuit. Besides coffee, Brand made very fine biscuits.

She supposed that, being an army wife, she must learn to cook, but somehow the prospect was daunting. She hadn't thought to pack one of Hattie's receipt books, but frying slices of jerky couldn't be too difficult, could it?

Brand appeared to be in a real fizz to be on their way. He packed up both bedrolls, fed the horses and hovered at her elbow while she finished the last of her biscuits. Before she swallowed the remains of her coffee, he tramped off to the creek to wash the tin plates, then packed them into his saddlebag.

She had to scramble to fit in her necessary morning stop and splash cold water on her face before Brand herded her over to the mare.

"Want a boost up?" he asked.

"No, I do not. Why are you in such an all-fired hurry this morning?"

"No reason." He wouldn't look at her, so she knew he was lying. Something was wrong. Her heart skipped some beats.

She pulled herself up into her saddle and shot him a look. "We are not being followed, are we?"

"Nope. Just want to get to Oregon before Christmas."

"Christmas! Brand, for heaven's sake, Christmas is days from now."

He didn't answer, just mounted and reined away. For the next three hours he rode ahead of her, and each time she tried to draw abreast of his black horse, he sped up.

"Brandon Wyler," she called after him. "You are no gentleman."

"You're sure right about that," he said. "You've mentioned that already."

Oh, for mercy's sake! She had to content herself with riding in his dusty wake, but under the calm, unflappable exterior she was trying so hard to maintain she was working up what Mama used to call a Suzannah-size head of steam.

When he started whistling "Oh, Susanna" between his teeth, the steam boiled over.

"Stop that!" she screamed. It was a most unladylike thing to do, but it did the trick. He hauled on his reins so hard his horse reared.

"What the hell is the matter?" he shouted.

"Everything!" she yelled back.

He turned his mount in a circle and trotted back to her. "Like what? Are you hurting?"

"No."

"Thirsty?"

"No."

"Need a private minute behind a bush?"

"No."

He narrowed his eyes. "Well, what, then?" His voice was like sand on steel, raspy and rude.

"I want you to slow down," she said through gritted teeth. "I am tired of eating the dust your horse kicks up."

"Okay. Trail widens out up ahead." He turned another circle, fell in beside her and again started on "Oh, Susanna."

"And stop whistling that song!"

This time when he drew rein he turned very slowly in his saddle and pinned her with eyes like two granite stones. "Can you say *please*?"

"Brand, so help me..."

"Drivin' you crazy, am I?" Inexplicably he smiled. "Know what's wrong with you, Suzannah?"

She stared at him. "There is nothing wrong with me that finally reaching Fort Klamath won't cure."

"Same here," he said with a laugh. "Seems like a real long way to ride for improvement, though, doesn't it?"

"It feels like going to the moon!"

He lifted the reins, then leaned sideways and laid

a hand on her tense shoulder. "I figure this trip is hard on you for one reason, and hard on me for another. I'm tryin' to make the best of it."

Instantly she was curious. Hard on him for *what* reason? Because he wanted to be rid of her? Because he didn't like her? A little pain lodged behind her breastbone.

The hurt was unexpected.

Chapter Thirteen

The trail grew steeper as it climbed into the foot-hills of the Bitterroot range, and it grew colder. The trees were taller and had thicker trunks; the bushes were greener and some had tiny flowers of pink and scarlet and deep gold. Suzannah wished she knew the names; she would love to have a garden when she and John set up housekeeping.

They climbed higher into the mountains and the path narrowed until the ruts that the pioneers' cov-ered wagons had cut into the earth were over a foot deep in places. The ground was rust-red and so hard the horses' hooves sounded like gunshots as they clattered over it. The air felt crisp and the wind was sharp.

Up ahead she could see the way was wide enough for only one horse. Any minute now Brand would motion for her to ride single file, and she steeled her-self for more dust. In anticipation she tied her red bandanna over her nose and mouth.

When he called a halt she willed herself not to complain but to accept the rear position with the grace her mother had instilled in her. At any rate, she would try. She sat her mare in the shade of a spread-ing larch and arranged her face to reveal nothing but acceptance with calm fortitude.

"Ride in front," Brand called, tipping his canteen to his lips.

She blinked. "Really? Do you mean it?"

"Sure, I mean it. I don't say things I don't mean." He poured water into his palm, removed his hat and slapped the liquid over his face and throat.

"Thank you, Brand."

He didn't answer, just replaced his sand-colored hat and motioned her ahead of him.

An hour later it started to rain. Fat wet drops splatted onto the ground and dampened her jeans and shirt until she felt cold and sticky all over. The trail grew wet, then slick and then muddy as water collected in the ruts and spilled over.

They were still climbing, and she slowed the mare. Behind her Brand started to whistle, broke it off and began again. It wasn't "Oh, Susanna" this time, and she had to smile. Even if she had screamed at him a while back, it was good to know the man wasn't deaf. He had heard her. He was paying at least *some* attention to her.

The rain increased. The drops fell harder and pounded onto the muddy ground until wide puddles bloomed on the trail. The horses moved even slower. Surely it was only a thundershower? Any minute it would cease.

But it didn't. Instead, the heavens dumped buckets of water down on them, the veil of water so thick she could scarcely see ahead.

"Rein up at that grove of trees ahead," Brand shouted. She pulled off the trail, halted her horse under a canopy of dripping oak and maple leaves, and waited for him.

"We'll camp here," he said when he rode up. "It's as protected as any place."

"Protected? Brand, raindrops are pounding those trees." She pointed upward. "It sounds like a Gatling gun."

"Now, how would you know what a Gatling gun sounds like?"

"My John demonstrated it with vocal sounds after supper when he visited."

"Bet that made scintillating conversation." He tipped his head at a spot farther off the trail and deeper in the trees. "Over there."

Suzannah stared in dismay. The rain was so heavy the trees were shrouded in thick mist. Every square inch of ground was wet, and the tree leaves jerked and spun as the falling water hit them.

Brand dismounted and tramped to a likely spot under a huge big-leaf oak. Good enough.

"I've got a tent, Suzannah. Take me a minute to put it up." It was his army-issue tent, made of tight-woven waterproof canvas. At least it'd been water-proof the last time he'd used it. "Stay under that tree and see if you can wrestle your poncho out of your saddlebag."

"I don't have a poncho."

"Well, I sure as…I bought one for you back at Fort Hall. What happened to it?"

"I didn't bring it. I left it at Colonel Clarke's house."

He looked at her so long she shifted nervously in the saddle. Well, hell. He rummaged in his own saddlebag for his poncho, shook it out and walked over to her.

"Put this on. Stick your neck through the hole and fold the flap over your head."

"But this is yours. What are you going to use?"

"A little water never hurt me."

"It isn't a *little*, Brand. It's a *lot* of water."

"Yeah, well. I won't wash away." He wrestled the tent out from behind his saddle, smoothed out the creases and set it up under the driest-looking tree.

"Not gonna make a fire," he announced. "Wood's too wet."

"What about our supper?"

He sighed. "Cold biscuits and—"

"Jerky," she finished, her voice resigned. "I might have guessed."

Brand stepped back to assess the water dripping from the tree leaves onto the tent and closed his eyes with a groan.

"What's wrong?" Suzannah demanded.

"My tent is, uh, kinda small." His army tent was big enough for one man. Just one. He slung his saddlebag inside and went to unsaddle the horses and untie both bedrolls. *Hell's bells, only gonna need one set of blankets tonight.*

"Look, Suzannah, it's—"

"I know," she said quietly. "We'll have to squeeze in together."

Squeeze. Did she say *squeeze*? He had to hand it to her. Another woman would get all fluffed up about the sleeping arrangement. Suzannah seemed to be taking it in her stride.

Now that he thought about it, she'd put up with everything except "Oh, Susanna" since they started on this trip. Those still Confederate waters sure ran deep.

He knelt at the tent entrance and unrolled the blankets so one layer of canvas was underneath and two dry blankets were on top. She had dismounted and now stood at his elbow, shielding his back and neck with one corner of the poncho. His throat got so thick he thought he'd choke.

"I'll picket the horses." He finished smoothing the blankets and looked up at her. "Crawl in there."

Without a word she stripped off the poncho and draped it over his back, then bent down and crawled on all fours into the sturdy little canvas shelter.

Brand watched her and gave up trying to swallow. Suzannah was surprising. Unsettlingly surprising.

He made quick work of feeding both horses a handful of dry oats, tied them to a thick pine branch and covered them as best he could with the poncho. Then he took a deep breath and crawled into the tent after Suzannah.

Chapter Fourteen

Suzannah scrunched herself up in one corner of the tiny tent, her knees tight against her chest.

"You won't be able to sleep sitting up like that," Brand said. He'd flattened himself out on the blankets, but she saw instantly there wasn't enough room for them both.

He turned onto his side and patted the space next to him.

She couldn't. She simply couldn't. Mama would simply die if she saw her now.

"Come on, lie down," he said, his voice tired. "I'm not gonna attack you. Isn't room enough."

A strangled laugh escaped her. Then she sniffled once and very, very gingerly stretched out beside him, making sure no part of her touched any part of him.

"Sure is small quarters," he mused.

She said nothing.

"We're both wet and tired and hungry, but at least we're dry," he said. "Sort of."

"Where is your saddlebag?" she asked. "I saw you toss it in here, but I don't see it."

"It's underneath me. Why?"

"Supper. You mentioned biscuits and—"

"Not gonna be many biscuits."

"Jerky," she finished. "I'm starving."

They devoured the six remaining dry, crumbly biscuits and the jerky rounds Brand sliced off with his pocketknife and washed it down with water from his canteen while the rain plop-plopped onto the canvas over their heads in steady, rhythmic patterns.

They didn't talk. Little by little it grew dark outside and the forest around them fell silent except for the sound of the rain. The wind picked up, swishing through the tree branches like a chorus of hisses.

Brand closed his eyes. Despite being jammed in here together like two tinned sardines, he felt oddly content. It wasn't a bad way to spend a rainy night, lying next to an intriguing woman. Damn, he hoped it wasn't going to snow. Wouldn't be unusual, this high up in the Bitterroots. And if it did…well, he guessed they'd eat some more jerky.

"I like listening to the rain," she said suddenly. "It's peaceful when it rains."

"No battles when it's raining," Brand said.

"Oh. I hadn't thought of that. Back home it meant we'd have chicken for supper. Before the war, that is. During the war we ate parched corn and a few scrawny quail our overseer killed."

"Rain for me means riding on patrol at all hours of the day and night and watching the tracks I'd been following disappear in the mud."

Again she said nothing, just lay beside him, listening.

"What about when you were young?"

"When I was young rain meant finding a stable or a barn to sleep in."

"You had no home then?"

"Nope."

"We surely had different childhoods," she said.

Brand noticed her bent knee was touching his thigh and wondered if she realized it. Probably not.

"You ever wonder whether you wanted the life you were born into? Servants and fine china and lace curtains on the windows?"

"Even poor people have curtains on their windows, Brand. And no, I never wondered about it, not until I started off with the wagon train in Missouri. Actually, even then Mr. Monroe took such good care of me I never wondered too much about anything. I never thought about such things until you and I started riding west together."

"You sorry?"

She waited a long, long time before answering. Just when his nerves were beginning to fray, she spoke. "No," she said. "I am not sorry. I have learned a great deal, and—" she hesitated, and his nerves stretched taut again "—and I am not sorry that I met you."

Her voice was beginning to sound drowsy. With any luck she'd drop off to sleep and he could shift his weight off his aching shoulder.

"Brand?"

"Yeah?"

"Are you warm?"

"Yeah."

"Then could you put your arm around me? I'm getting cold."

Oh, hell, yes he'd put his arm around her. He rolled toward her, slid one arm under her shoulders and pulled her flush against him. She gave a sleepy little sigh and snuggled her head under his chin.

"Suzannah?"

"Hmm?"

"Are we friends or enemies?"

"Friends, I think. Even though we don't get along sometimes, we are friends. I think so, anyway. Do you think so?"

He didn't know what the answer to that was. But he sure wished he had some whiskey hidden in a flask somewhere to help him think about it.

Somewhere around midnight, he guessed, Suzannah gave a soft sigh and wriggled even closer to his rigid body. Made him feel almost poetic inside, something that might be described as sweet agony. He wrapped both arms around her, rested his lips against her hair and finally let himself drift off to sleep.

At first light he woke with a start to find her propped up on one elbow, staring down into his face with eyes that were soft as moss.

"I watched you while you were sleeping," she said.

He'd watched her, too, in the long, dark hours before she'd moved smack up against him. She looked beautiful. And sweet, like a child.

He took a careful breath. "Yeah? Do I snore?"

"No, you do not." Then her face changed and a little frown wrinkled her forehead. "Do I?"

"No. You talk in your sleep, though."

Her impossibly green eyes widened. "Oh, land sakes alive, what did I say?"

"Nuthin' much. Something about your momma

and some. about this John you're so all-fired up to see."

"Wh-what about John? What did I say?"

Brand would be damned if he'd tell her. What she'd uttered was a bunch of noes and something about her horse.

"You said, 'Good evening, John. Welcome to Marlborough.'"

"That's our plantation. I guess I was remembering back when he visited. It seems like eons ago."

"The rain's stopped," he said to change the subject. "Hear the birds? Chickadees and sparrows."

She cocked her head to listen. He loved hearing birds sing in the morning. Even dead tired after a long patrol, if he woke up to a meadowlark or some chattering finches he didn't feel as lonely as he sometimes did. Sometimes, after days of nothing but hard riding and drunken talk at night, he felt so empty inside he ached. He'd never known what it was he was missing.

Until now.

"Suzannah, let's crawl on out of here and get going. We've got almost four days' hard traveling between here and Fort Klamath."

"Ye-es," she said slowly. But she didn't move.

"Suzannah?"

All at once she bent her head and brushed her lips over his. "Brand, there's something I want you to know."

He reached to the back of her neck and held her there, an inch from his mouth. "What is it?"

"Even with all your rough edges—and they are very rough indeed by Southern standards—I think that you are a fine man. A wonderful man, in fact. My papa would have liked you."

God, he wanted to kiss her so bad his arm shook. "You know, you're gonna waste yourself on your lieutenant. Next time he kisses you, I want you to remember this."

He pulled her head down to his and kissed her long and hard. Then he did it again, softer and even longer. She made him weak with yearning and hard with wanting. Four more days of this and he'd be nothing but a shell of himself.

When he released her, she gave him a long, puzzled look and scooted backward out of the tent. He lay there another full minute, feeling dazed and hungry, and then he followed her out into the wintry sunshine.

She'd disappeared behind a bush. He allowed a few minutes before he went to check the horses.

When she reappeared her face was dripping wet. "There's rainwater everywhere," she announced. "Little pools under those leafy shrubs, what are they called?

"Salal. You can eat the berries."

She grinned at him and clapped on her hat. "I already did."

He strode off to tend to the horses, and when he returned she had rolled up their blankets and dismantled the tent and folded it up. Lord God, she was an unusual woman. Surprising. Resilient. Adventurous. And, oh, she was desirable as hell.

Suzannah spent all morning on the trail thinking about Brandon Wyler. Why did kissing him make her feel all shaky and happy inside? She had kissed

John only twice, once when he proposed and again when he'd ridden away from the plantation, but neither kiss had felt anything like Brand's.

She puzzled over it as she rode, and by noon, when the horses were struggling up the last steep switchback before reaching the top of the mountain, she had sorted it all out.

She was attracted to him. More than attracted. When he smiled at her, her breath came short, and when he shouted at her she wanted to crawl behind a rock and hide. But when he just rode along ahead of her, as he was doing now, she could study him, the tall frame and broad shoulders, the wide-brimmed hat he never took off except when he slept, the easy, loose-jointed way he moved with his horse. His voice, all rumbly when he was tired. And the look he sometimes got in his gray eyes, as if waiting for something.

And the exquisite, trembly feel of his mouth on hers. That she mulled over more than anything.

But remember, Suzannah Cumberland, you are already spoken for.

"Dismount," Brand suddenly ordered. "Stretch your muscles. And look at the view from up here."

She scrambled off her mare and gazed past him. From the top of the mountain, forested hills and green valleys seemed to roll on forever. Oh, it was lovely!

"This is beautiful country," she breathed.

"See that river down there? We'll be crossing it today."

Suzannah stared at the silvery ribbon winding

through a flat green valley below them. "That is beautiful, too."

"You might not think so when we reach it. Probably swollen because of the rain."

Before she could question him, he'd started on down the other side. Whistling.

The three men halted and drew their horses into a circle. "That her?"

"Yeah. Looks diff'rent in them jeans, but that's her, all right."

"She carry the money on her?"

"Nah. Too heavy. Prob'ly in that saddlebag."

"She sure ain't headin' to Texas, like that feller said. They're headin' west."

"Thought the guy you shot was dead, Shorty. The man with her looks suspiciously like him."

"Guess I only winged him, Red. Coulda' sworn—"

"Aw, ferget it. We've got her in our sights now. Just a matter of getting the drop on 'em."

"And getting our hands on that money."

The man called Red scratched his bristly chin. "So, what do we do now?"

"Follow 'em. Wait fer a chance to…you know, get our hands on the woman, and then…"

"And then what? We gonna kidnap her?"

"Maybe."

"What about the guy ridin' with her?"

"Well, hell, Red, you shot 'im once, now you're gonna get a second chance."

Brand reined up on the riverbank and sat studying the situation. *Swollen* wasn't even half-accurate.

What had been a lazy, meandering river when he'd returned from Marcy's funeral a little while ago was now a raging froth of brown-green water with cross-currents and swirling eddies that swept along small logs.

He'd seen it like this before. It usually took two or three days for the water to recede, but he didn't have two or three days. He had to get Suzannah to Fort Klamath intact before he lost his head and jumped her while she lay beside him some night.

He'd never ravished a woman before, especially not a virgin who was engaged to another man. But the truth was he didn't trust himself to wait another two or three extra days, and nights, for the Snake River to drop to its normal level. He'd look for a place where they could get two horses across.

After riding along the bank two miles in each direction, he found it. Wasn't pretty, but it looked possible.

"Can you swim?"

She shot him a frowning look. "N-no."

Brand swore under his breath. Couldn't cook. Couldn't shoot. Couldn't swim. She didn't belong out here in the West; she belonged down south on a plantation where life was slow and easy and servants did everything.

"We're gonna ride our horses into the water, and when it gets deep enough they'll start to swim. All you have to do is hold on tight and let the horse do the work."

Her face looked white and drawn with fear.

"Think you can do that?" he asked.

First she shook her head, then after a moment she

nodded and tried to smile. "A-all right. I suppose I can do that."

Brand groaned. For damn sure she didn't want to. "Suzannah, as long as you don't lose your nerve, you'll be safe."

"I w-will not lose my nerve," she said. "I promise."

He couldn't look at her. "I'll go in ahead of you. You follow exactly where my horse goes, you got that?"

She nodded and grabbed her reins in a death grip.

Brand started down the bank and splashed into the river.

Chapter Fifteen

Suzannah kept her eyes on Brand's black horse as it moved forward into the raging water, gripped the reins tight and urged her mare to follow. With each step the water grew deeper and deeper, tumbling around the animal's legs, then rising to its hindquarters. The urge to shut her eyes and pray was overwhelming.

When the roiling water reached her knees, she felt the mare stop all motion, and suddenly she realized it was floating. No, she thought in amazement, it was swimming! At least, she prayed it was swimming. The river swirled over her thighs, and she held tight to the reins and tried desperately to remember what else Brand had said.

He was ahead of her. She must have cried out because he twisted in the saddle to look back at her. "Grab onto the mane," he shouted.

She kept hold of the reins but bent forward and dug her fingers into the mare's coarse neck hair. All at once one of her boots slipped out of the stirrup, and the next thing she knew she started to tilt.

"Brand!" she screamed.

Before she could draw breath she felt the icy water close over her head. She clawed her way up until her head broke the surface, and then Brand was there, hoisting her up out of the river and onto his lap.

With his reins in one hand he wrapped his other arm around her, and she clung to his safe, solid body.

"Think I ripped your shirt," he shouted.

"What?" His horse was swimming along toward the opposite bank, and she saw that Brand had hold of her mare's reins and was pulling it along beside them.

"Your shirt," he yelled over the sound of the rushing river. "I grabbed the neck of your shirt to haul you out. Think it ripped."

"Doesn't matter," she screamed near his ear.

"Does matter. I paid for it!"

She couldn't suppress a choked laugh, and all at once they were sloshing out of the river and clambering up the bank onto solid ground. He dropped both sets of reins, slid her off his lap onto the ground and dismounted.

She was so jelly-legged she couldn't stand. Brand grasped her shoulders to steady her. "You okay, Suzannah?"

"Yes, but I can't seem to stand up."

He scooped her up into his arms and carried her across a marshy flat to an expanse of gray-green sorrel and tule grass.

"I'll build a fire. You need to get out of those wet things."

"Out here?" She stared at him. "But it—it's so flat. Someone might see me!"

He had to laugh. "Which would you rather be, embarrassed or down with pneumonia?"

He had to scout a ways in ever-widening circles

before he found wood, and even then the branches were spindly and not too dry. When he returned to Suzannah, she was shaking with cold and her teeth were chattering.

"Strip," he ordered.

"Oh, but—"

"You want to die of pneumonia? I said strip!"

She turned her back and began unbuttoning her shirt, then unbuckled her jeans. By the time she'd pared down to her underthings he had a fire going.

He rustled one of his clean shirts out of his saddlebag.

"Put this on."

"Y-yes, s-sir." She buttoned his shirt up to her chin and managed to wriggle out of her wet camisole and drawers. The shirt came down below her butt, but he turned his back anyway.

"Don't put the socks on yet," he said over his shoulder. "Gotta dry out your boots first."

He undid his bedroll and wrapped her up in a dry blanket, sat her down on a log by the fire and went to look for some sticks to prop her boots on. Finally he squatted down on his haunches in front of her.

"Getting warm?"

She nodded and tugged the blanket tighter around her shoulders. "Brand, you are soaking wet, too."

"Not too much. My jeans'll dry out and I'll prop my boots next to yours."

She looked up, her face pinched. "What are we going to do now?"

"Now? Sit here until we're dry, then we move on."

"Could we stay here? Pitch your tent and—"

"Nope." He'd be damned if he'd risk another night scrunched up next to her in his tiny little tent.

"But—"

"No."

Both sets of boots started to steam. Brand tried to calculate how long it would take to get them reasonably dry and how many hours of daylight they had left. Boots first, he figured.

To keep himself too busy to admire Suzannah's long bare legs poking out from the blanket, he rubbed down the horses with dried tule grass, unpacked the coffeepot and boiled up some double-strength coffee, and sliced off some jerky for lunch. Then he checked the bedrolls and repacked both saddlebags.

When he finished he turned toward the fire and allowed himself a good long look at her. Her braid had come undone and her hair was beginning to fluff around her face. In the late-afternoon sunlight it looked like spun gold.

He clamped his jaws tight and looked away.

Suzannah sat on the log in front of the fire for as long as she could stand it, then sprang to her feet. "Stop pacing around like that! Come and sit down by the fire."

"Can't" came his terse reply.

"Why can't you? It's not going to make my clothes dry any faster if you keep walking about. Watching you is making me dizzy."

"Then don't watch."

"Oh, for mercy's sake. Why are you so bad tempered? You would think I fell in the river on purpose."

He didn't answer. Maddening man! That's what

he always did when he was angry about something and she was being logical—he answered in monosyllables and refused to look at her. Finally he paused in his pacing to run his hand over the shirt and jeans he'd draped over the bush.

"Are they dry?" she called.

"Dry enough. Get dressed."

She gritted her teeth. Brand issued orders just like an army officer. Well, of course he *was* an army officer, or he had been one. She guessed the military discipline never rubbed off.

He snatched her outer garments off the bush, stalked over to where she sat enveloped in his blanket and dropped them at her feet. Then he strode off to the other bush and, with just his thumb and forefinger, lifted off her muslin drawers and camisole as if they were red-hot. These he carefully laid on top of the pile in front of her.

She shrugged out of the blanket. "I'll just go over behind that bush and—"

"I'll turn my back."

She bent to gather up her dry clothes. "How do I know I can trust you?"

Very deliberately he faced away from her and propped his hands at his waist. "Trust is a funny thing," he said. "Takes time to build it, and it can all crumble in a split second."

She had no answer to that. She moved behind the largest bush, stepped into her drawers and hiked them up. "Is your back still turned?"

He snorted at that. "I may be a lot of things, Suzannah, got rough manners and not much book learnin', and I have a healthy dislike for most people, but I'm not dishonest. Sometimes I wish to God I was."

"Yes," she said quickly, "I understand. I truly do understand." She drew her camisole over her head and tied the ribbon.

"We've been on the trail together for over six days now. Ridin' together. Eatin' together. Even sleepin' together, in a general sort of way. I haven't done one damn thing to cause you to distrust me, have I?" He was addressing the horses, tied up opposite the bush she was dressing behind.

"N-no," she said uncertainly. She pulled on her almost dry jeans. The cloth belt with all her cash had been dried right along with her jeans. She'd forgotten about it, and now she prayed her money was all there.

"Brand, did you find—?"

"Yep. It's all dry and none's missing. Kinda thought you'd ask about it before now, Suzannah. Kinda careless of you."

She bit her lip and buttoned up her shirt. "I did not ask you because...I...I guess I do trust you. Otherwise I suppose that would have been uppermost in my mind."

"You decent yet?"

"Yes, except for my boots."

He pivoted, snatched her boots off the sticks propping them before the fire, then snagged her socks off the hot rocks and tossed them to her.

The socks felt deliciously warm. The boot leather still felt damp and the fit was so tight she couldn't tug them on. This must be why cowboys out west preferred riding to walking; the thought of another set of blisters made her stomach tight.

Brand squatted next to her. "Give me your foot." He massaged her cold toes with his strong, warm hands, then slid her foot into the boot and yanked it up tight. After he drew on the second one, he stood up.

"Stomp around some, see if they're on right."

She laughed. "I have not 'stomped around' since I was seven years old."

"Do it anyway."

She made a quick circuit around the fire pit. "They fit all right, but they feel a bit tight."

He nodded and handed over her money belt, which she tied around her waist. Then she turned away to retuck her shirt in to hide it.

Yes, she did trust Brandon Wyler. And that was "perplexin' strange," as Hattie used to say. He was as different from a Southern gentleman as dawn from midnight, but she did trust him. After all, he carried four hundred dollars' worth of her gold, wrapped up in a sock in the bottom of his saddlebag.

Chapter Sixteen

Brand reined in and stopped. He felt someone watching him; couldn't say why, just that for the past two hours he'd been aware of prickles along the back of his neck. He pulled up and sat studying the winding trail ahead.

"What's wrong?" Suzannah called.

"Don't know, exactly. Maybe nothing." He surveyed the clear blue sky overhead, where a buzzard soared over the treetops. As he watched, it gradually circled lower. The air smelled of pine and something else he couldn't put a finger on. Something sharp and raw. Smoke? An Indian camp?

He started forward again. It didn't help that they were riding into the sun. Ahead was a stand of thick woods, and as they moved into it he thought he heard something. He reined in, motioned for Suzannah to stay silent and listened.

Crows screamed overhead. "Must be a rabbit or something," he said at last. "Suzannah, ride ahead of me." He didn't want her behind him where he couldn't keep track of her. It was bad enough being out here in the wilderness with nothing but his instincts and a rifle, but Suzannah added another dimension. He felt responsible for her. He wanted to protect her.

Face it, Wyler, you'd die to keep her safe.

Well, hell. When had that happened? When had her well-being become more important than his own?

They rode for some time without talking, and little by little he realized she was as wary as he was. Did she also feel like somebody was watching them?

He stared hard at every clump of bushes and shady spot under the alder trees until his eyes burned. Nothing. When night fell he wanted to be out of these trees.

"Let's move a little faster," he called.

She nodded and nudged the mare into an easy canter. When they stopped to water the horses, he snared a trout in the brook and after another hour of traveling he called a halt.

"We'll camp here." They were almost out of the trees, just coming into a long valley dotted with camas and sprangly wild roses. Dusk sent gray shadows across the trail and the sky turned red-orange and then purple as the sun sank behind the hills to the west. Pretty, but it sure was cold.

Suzannah slid off her horse and immediately made for a copse of leafy ash trees while Brand unsaddled both horses and started a fire. He'd just gutted the fish and knelt to set the coffeepot on the fire when he heard an odd sound.

He cocked his head. "Suzannah?"

No answer.

Didn't take a woman that long to… He stood up and moved slowly toward the trees where he'd last seen her.

He jerked when he saw her, butt down in the dirt,

pinned between a scruffy-looking man's knees. A dirty hand was clapped over her mouth, and her eyes were wide with fear. Automatically his right hand twitched toward the Colt on his hip, then he felt the hard barrel of a gun at his back.

"Don't do anything sudden, mister." The voice came from his left. So there were two of them. He studied the man holding Suzannah. The same fat guy he thought he'd sent off to Texas. Then he remembered there had been three of them.

Someone lifted his revolver out of its holster and shoved him forward. "We was just askin' the lady 'bout all that money."

"What money?"

"The money the lady brought with her from Missouri."

"She doesn't have it any longer. Left it with the sutler at Fort Hall."

"Nah, she didn't." The man on his left, the one with the bristly chin, nudged him down beside Suzannah. "She's payin' you with something, ain't she?"

"Nope. Let her talk, she'll tell you she's not payin' me anything."

The man removed his meaty hand from her mouth. "That right, honey? You ain't payin' him?"

She wiped her hand across her lips. "That is correct. The major was…was ordered to accompany me to Oregon. Payment was not included."

"That right?" Quick as a flash he twisted her arm behind her back and yanked upward. "You sure that's right?"

She cried out and Brand clenched his fists.

"That is correct," she repeated. "I told you that before."

Another yank on her arm, and her breath hissed in.

"Let her go!" Brand shouted. "Only a coward would hurt a woman."

He twisted her arm higher. "Yeah? Well, I guess I'm a—"

Brand launched himself sideways at the man, but the other two pounced on him and dragged him off, then pinned his arms behind him.

"I asked you where it is, honey. It's only gonna get worse if you don't tell us." He tightened his grip and she gasped.

"All right, I'll tell you," she cried. "It's…it's hidden in my saddlebag."

Brand blinked. It was no such thing. He'd dropped all her gold coins into a clean sock, knotted the top and shoved it in *his* saddlebag. In a special secret rawhide pouch he'd personally stitched into the lining before they'd left Fort Hall. So why…?

Because, you idiot, she wants to distract them.

Fatso released her and stood up. "Okay, lady, let's go get it. You first."

Suzannah stumbled to her feet and took a step forward. Brand leaped up and grabbed her shoulder.

She looked straight into his eyes. "I'm sorry, Brand. I didn't want to tell them, but…" She gave a convincing sniffle.

He snaked his arm around her shoulder. "You couldn't help it," he said loudly.

She leaned into him. "Get ready," she breathed.

In answer he tightened his fingers about her shoulder and squeezed once.

They emerged into the clearing where the horses stood waiting, and suddenly Suzannah's legs buckled and she sank to the ground directly in Fatso's path. When her knees connected with the spongy forest duff, Fatso checked his stride to avoid stepping on her, and in that instant Brand reached behind him, closed his hand around the barrel of the rifle pressing at his back and jerked it forward. Off balance, the man stumbled forward.

Brand then swung the barrel wide and rammed the butt backward into the man's belly. He doubled over, and Brand yanked the rifle out of his hands, spun and leveled the weapon at his chest.

In the same instant Suzannah reared backward, knocked Fatso's revolver out of his hand and pounced on it before he could recover. She fired a shot at him, but it went wide and just nicked his upper arm. Fatso backed off, hands raised, and she fired again. This time she hit his shoulder.

"What the—?"

The third man, bringing up the rear, went for his holster, but Brand put a bullet into the pine needles at his feet and he froze. Suzannah stepped forward and lifted away his gun.

"Turn around," Brand ordered. "If you want to ride out of here in one piece, keeping moving toward your horses."

"You gonna shoot us?" Fatso panted.

Brand spit off to one side. "Maybe." He herded the three men into a tight knot. "Take off your boots and your pants, all of you. Throw them over here."

"Hell, we cain't go nowhere half-nekkid! Cain't ride with no boots, neither."

"Should have thought of that before."

Hesitantly Fatso unbuckled his belt, let his jeans drop to his hips, then turned away from Suzannah. Brand had to laugh at that. The other two men stripped in front of her, and the pile of clothing at his feet grew.

"Now, mount up."

The three half-dressed outlaws lumbered awkwardly to their horses and dragged themselves up into the saddle, where they sat nervously eyeing Brand's rifle and the revolver in Suzannah's hand. Fatso leaned down and suddenly made a grab for it, and she fired a bullet into the meaty part of his other shoulder.

"Keep movin," Brand snapped. "If you're real lucky that band of Indian braves won't pick up your trail."

"I-Indians?" Fatso stuttered.

"Yep. All painted up like Christmas," Brand observed thoughtfully. "Might be a war party."

"C'mon, boys, let's get outta here!"

"I wouldn't go anywhere near Fort Hall if I were you," Brand said, his voice lazy. "Soldiers are out lookin' for whoever shot Mr. Monroe."

"You ain't sendin' us out there with no weapons, are ya?"

"Damn right," Brand snapped.

Suzannah watched the dust puff after the three pounding horses and all at once she got the shakes. Brand lifted the revolver out of her grasp, stashed the extra rifle across her saddle pack and slid both revolvers into his saddlebag.

"Feel like some supper?"

Chapter Seventeen

All through supper, while they ate the fish Brand fried and drank the coffee he made, he studied the woman across the campfire as if he'd never seen her before. Finally Suzannah couldn't stand it any longer.

"Would you mind telling me why you keep staring at me? Is there dirt on my face?"

"No, there's no dirt on your face. It's what's on the inside I'm puzzling over."

"Well, what? What is on my inside?"

He tossed the dregs of his coffee into the fire. "Not sure. Thought I had you pretty well figured out, but now I'm kinda puzzled."

"I would venture to say that no man is ever sure what a woman is really like on the inside."

He blinked. "Works two ways, doesn't it? Does a woman ever know what a *man* is really like on the inside?"

"Why, of course she does! Girls learn those things practically from the cradle. At least Southern girls do."

One eyebrow quirked. "First you fake a fainting spell and grab Fatso's revolver, then you put a bullet into his arm. And then you do it again. Are all Southern girls that brave?"

"I was not brave," she admitted. "I was frightened to death."

"Can't imagine how the South lost the war," he murmured.

She grimaced. *The war.* No Southerner would ever forget the War Between the States, the men who would never come home, the women who starved and made do with scraps of food and rags on their backs.

"Well, to be honest, I *was* frightened. That does not mean I was helpless."

He just looked at her, then shook his head. "You know something? If you think you're frightened, you're lyin' to yourself, Suzannah. Either that or you're lyin' to me."

She was quiet for a long moment. "I want to tell you something, Brand. About the war. About me. We call it the War of Northern Aggression. Did you know that? We, the women at home, had to learn to be strong. We had to, otherwise we would have died. We learned how to endure—that is different from being brave. We lived with fear every minute of every day for four long years. We did it because we had to."

Again he shook his head, but there was an expression in his eyes she could not read. It didn't change when he rose and stowed the supper plates in his saddlebag, or when he rolled out his bedroll beside the campfire and shucked his boots. He stretched out with his hands locked behind his head and kept looking at her.

It made her nervous in a funny way, as if he could see all the way inside her. She wondered if he liked what he saw.

Brand watched her smooth out her blankets on the opposite side of the fire and arrange her saddlebag to use as a pillow. *Who was this woman?* She was slim and delicate looking. Only came up to his chin, and he would swear her hands had never done a day's work in her life. But when push came to shove, she sure stiffened her spine. She'd showed real ingenuity, too, faking a fainting spell and snatching Fatso's revolver. And guts.

He couldn't stop thinking about it. Sure was glad she was on *his* side; he'd hate to think how fast she could tie his spurs in a knot.

In the morning he stirred up the coals, made coffee and waited for the sun to come up. The sky turned pink before Suzannah woke up; by the time she sat up and yawned, it was like a big blue bowl over their heads.

She was rumpled and her hair tumbled haphazardly about her shoulders, but God in heaven, she was so beautiful it made his throat ache. Sure hoped the man waiting for her in Oregon appreciated what he was getting. And he'd better be something special enough to deserve her.

"Coffee?" He set a mug near her elbow. She gulped it down while he rolled both bedrolls, fed the horses and packed up the coffeepot.

Then he started toward the saddled horses. "Let's mount up and—" His words stopped and he looked beyond her, his eyes narrowed.

A puff of gray dust rose across the wide valley before them. Brand swore and ran for his rifle.

"Get over there behind that bush," he said sharply.

Hoofbeats drew close, and Suzannah peered out

between the branches. A very young man, too skinny to fill out his blue army shirt, hauled his winded horse to a stop and bent over the saddle horn, panting audibly.

Brand lowered his rifle. "Where ya goin' in such a hurry, son?"

"In-Indians," the kid gasped. "Lots of 'em. Moving south and heading this way."

"What kind of Indians?"

"Kind? Whaddya mean, *kind*, mister? Indians are Indians."

"No, Indians are *not* just Indians. You think all white men are the same? I mean what tribe," Brand said calmly.

"Dunno. Got red skins an' paint on their faces. I'm ridin' to Fort Klamath to report 'em."

"Nez Perce, most likely," Brand said. "They head south from Canada about this time every year."

"Oh. Well, I gotta report 'em anyway." Without another word the boy reined away and kicked his mount into a gallop.

"Brand? What should we do?"

"Nuthin'. If it was a war party, you wouldn't see hide nor hair of them until it was too late. If it's the Nez Perce on the way to their winter camp, nuthin' to do but watch 'em."

"Are you sure?"

"I'm sure. Don't you trust me?" he added with a chuckle. "Mount up."

He rolled up the blanket behind his saddle, kicked dirt over the fire and pulled himself onto the horse next to her, still laughing.

Chapter Eighteen

At noon two days later, they rode past the sentries into Fort Klamath. Despite being one of the oldest forts in the northwest, it was well preserved, with white-painted buildings, a well-maintained, grassy parade ground and a prosperous-looking sutler's store.

Brand walked up the wooden steps to the corporal's office with Suzannah at his heels. The officer behind the battered desk leaped to his feet and saluted him. Guess he was still known out here.

When the man laid eyes on Suzannah, the cigarette he was nursing almost fell out of his mouth. "Ma'am. Miss. Uh, Missus—"

"Don't go there, Corporal," Brand said. "Miss Cumberland isn't married. Yet."

Brand took her aside. "You want to find your intended right away?"

"Oh, no," she whispered. "I need to bathe and don fresh clothes first. I would never want John to see me like this. I have a dress in the bottom of my saddlebag."

Brand turned back to the officer. "Corporal, Miss Cumberland will be staying with Colonel McLeod and his wife."

"Very good, sir. Shall I—?"

"No, I'll escort her over myself."

"Colonel McLeod's hosting a Christmas Eve ball for officers and their wives this evening, Major. I'm sure Miss Cumberland would be an honored guest. And you, too, sir," he added hastily.

Brand gave the man a long look. He hadn't been an *honored guest* at any social gathering for years, ever since he'd knocked out an overbearing soldier for pawing a young woman guest.

"Could someone see to our horses?"

"Of course, sir."

Suzannah tugged his arm. "Brand, I need my saddlebag."

He grabbed it off her mare before the young soldier led both mounts off to the stable. It was the same young man who'd warned them about the Indians, and he sent Brand a sheepish smile.

Brand walked Suzannah over to Colonel McLeod's quarters, a white-painted house with a wraparound porch and red roses climbing up a trellis. A wreath of dark green holly hung on the front door. At the bottom of the wide wooden steps, Suzannah again tugged his arm.

"Brand, will you stay?"

"Stay? You mean at the colonel's house?"

"No, I mean for the ball tonight? You see, I don't know anyone."

"Except for John."

"Oh, please, Brand. Just for tonight. Now that I am really here, for some reason I am feeling very unsure of myself."

Brand looked down into her moss-green eyes. The last thing he wanted to do was ride away from her. He'd dreaded it ever since that first night on the trail when he'd dropped her into the creek. Somehow he'd known even then that this was different, that *she* was different.

And the first time he'd kissed her and felt her heart flutter against his chest, he'd felt something move deep inside him that had never been there before. Every hour since that moment, he'd been lying to himself. Now that it was here, now that he had to leave her, he was damn sure he didn't want to. In fact, he wasn't sure he'd be able to.

"All right, Suzannah. I'll stay. Just for tonight." He turned her toward the colonel's front door.

"Will you come to the ball tonight?"

"To be honest, I don't want to. Hate crowds of people in stuffy rooms and—"

"Can you dance?"

"What? Oh, sure, but—"

"Then I will see you tonight, Brand." With that she walked up the steps to the front door. Brand knocked, and when the door swung open he found himself instantly enveloped in a floury embrace.

"Brand! What in the world are you doing here?"

"Delivering someone." He gestured to Suzannah. "Violet, this is Suzannah Cumberland."

Mrs. McLeod's bright blue eyes widened. "Why, my dear, I took you for a boy in those duds! My heavens, wherever did you come from?"

"South Carolina, Mrs. McLeod."

"Oh, surely not!" She inspected Suzannah's wrinkled shirt and dirty jeans.

"She started off in Missouri," Brand volunteered.

"On a wagon train. We came from Fort Hall on horseback."

"I have come out west to marry my fiancé, Lieutenant Walters."

The older woman's face changed, but she quickly recovered. She turned to Brand, whose attention just at that moment had been caught elsewhere. "Brand, I haven't seen you in years."

Mrs. McLeod led the way to her front parlor, where a huge decorated Christmas tree stood in one corner. Both Brand and Suzannah declined the offer of a velvet-covered chair.

"Trail dust," Brand explained.

"Oh, of course. My dear, I'd wager you would like a bath?"

After the colonel's wife had shown Suzannah upstairs, Brand went off to the sutler's for a bottle of good whiskey and then headed for the officers' barracks.

Violet McLeod patted Suzannah's cold hand. "Why, of course we know your lieutenant, my dear. Would you like to reunite with him now? Or would you prefer to freshen up some first?"

All Suzannah could do was nod. She must look sadly trail weary—filthy, even. She wanted to look beautiful for John. That was one of the things he had complimented her on.

Oh, if only she didn't feel so alone! If only Brand…

If only Brand what?

An hour later she sat up in the tin bathtub and

buried her face in her hands. If only Brand could stay forever.

But I will be married soon. I will have no need of Brand.

The thought of her marriage brought her no comfort. She sat motionless in the tepid water for a long half hour, then busied herself scrubbing her sun-browned skin and washing her dirt-encrusted hair.

Just as she finished combing out her wet curls, Mrs. McLeod poked her head into the guest bedroom. "Miss Cumberland, your young lieutenant is downstairs in the parlor waiting to see you." The older woman's smile made her wrinkled face seem almost youthful.

Suzannah's thoughts flew into a frenzied jumble. "Oh! I— Well, I did not expect him so soon."

"My dear, the corporal on duty sent word to him. I am quite sure the moment your fiancé heard you had arrived he lost no time in—"

"But I am not ready! I brought only one dress, and I was saving that for my wedding. All I have to wear is what I wore on the trail, my jeans and a boy's shirt."

"I think Lieutenant Walters will not mind when he sees you at last. It has been many months, has it not?"

"Almost six months, yes." Six long, unsettling months. She scarcely felt she was the same person she had been before she left South Carolina.

"I will ask him to wait, shall I?" Mrs. McLeod pursued.

"Y-yes. Tell him…tell him I will be down directly."

The instant the door closed Suzannah dashed

to the mirror over the maple chest of drawers and peered at herself. A stranger looked back at her. A stranger with tanned skin, a sun-reddened nose and strands of wet hair hanging to her shoulders.

Heavens, her hair! Should she braid it, as she had while traveling? Or perhaps pile it up on top of her head, as she had worn it at home? She grasped a handful of her shiny blond mane and studied it. It was too long to pin up. Quickly she plaited the thick tresses into a single fat braid and secured it with the yellow ribbon she'd hidden in her saddlebag.

Then she pulled on her jeans and a clean blue-checked shirt, pinched her cheeks and drew in a shaky breath. She was terrified, and she had no idea why.

Lieutenant John Walters, here I am at last.

She walked slowly down the staircase to the McLeod's parlor and tapped on the open door. The slim young man in an army uniform jolted to his feet and stood staring at her with his mouth open.

"Miss Cumberland?"

"Yes, John, it is I."

He swallowed audibly. "Miss—Suzannah, is it really you? You look, well, you look an awful lot different."

"That is not at all surprising," she said, hoping she sounded calm and dignified. "I have been traveling for the past six months to reach you."

"Have you?" His gaze moved from her shirt to her jeans. "You're dressed kind of strange."

"Well, yes. I have been traveling, as I said. A dress was not practical on the trail."

He glanced down to the hem of her jeans. "You're barefoot!"

Suzannah gulped. In her haste to dress, she had forgotten her boots. And her socks. Her bare toes curled under on the polished wood floor.

"John, are you not glad to see me?"

His expression changed. "Yes, yes, of course I am. Of course. But…" He peered at her face. "I didn't expect you to look so, um, different. Your face is all suntanned."

"My hands and arms, too." She extended them for his inspection. "I wore a hat, but it didn't help all that much."

"I see. Yes, I do see. Your nose is sunburned, too. Women should not be allowed to be out in the hot sun."

Allowed? A flash of irritation poked at her. Why did he not ask if she was in good health? Or if the journey had been comfortable? Or if she were well rested?

Why does he not kiss me? Or at least take my hand?

"You look just the same," she said. "Just as I remember you." In truth he was shorter than she remembered, but he had the same crisp uniform and the same reddish-brown hair and brown eyes.

He said nothing, just kept staring at her.

The door opened and Mrs. McLeod set a tea tray on the low table, then retreated without a word.

"Would you care for some tea?" Suzannah asked in her most polite, entertain-her-guest voice.

"What? Oh, sure. Tea. Of course." He sank down onto the settee. Suzannah moved forward, settled herself beside him and lifted the teapot. At least she had not forgotten her manners.

"Would you care for milk? Or sugar?"

"What? I, uh, Miss Cumb—Suzannah, you look quite…different."

"I will look more like myself tonight at the ball. I will be wearing a dress, one you may remember. Yellow, with flounces at the hem." She waited.

He looked blank.

As calmly as she could manage, she poured a delicate blue-flowered cup full of tea, settled it on the matching saucer and handed it to him. Her hand shook.

"Men don't, uh, remember dresses," he said at last. "Men remember mountain trails and Indian villages they've burned. And other things like that. Not dresses."

Suzannah blinked. Did he not remember the night he had proposed? The night she had worn her favorite yellow dress? He had said she looked beautiful—"pretty as a jonquil" were his words. Surely it would all come back to him tonight when he saw her at the ball?

"These garments I am now wearing must look odd to you, John. I had to wear them because we— that is, Major Wyler and I—traveled from Fort Hall on horseback."

"Fort Hall, huh? You rode all the way from Fort Hall?"

"Yes." She poured herself a cup of tea and took what she hoped was a ladylike sip. How she wished she could add some of Brand's whiskey! "It took us almost ten days to reach Fort Klamath."

"I see. I didn't know you even rode a horse, Suzannah."

"Well, to be truthful, I didn't. At least not at first. So I learned."

"A woman's proper place is not on a horse. It is in the parlor. Or the kitchen."

In the kitchen? Whom did he think he was marrying?

He hadn't touched his tea, she noted. The flowered china saucer sat balanced on his knee, held in place with a forefinger touching the cup.

"John, you are pleased that I came, are you not?"

His cup rattled. "Oh, sure. Sure I am."

"Are you surprised?"

He looked stricken. "I am, yes. Actually I'm…in shock, I guess."

"But you did expect me, did you not?"

"Uh, sure I did."

She felt a little sorry for him. She guessed it wasn't every day a man's fiancée turned up so unexpectedly. She rescued his cup and saucer and offered him the plate of iced Christmas cookies.

But he *had* invited her to come out west to marry him! When she assumed the duties of an officer's wife, he would be glad she had come.

Tonight she would make sure he remembered her yellow dress. And her. They would dance together again, as they had on that moonlit night back in South Carolina, and he would realize…everything.

She rose. "I must retire and rest." She turned her most gracious smile on his reddened face and smiled. "Until this evening, John."

Chapter Nineteen

Brand shook his head to clear away the whiskey-induced fog in his brain. After dropping Suzannah off at Colonel McLeod's, he'd downed more than a few, and now he had to pull himself together to attend Charlie and Violet's Christmas Eve ball. He rolled off the cot and stood up.

The china pitcher and basin on the bureau across the room beckoned. Sure would like a bath, but he guessed he'd have to make do with sponging off. He shrugged off his tan shirt and began to unbutton his trousers.

Half an hour later he'd scrubbed off the worst of the sweat and grime from the trail, shaved and slicked back his dark hair. He hoped he looked halfway civilized; he wanted to leave Suzannah with a decent image of him.

Suzannah. Oh, damn.

Tonight would be the last time he'd ever see her, and the thought put a rock in his belly as big and sharp-edged as a craggy mountaintop. Funny how she'd grown on him in just ten days. Not so funny how much he wanted to keep her by his side. He'd never wanted to do that before with any woman; now he wanted it so much it made him ache.

Ah, hell, Wyler, what'd you expect? You let your

guard down with a woman like Suzannah and wham!
Your heart gets clobbered.

He stuffed his clean shirt into his jeans and gave
himself one last look in the wavy glass over the
washbasin. A damn fool stared back at him.

The ball was well under way by the time Brand
entered the overheated, heavily perfumed room on
the first floor of the officers' quarters. Mistletoe
hung from the ceiling, and the musicians' stands
were festooned with bright, shiny red ornaments.
Two fiddle players and a cornet pumped out waltzes
and reels, and a long cloth-covered table held cakes
and pies and cookies shaped like Christmas trees.
And whiskey, he noted. It wasn't near enough for
the thirst he was working up.

"Brand," Violet McLeod sang. "How nice that
you could join us."

Brand inclined his head. "Mrs. McLeod."

"Oh, for gracious' sake, Brand, I've known you
for at least a decade. Call me Violet. Charlie's over
there by the chocolate cookies." She waved her hand
vaguely toward the refreshment table and turned to
greet a captain and his lady.

"Brand!" Colonel McLeod gripped his hand in his
big paw. "Good to see you. Any time you want to
come scout for me, you just say the word." He nodded his graying head and slapped Brand's still sore
shoulder. "Any time."

Brand tried not to wince. "Don't think so, Charlie."

"Oh? Why is that?"

"I'm finished with army life."

The colonel turned his lined face toward him. "What do you plan to do instead?"

Brand opened his mouth to reply, but just then he caught sight of Suzannah coming through the door. She wore a yellow dress with ruffles around the hem, and she looked so beautiful his heart turned a big fat somersault inside his chest.

"Brand?" the colonel said.

Brand tore his gaze away from Suzannah and focused on the man prodding his arm. "Sorry. What did you say, Charlie?"

"I asked what you plan to do."

"About what?"

The colonel followed his gaze straight across the room to the vision in yellow silk. "About *her*, I'd guess. Brand, in all the years I've known you, I've never seen you look at a woman like that."

"Yeah?" He swallowed. "Well, in all the years I've known you, and Violet, and the army, I've never known a woman like Suzannah Cumberland."

"Ah. You know that Miss Cumberland is engaged to marry one of my lieutenants?"

"Yeah, I know."

The colonel coughed. "You want to meet him?"

"Hell, no. Well, maybe I do. Want to be sure the man deserves her."

Charlie McLeod gave him a considering look and scanned the room. "He's over there, by the musicians. Come on."

Brand sized up the slim young soldier across the room in one glance. Not good enough. Not near good enough for Suzannah.

"Major Wyler, I'd like to introduce Lieutenant John Walters."

Brand jerked his head up at the name. *Walters!* Was this the man Marcy had written him about? The man who'd stood her up at the altar? His name had been Jack Walters.

"Lieutenant," the colonel went on, "meet Major Brandon Wyler. He's with Colonel Clarke at Fort—"

"You got a brother named Jack?" Brand interrupted.

A frown crossed the young officer's forehead. "No. Sometimes I go by Jack, though."

"You ever know a girl named Marcy Wyler?"

"Yeah, I think so. Some time back."

"Walk outside with me," Brand ordered. He turned toward the doorway.

The minute Walters reached the wide front porch, Brand pivoted and laid him flat with one punch. "Lucky I'm not armed," he said, "or you'd be a dead man."

Walters lay half-conscious on the plank floor, and Brand strode back inside. "Charlie, I need a word with you."

The colonel followed him to a quiet corner of the room and listened intently, his expression growing increasingly grim with every word Brand spoke in his ear. Finally he nodded.

"All right. Dammit all, sure am sorry about Marcy."

"Give me ten minutes, Charlie. One dance, all right?"

"All right."

Brand turned away and watched Suzannah across

the room, dancing a Virginia reel with a lanky captain. He headed straight for her. He waited until she and her partner sashayed down the double row of couples and then he moved forward, elbowed the captain out of the line and stepped in to swing her in the center.

"Brand!" She went white, then rosy-cheeked. He grabbed her hands and they began circling.

"I'm cutting in," he intoned. "Look natural."

"But—"

They parted, each retreating back to the line of dancers, where they stared at each other across the expanse of polished wood flooring. The reel ended and he marched across the narrow space separating them.

The band struck up a slow two-step, and Brand pulled Suzannah into his arms. Her hair was caught up with a yellow ribbon; it smelled of violets.

"Brand...?"

"Don't talk, Suzannah. Dance with me."

He held her too close, but he didn't care. She was warm and alive and he couldn't have uttered another word if someone held a gun on him. He just wanted to hold her. Touch her.

"I want you to meet my fiancé," she whispered.

"Already met him." He sucked in a breath. "Don't marry him, Suzannah."

"But I've come all this way, nearly three thousand miles."

"Doesn't matter. He's bad news."

"Brand, it *does* matter. You don't know him. Besides, I made a promise to marry John. A lady does not break a promise."

"Break it anyway."

She looked up into his face. "I cannot. People would know, and I would be ruined, don't you see?"

"Nope. Women out here in the West don't ruin so easily."

"I cannot go back on my word. I simply cannot."

"Yeah, you can. Nobody would know."

"*I* would know."

At that moment Lieutenant Walters reentered the ballroom, surreptitiously rubbing his jaw, and Colonel McLeod stepped to the refreshment table and rapped a spoon against a glass to quiet the crowd.

"Ladies and gentlemen, I have an announcement."

Here it came. Brand pulled Suzannah tight against him, dropped his head to brush her hair with his lips and released her. Charlie would make sure John Walters did not desert her at the altar as he had Brand's sister, Marcy. If she was still dead set on marrying the man, he could at least make sure Walters did not abandon her.

Charlie cleared his throat. "I have the pleasure of announcing the forthcoming marriage of Miss Suzannah Cumberland and Lieutenant John Walters. The ceremony will take place tomorrow morning, Christmas Day, at eleven o'clock in the post chapel."

Lieutenant Walters sent the colonel a startled look. Amid the cheers and bustle, Brand caught Charlie's eye and gave him a thumbs-up. It was a done deal. He'd protected Suzannah, but he felt lousy. Walters wasn't worth her little finger.

Before the lieutenant could reach her, Brand bent his head and murmured near her ear, "I'm not leavin' until this is over."

She raised her head. "But why?" she whispered.

"Because I care about you, dammit. I care what happens to you."

"Brand, would—would you give me away tomorrow? Please?"

He went dead inside. Give her away? That was the last thing, the very last thing, he wanted to do. He steeled himself to say no, but when she looked up into his eyes he couldn't do it.

"Yeah, I'd like to talk you out of this, but if you're really set on doing it, I guess I can walk you down the aisle."

As soon as the words were out, he set her apart from him and headed for the whiskey.

Christmas Day dawned clear and cold, with blue skies and a hint of snow in the air. Suzannah dressed slowly, wondering why her favorite yellow dress, now her wedding-day dress, felt so heavy, as if it were made of woven iron.

Today was Christmas! The holiday she had loved since she was a girl, before the war. Good things happened at Christmastime, even miracles. Gifts were exchanged, and today promises would be made.

She shook the thoughts out of her head, stepped in front of the mirror to arrange her skirts and pinched her cheeks to add color. Then, with a funny, trembly feeling in the pit of her stomach, she opened the door, stepped out and paused at the head of the stairs.

"Oh, my dear," Violet McLeod exclaimed. "You look perfectly lovely!"

Suzannah could only nod and press the woman's wrinkled hand. Her throat had been so tight all morning she couldn't speak, and now that it was almost time for the wedding, she had to admit she was frightened to death. Mama said all brides were nervous, but right now that didn't help one little bit. She felt so fluttery inside she thought she would be sick.

But at least she would not have to face this alone—Brand would be there.

She picked up the bouquet Mrs. McLeod had cobbled together out of roses and honeysuckle and took one last look in the mirror.

Did all brides look this pale? Her eyes were huge, and they looked haunted somehow. She glanced quickly away and moved to the door.

Brand was waiting at the bottom of the staircase, wearing an army uniform. When she reached him, his smile seemed a bit lopsided.

"Thank you for being here with me," she breathed.

He nodded, ran his gaze over her hair, her dress, on down to her shoes, and nodded again. "Suzannah, you look beautiful." He bent his arm and lifted her hand into the crook of his elbow.

The post chapel was next door to the colonel's residence. Very slowly Brand walked her to the entrance and paused at the door. He bent his head toward her.

"Don't do this, Suzannah. Don't throw your life away on this man."

"I must," she murmured. She forced herself to look down the aisle to the altar where John stood waiting with the chaplain. She did want to marry John, didn't she? After all, she had come three thousand miles to do so. She must see it through.

"I guess I am ready," she breathed.

"Well, I'm sure as hell not," he replied. She tugged him forward and started down the aisle, her hand resting on his arm.

"Just give me a sign and I'll stop this," he murmured.

"No."

"I have two horses saddled out front. Saddlebags and everything. Come with me."

"I cannot."

"Suzannah, I want you with me," he breathed. "I'll marry you if that's the only way I can keep you."

She bobbled her next step. "I cannot," she repeated. "You know that."

He took another step forward. "I love you, Suzannah. Never said that to a woman before, but I'm sayin' it now. I love you."

She bobbled that step, too. "Brand…stop."

"No. I won't stop. I'm fightin' for my life here."

Tears stung into her eyes. "I am f-fighting for my life, too."

"No, you're not. You're runnin' away from your life."

She couldn't have answered if she had wanted to. Her heart was splitting in two—one part was a woman who would be an army officer's wife, and the other was a woman who would risk everything for love with an unpredictable, bossy, rough-edged man who didn't know what he wanted in life.

They arrived at the altar, and he hesitated.

"Brand…Brand, you must let me go now." She stepped forward, away from him, and turned to face John Walters. Brand saw with satisfaction that the lieutenant's chin was cut.

Brand couldn't look at her. The chaplain cleared his throat. "Who gives this woman in marriage?"

Brand snapped his jaw shut and refused to answer. He'd be damned if he'd give her away like she was a sack of cornmeal.

The chaplain lifted his Bible. "Dearly beloved…"

Brand spun, retraced his steps back down the aisle and strode out the chapel door into the weak sunshine. He didn't think he could stand watching Suzannah pledge to love and honor that man. He felt sick when he thought about it.

He sagged against the trunk of a poplar tree and waited for it to be over. Minutes went by.

He closed his eyes. More minutes went by.

How long did it take to get married, anyway? Sure wished he'd stuck a whiskey flask in his back pocket. His shoulder hurt where it pressed against the tree. Funny, he'd forgotten all about that bullet wound.

A bird started singing over his head. Sparrow, maybe. Pretty. Made his eyes sting.

And then there she was, standing in the chapel doorway in that yellow dress, looking so beautiful it made him crazy. She was clutching her flower bouquet.

He straightened and pushed away from the tree trunk.

She was alone. Had something gone wrong? He took a step forward, and suddenly she caught up her skirt and started toward him. He met her halfway.

Half laughing, half crying, she threw herself into his arms and kissed him hard. "Brand. Oh, Brand."

"Suzannah," he whispered against her lips. *"Suzannah."*

"I couldn't do it. I couldn't marry him. I c-couldn't because it's you I want. And oh, Brand, could we leave right away?"

He swallowed hard, folded his arms around her and kissed her, then kissed her again. "Honey, this is one helluva fine Christmas gift we're giving each other. All I've got is whiskey and jerky for the journey back."

"I love jerky," she said dreamily. "And I love you, Brand. Imagine that!"

"That's good, because if you remember I only have one very small tent. Not really enough room for two."

"I remember," she sighed. "As I recall it was actually the perfect size."

The chaplain appeared in the chapel doorway, his face puzzled, his Bible still clutched in his hands. He watched the two figures on horseback as they moved away from the fort and headed south, and then he smiled.

One horse was riderless, and on the other sat a man engulfed in a cloud of yellow silk. Then a wide-brimmed tan hat sailed up into the air over their heads, and laughter rose into the warm, sweet air.

* * * * *

THE COWBOY OF
CHRISTMAS PAST

Kelly Boyce

Author Note

When my editor asked me to take part in this year's Christmas anthology I was thrilled! I had never written a novella-length story before, but was up for the challenge. It helped that I actually wrote the story over the Christmas holidays—a little hard *not* to get into the spirit with Christmas carols and tree-decorating going on!

The spark for Levi and Ada's story came to me while trolling Pinterest (I do this a lot…). I came across a picture of a cowboy on a horse, head down, riding into a fierce snow storm. I wondered what he was doing out in this storm. Surely only the direst of circumstances would bring someone out in such weather. Which naturally led me to wondering what those circumstances were, who this guy was, and where he was going. Or, maybe more important, *who* was he going to? And why?

From there, this story of second chances unfolded and I enjoyed my holiday spent with *The Cowboy of Christmas Past*.

For my sister Alyson—best bud, confidante,
partner in crime, and lover of all things Christmas.
This one's for you.

Chapter One

Colorado, December 1876

The cold air bit into Levi, icy talons cutting through
his sheepskin jacket, past the flannel shirt and underclothes he wore to slice at his skin. He urged his
horse onward. The mare's labored breathing gave
credence to the pace he'd set and the length of time
they'd been at it, but he had little choice. A storm
brewed at his back and the injuries he'd incurred had
done him no favors. He didn't have much time left. If
he didn't find the cabin soon, he might as well have
let the hungry bear finish him off.

"C'mon, Cleo. You make it up this last rise and I
swear it's a straight shot after that."

The horse snorted its displeasure, and he couldn't
blame the mare. He hadn't exactly planned on arriv-
ing at Ada's doorstep half-dead when he set out on
this journey. Originally, all he had wanted was to set
eyes on her, see her one last time before he headed
for Salvation Falls to start his life over now that his
prison sentence had been commuted.

A prison sentence he never should have served.

But things had gone awry from the moment he
arrived in Glennis Creek only to find she'd left town
and moved up into the mountains after the death of

her husband. Del at the livery wouldn't tell him any more than that. Instead, the old coot had counseled him to quietly move on out of town before the folks heard of his unwanted return.

He'd complied. Fact was, if Ada wasn't there, he had no reason to stay.

Widowed.

He shook his head. It changed nothing.

Liar.

The warm bundle hidden inside his jacket squirmed, interrupting his thoughts. A grunt escaped and pain shot through him like a jab from a hot poker as one little leg knocked against his wound. A couple hours' ride out of town he'd found himself face-to-face with a rather ornery bear. Cleo had bucked him off and run—not that he blamed her. He'd have done the same thing. He'd barely had time to scramble to his feet before the bear's sharp claws tattooed their intentions across the left side of his chest. His coat had taken the worst of it, but not all. It hurt like hell and wasn't getting any better.

"Hold still, will ya? We're almost there."

At least he thought so. It had been a good eight years since he'd traveled this terrain. A good eight years since he'd traveled anywhere, for that matter. Unless one counted the times they let him out of his cell to feel the fresh air on his skin and stretch his legs. He pushed the thought away. He'd spent far too long living a life forced upon him by the lies of others. He wouldn't give them another day.

Provided he had another day.

When he'd left prison ten days ago, he'd figured on heading to Salvation Falls, a burgeoning town with a rail stop. One of the men serving time with him had been from there. Abbott Connolly hadn't lived long enough to see it again, but he'd painted a real pretty picture, and after eight years of staring at prison walls for a crime he hadn't committed, Levi could do with something pretty to look at.

Maybe that explained why he'd headed for Glennis Creek instead. The prettiest thing he'd ever seen had been there, and some part of him that liked to rub salt in the wound wanted to see it one last time.

See her.

See what the years had done to her after he lost her to another man.

Levi pulled his glove off with his teeth and slipped a hand under his tattered coat to check his wound. Damp. He retracted his fingers, now tinged with his blood. He'd bled through his makeshift bandage.

He gritted his teeth and glared at the furry face that poked out from beneath the warmth of his coat. "Thanks."

There was no accounting for how much blood he'd lost, but it had been enough to make his head woozy and his reflexes slow. If he didn't find shelter fast, death would come courting and there wouldn't be a thing he could do about it. Maybe he should welcome it, but he'd never quite gotten the hang of giving up, and he wasn't up to learning anything new today.

The mare crested the hill and Levi's body shuddered along with the horse. Not much farther now. He peered across the white expanse in front of him. In the distance, the peaks of the mountains jutted into the late-afternoon sky, streaked with purple and orange and mottled with ominous, dark clouds.

"I promise there is a warm barn waiting for you at the end of this." He nudged Cleo with his heels and the mare reluctantly trudged on. They'd been riding for most of the day, first to Glennis Creek and then away. The ride up the mountain should have taken two hours at best, but the bear attack had waylaid him and after he managed to pick himself up and put himself back together, he had to track his horse through deep snow. He'd found her by the creek, none the worse for wear. Unlike him.

He'd pushed the horse to her limits and owed her a decent time to recuperate before heading on to his new life. A home where the view wasn't restricted by metal bars and high walls. A decent job with a regular wage. Permanence. A house to call his own.

An empty house.

His jaw tensed and he shook the thought away, but the anger that came with it lingered. Nine years ago, he'd held all of those things in the palm of his hand. He'd turned over a new leaf, given up his outlaw ways, the only life he'd ever known. Told his pa to take his band of idiots and desperadoes and move on to another town without him. He'd wanted no part in it. Never had.

His pa hadn't taken the news well.

You'd think after twenty-three years of living with the man he'd have caught on to the fact Delroy MacAllistair didn't cotton much to being told what to do. Even less to having his only son turn his back on the family business. If one could call robbing and looting a business. His father had, but it had hardly been a lucrative one. It seemed they were always scrabbling to get by, dividing up the take between the group until there was barely enough left over to get a decent meal, a cheap bottle of whiskey and a roof over their heads. More often than not, Levi had spent his nights under a blanket of stars, shivering in the cold and damp and wishing for all he was worth for a home like regular folk. A place to put down roots and make a life.

Then he'd met her.

Ada Baxter.

He closed his eyes and smiled past the pain at the memory of her beautiful smile, but the image wavered and twisted like a bad dream. He opened his eyes but the image remained fixed in his mind.

Pa's retaliation had been swift and ugly. He'd robbed the Granger bank and killed a man. The sheriff had caught and hanged him, but not before Delroy had claimed Levi had been a part of it. He'd been lucky enough not to hang, but they still sent Levi up the river with a sentence that'd put him close to middle age by the time he got out.

And while he wrestled with the new fate that had destroyed the future he'd intended, Ada had turned her back on him and married another man.

It made no sense why he wanted to see her again. Vindication? To prove to her she'd been wrong? He shook his head.

What did it matter now?

Except that it did. Which likely made him the biggest fool in the state.

"Ma?"

Ada turned from the pot of stew she was stirring to glance at her son, who had climbed up on the sofa to peer out the window. Frost covered its edges and immigrated inward. Micah placed a hand over it and let his body heat melt it away.

"What is it, honey?"

"Rider comin'." He met her gaze. Fear lodged in her throat. She tried to hide her concern, but failed. "You want me to get the gun?"

She swallowed and stopped stirring, setting the spoon on the counter. "No, sweetie. Come away from the window." The last thing she needed was an eight-year-old playing defender of the castle. Not that the small two-room cabin was much of a castle, but it was all she had.

In truth, she didn't even have that. Like everything else Harlan had owned, he'd left it to his mother upon his death.

She shooed Micah back and took his place at the window. In the distance, a dark form dotted the white horizon where the snow on the ground meshed with the fat flakes falling from above. The rider had hunched over the horse, likely to blunt the cold. What in heaven's name brought someone out in such weather? Not that it mattered now. She judged him a few minutes away and heading straight for them. She didn't have much time. She pushed away from the window. "Go to your room, Micah."

"But Ma—"

She cut him off with a glare. "Go to your room. And stay there until I tell you to come out. Don't light a candle and if you hear me open the door, get under the bed. You know what to do after that, right?"

Micah let out a huff of breath and rolled his eyes. "If anything happens to you, I take Moony and ride to Grandma's. I go as fast as I can and I don't look back."

She hated the lessons she'd had to teach her son, but since Harlan's death two years ago and her exile to this cabin in the middle of nowhere, she'd had little choice. Anything could happen and she needed him to know what to do, to be prepared. She'd learned the hard way what could happen if you weren't.

"Go." She waited until his bedroom door closed, then removed the stew from the stove and grabbed the rifle from the rack next to the door. She kept it loaded, ready to shoot. Just in case.

The frost on the window made it difficult to see. The rider grew closer. His image wavered in and out of the squalls of snow that kicked up with each gust of wind. Maybe the fool would freeze to death before he reached the cabin. Her fingers flexed against the rifle and she ignored the fear rippling in her stomach. She glanced toward Micah's door. She couldn't afford fear.

"Just breathe," she whispered. "You can do this."

She'd never killed a man before, though there had been a few times when she'd have liked to. The rider drew closer and Ada scurried off the sofa and away from the window. It was too late to smother the fire. If the rider sought shelter, he would have seen the smoke drifting up from the chimney and known someone resided inside.

She jumped back as the door reverberated from a loud pounding on the other side. Her heart leaped into her throat. She wanted to scream but knew she couldn't.

"Who's there?" she shouted, but the wind's howl whisked away any response.

The door shook again. A squall buffeted the cabin, causing the glass windowpanes to rattle in their frames.

Her hands shook where they gripped the rifle, her palms slick. What should she do? If she left him outside, he likely would die. The temperature had dropped considerably and the snow and wind had picked up. It was at least a three-hour ride into town over rough terrain in the dark. It would be suicide to attempt such a thing.

The latch on the door lifted. She'd forgotten to throw the bolt. She took a fortifying breath and lifted the rifle butt to rest against her shoulder, sending a quick prayer to anyone who cared to listen and perhaps offer a bit of help.

The door edged open and her finger twitched near the trigger. Instinct made her step back as cold invaded the room. The fire in the hearth billowed from the influx of air as the door opened wide, revealing the rider.

She froze. It couldn't be. Fear must have addled her brain.

"Hey, there, darlin'."

He smiled at her, that half lift at the corner of his mouth. The smile she remembered. The one that had made her fall in love with him in a fast minute. The one that had haunted her dreams every night for the past eight years.

"Levi." She hadn't spoken his name since the day she'd left him. She had buried the sound and taste of it deep down inside where she wouldn't be tempted to go looking for it.

"Fancy meeting you here."

His words washed over her and filled in all the cold spots with lingering warmth. She closed her eyes for just a moment and wallowed in the sensation. Then did the only thing she could think to do.

She lowered the gun and strode forward, determination in each step.

Then she slammed the door in his face.

That had gone well. At least she hadn't shot him, though for a second or two he had thought she might. Funny, since he was the injured party. In more ways than one. He tried to resurrect the pool of anger that had fueled his journey from prison through Glennis Creek and up onto this godforsaken mountain, but he couldn't find it.

Turned out his mind was too fixated on the fact she was a far sight prettier than he remembered. And he'd had a lot of time to ruminate on those memories. Years of imagining her soft skin and full lips. Day upon endless day of reliving every slope and curve of her delicious body, each one that made a man happy to be alive so that he could witness such beauty.

Although *happy* wasn't a good description of her expression when he'd opened the door. A door he now stared at from the outside. A bitter wind blew down the collar of his jacket and through the openings cut into it by the bear. His body shuddered. At least if she'd shot him it would have been a quicker death than turning into a block of ice on her front step.

He looked to his left. He could see the faint outline of the barn hiding behind the heavily falling snow. It wasn't too far off. Maybe he could bunk there for the night. It wasn't ideal, but he had to get out of the cold. The sooner the better. He could barely feel his legs. Or anything, for that matter, save for the wound in his side, where the life continued to leak out of him.

He tried to turn but his legs refused to move. And his arms...they weren't exactly cooperating, either. The fuzziness in his brain grew, dulling the edges of his mind. He felt...strange. Light and heavy at the same time. He glanced up. It sure had gotten darker in the past few minutes, too. He squinted into the blowing snow, except then his eyes closed and they didn't want to open.

Was he dying? Didn't that just beat all? He made it all the way here through the cold and snow, got up close and personal with a bear that insisted on leaving its calling card on his side, only to die on her doorstep. What did they call that? Poetic justice? Irony?

The snow spun around him. Or was that just in his head? Maybe if it stopped he could get his bearings. Make it to the barn and—

His kneecaps thudded against the small doorstep. He hadn't even felt his legs give way. Was this God's way of trying to get him to pray? He wondered if he should tell him he'd given up praying shortly after he got locked up for a crime he hadn't committed.

He fell backward, unable to stop his body's momentum. Snow sprayed around him as he sank into a low drift. The bundle beneath his coat squirmed and a head poked out. He managed to fumble with his arm enough to shove the head back in. No point in both of them freezing to death.

"Ada…" Her name escaped from him like an accusation. And a benediction. She had been his savior and his destruction.

Blackness crept into the edges of his vision, bled through him, then stole him away.

Chapter Two

"Mama?"

Ada's heart pounded in her chest. The rough wood dug into her hand where it still rested on the door. She couldn't speak. Couldn't get her mind to work. It couldn't be him.

Levi MacAllistair was serving time for robbing the Granger Bank. He could not be standing on her doorstep. She shook her head but kept her hand in place, afraid to remove it, afraid the memories of her past would rush in with the storm and she'd be lost to them forever.

"Mama!"

The urgency in Micah's voice punched through the mess in her mind. She looked to his bedroom door, but he had returned to his perch on the sofa. Did the boy never listen to her?

"Get away from the window."

He stayed put and for a brief moment anger cut through the miasma of emotions choking her. It had only been a vision. A ghost from years gone by. But Micah's next words ruined that notion.

"There's a dead man on our step." Micah's dark blue eyes grew wide and he looked at her. "Did you shoot him?"

She shook her head, in answer to both his question and his claim. Levi MacAllistair had stood on the other side of that door alive and well, wearing the same smile he'd worn when he'd run into her as he stumbled out of the Broken Deuce Saloon nine years earlier. She would have fallen had he not caught her in his arms. They had done an impromptu dance in the middle of the street until he'd found his balance. Then he'd looked down at her and smiled.

And she'd been lost.

In one swift second, that smile had made her forget all about Harlan Baxter. All about the debt she'd owed his family when his mother had taken Ada in years earlier, after her own parents had died within months of each other, leaving her alone. And all about the expectation that she would marry Harlan and make her position in the Baxter family a permanent one.

The minute Levi entered her life, he'd turned it upside down, and she'd never quite figured out how to right it once he'd left.

"We ain't gonna leave him there, are we?"

"Aren't," she corrected Micah. As to his question, she didn't have an answer. She crossed to the window, cleared the frost and peered out. Micah had the right of it. Levi's tall, lean form lay on its side on the ground, unmoving save for the shock of dark hair pulled to and fro by the wind. His Stetson had blown off and was stuck in the drift next to him.

Micah turned to her in all seriousness. "Ma, we can't leave a dead man on our doorstep. It's Christmas."

Ada wasn't sure what one had to do with the other, but Micah was right. She couldn't leave him there.

She set the gun down and moved to the door. With a deep breath, she opened it wide and let the storm blow in as she rushed out.

The cold stole her breath away and a strong gust knocked her to her knees next to his prone body.

Levi.

Denial fled. Any hope that he'd been an unwanted figment of her imagination retreated.

Why wasn't he in prison? Had he broken out? Come all this way to demand an explanation? And what would she tell him? What *could* she tell him?

Micah's head poked through the open door. "Is he dead?"

She pressed her fingers against Levi's neck. His skin held little warmth, but a pulse beat beneath her fingertips. "No. He isn't dead."

His chest rose and fell. She tilted her head. In truth, his chest did more than that. It…moved.

A lot.

She pulled her hands away and he rolled onto his back. Her eyes widened as the front of his coat shifted and a small furry head popped out of the opening just beneath Levi's bare neck. The man didn't even have the good sense to wear a proper scarf.

"It's a dog!" Micah ran from his perch on the doorstep and dropped to his knees next to Levi, reaching for the small animal. He pulled it out and cuddled the squirming pup against his chest. "You think he's got a name?" He laughed as the dog lifted its head and licked the snowflakes as they landed upon Micah's face.

Perfect. Micah had been bothering her for a puppy

since last summer, but their limited funds hardly allowed for another mouth to feed. "I don't know. Now set the pup down and help me get him inside."

Micah reluctantly did as he was told, but not before shooing the dog inside first.

They wrestled with Levi's large form, dragging him with great effort. By the time they managed to pull him inside next to the fire, Ada's muscles quivered and sweat trickled down her back. She crouched by his hip and tapped his face, the bristle of unshaven skin tickling her hand.

"Levi? Levi, can you hear me?"

Micah stopped playing with the dog that tugged at the sleeve of his shirt as if it were a life-and-death struggle. "You know him?"

She didn't meet her son's gaze. "I used to." Once upon a time.

"Can we keep him?"

Her head shot up. "Levi?"

Micah wrinkled his freckled nose. "The dog."

Her face flushed. "No. The dog belongs to Levi and neither of them will be staying long. Don't go getting attached, you hear me?"

She wished someone had given her the same advice years earlier. It would have saved her a world of hurt.

Micah huffed and shot her an angry look. She'd been getting a lot of that lately.

"Take his horse down to the barn and see that he's brushed and fed. Make sure you use the rope to guide your way. Weather's kicking up in earnest now." She'd tied a rope from the corner of the house that led to the outhouse and then on to the barn. It had proven a godsend on more than one occasion.

"Can I take the dog?"

"Fine, but don't lose him in the snowdrifts." The dog was the size of a large barn cat and though it bounded around as if it had springs on its feet, the drifts were deep. She didn't want to have to explain to Levi that she'd lost his dog in one of them when he came to.

If he came to.

She waited until Micah closed the door behind him before she unbuttoned Levi's sheepskin coat. Dark stains were dotted around the tears on his left side. Blood? She shook her head and pushed the coat open. He had filled out since the last time she'd seen him. His body hardened and defined by the years and his circumstances. She glanced at his face, at features honed by the passage of time. Though some softness remained. In his lips, and the thick dark lashes that cast a crescent shadow against sharp cheekbones.

Time had only made those more prominent. More tempting. "You stop that right now," she admonished. "You don't need to be walking that road again."

She'd been down it once already. Only heartbreak and misery waited at its end.

She reached for the buttons on Levi's red flannel shirt. Firelight danced shadows across him, but not enough to hide the fact the shirt had met the same fate as his coat, though the dark stains were more prominent here, stretching down the length of his shirt to pool at the waistband of his denims. White poked out beneath the shirt where he'd tried to bandage the wound, but it had not been sufficient to keep the blood from oozing out.

Her hands shook as she hovered over the tattered remains of his shirt, unsure of what to do. For the first time since he'd collapsed on her doorstep, fear crept in and whispered the possibility that he could die here, on her floor. She gave herself a mental shake and pushed the whispers away.

The buttons of his shirt and undershirt gave way beneath her hands until the broad expanse of his chest and the defined ridges of his abdomen glowed in the firelight.

"What in heaven's name did you run into?" A mountain cat? A bear?

She had no answers and Levi was in no condition to provide them. Might never be if she didn't do something to stanch the seeping wounds and keep them from becoming inflamed. She pushed herself to her feet and fetched a bottle of whiskey, a washcloth and basin of water. She needed to get him fixed up before Micah returned. This wasn't something a child needed to see.

She struggled to get him out of his coat and shirt, then cut away the makeshift bandage. Steeling herself, she dragged the damp cloth across his chest and down his hard belly. The ridges of muscles tensed beneath her ministrations, then relaxed.

Memories assaulted her, pulled and grabbed and tried to tangle their roots into every dusty corner of her mind. She braced against them, pushed them back. A low groan emanated from his lips and strain etched into the bones of his face, stretching the skin taut as she drew closer to the wounds. Three gashes cut through the skin of his biceps and across his rib cage. The two outer ones were ugly, but not deep. The middle one, however, gave her concern. Blood trickled from its edges and it stretched across his ribs to stop at the upper point of his abdomen. Its edges were inflamed, red and ugly.

She brushed her fingers over his brow, down his cheek, over the several days' growth of beard. His skin had warmed, though whether from fever or the fire she couldn't say. She had never thought to see him again, had tried to tell herself it was for the best. But telling wasn't the same as convincing. Many a night she had stared up at the night sky and wondered if he looked at the same stars. She wondered if he had forgiven her for what she'd done—not that she'd had much of a choice—or if he hated her for it.

Still, the guilt of it bit into her and cut as deep as the wounds gashed across his flesh.

"I'm sorry," she whispered.

"Sorry for what?"

Chapter Three

Ada's hands flew away from his face and Levi silently cursed himself for not holding his tongue. He'd been awake since she'd shooed the boy out of the house. How could he not be after the way they'd dragged him across the floor like a carcass? He'd tried to rouse himself as she cut away his clothing and pulled the cloth down his bare skin, but his body refused to cooperate.

Well, most of it had refused. Some parts, however, had responded quite readily to her touch. To the unexpected apology whispered across his skin.

"You're awake?" That wasn't happiness he heard in her voice.

Levi opened his eyes. Lord, but she was a beautiful sight. No matter that she was a mess, the knot of hair at the base of her neck having mostly given way to the weight of the golden waves that now dangled over her shoulders and curled around her breasts. He swallowed. Bad idea looking there. He shifted his focus back to her face. To those pale green eyes that he'd lost himself in. Found himself in. Eyes that had allowed him to envision a future men like him didn't often get.

Turned out he was right on that account. But for a little while, it had been nice to believe otherwise.

"What are you doing here?" She held his gaze for a fleeting moment, anger burning in those beautiful eyes that had once promised him the world before tearing it away.

"I could ask you the same question," he said.

She looked away and the damp cloth stroked across his chest in smooth, even strokes, carefully avoiding the cuts left behind by the bear. He marveled at how something that hurt so much could feel so good.

"I live here."

"Figured that. I'm asking why you aren't living in town. Your husband had a big house on the hill, if I recall." He couldn't help the anger that curled against the title that should have been his. He tried to lift himself up on his elbows to get a better look at her, but his head spun and she placed a warm hand on his shoulder and pushed him back down.

"Stay put. Harlan died two years ago—his heart gave out."

Levi hadn't been aware the man had had a heart, but he kept that observation to himself. Likely he was biased against the man Ada had abandoned him for. "Guess I'm sorry for your loss."

She gave him a look he couldn't decipher. "I doubt that."

He didn't try to refute it. Deceit had never been his strong suit. Truth of it was, Harlan hadn't deserved her. Then again, neither had he. "That doesn't explain why you aren't in town."

Her lips pursed and she bent closer to inspect his wounds. "Harlan left everything to his mother. She allows us to stay here."

Us. He'd heard another voice. A younger one. The one she'd sent to the barn with his horse. He didn't have time to ruminate on it as her fingers pressed against the edges of the middle gash, causing his body to buck.

"I'll need to stich these up."

Fantastic. He eyed the whiskey bottle she'd set near his head. Half-full. He tried to distract himself. "Why did Harlan leave everything to his mother and not you?" It seemed a strange twist of irony that she left him for a richer man and got nothing in the end.

She turned to the basin and dropped the cloth into it. The water turned a pinkish red. She wiped her hands on her apron. "We had a bit of a falling-out."

"Over what?"

Firelight caressed her skin, illuminating her profile. The years had been kind to her, turning her from a pretty young girl into an even more beautiful woman, but the life that had once shone brightly in her eyes had dimmed.

"That's none of your concern."

He didn't press her. "The boy's your son?"

She hesitated before nodding. "Micah. He took your horse down to the barn. The dog followed him. You mind telling me what you're doing here?"

"I was heading to Salvation Falls." Not entirely a lie, just not entirely the truth.

He glanced around. The cabin consisted of two rooms. The one they were in served as the living space, kitchen and bedroom, if the bed behind her was any indication.

"You want to tell me why you're anywhere other than prison?"

He glared at her, old anger burning through his veins. He had sworn to her he was innocent, but it hadn't mattered. She'd up and married Harlan anyway. Left him to rot. "My sentence was commuted due to lack of evidence and new testimony."

His pa's cousin, Lucky Stoker, had ridden with them for as long as he could remember. A hard-nosed criminal, he'd possessed a strange sense of justice. But it had taken him a good eight years to find religion and then his way to the courthouse in Laramie, where he'd given long overdue testimony that Levi hadn't been involved in the robbery of Granger Bank.

"And so you came back to Glennis Creek?" If the news of his commuted sentence surprised or disappointed her, he couldn't tell.

He paused, not wanting to admit he'd come to see her. To give his eyes one last chance to rest upon her before leaving for good. "I'm on my way to Salvation Falls, just west of here. Met a man in prison by the name of Abbott Connolly. He told me about it and it sounded like a nice place to settle down and start over."

Was that disappointment written into her features?

"If you were headed to Salvation Falls, you're a bit off track."

"I met a rather large bear who thought he'd put a crimp in my plans."

"Where is the bear now?"

"Run off. The dog followed me from town. A stray, I guess. Either way, he proved too much of an irritant to allow the bear to enjoy his meal, so he lumbered off."

"You're lucky. Can you make it to the bed?"

Her lack of response to his near-death experience grated. He raised an eyebrow and smirked. "That's rather forward of you, Miss Dunlop." He couldn't resist using her maiden name, the one she'd had back when he used to believe in hope.

She glared at him but held her tongue, her lips twisting to one side. If he didn't know better, he'd almost guess she held back a smile. But he did know better. Ada hadn't kept any smiles for him.

She knelt next to him and put her shoulder under his arm. He winced as he staggered to his feet, leaning heavily on her as they made unsteady progress across the room to the bed. Despite her small stature, she held steady, demonstrating an underlying strength that hadn't been there before.

She put his shirt beneath him as he lay down and, with her assistance, pulled his feet up onto the bed. With efficient movements, she removed his boots, then came back to stand at his side. "I'll need to stitch the wounds before I bandage them again."

"You plan on lettin' me have some of that whiskey before you get started?"

"A little. I'll need to pour some into the gashes. It helps fight the inflammation."

She poured him a glass and slipped a hand beneath his head to lift him up far enough so that he could drink. He gulped the amber liquid like a greedy man dying of thirst, trying to blot out the pain. To erase the feel of her fingers threaded into his hair. The absence created when she let his head ease back onto the pillow.

Ada prepared the needle, then gently probed the area around the wound. He gritted his teeth and fisted his hand into the quilt beneath him. It hurt like the devil, then hurt even worse when she slid the needle through his flesh and pulled the thread taut.

He grunted and his head went fuzzy. She hesitated for a heartbeat.

"Keep going," he said. It had to be done.

The fuzziness in his head grew and the room dipped and swayed. He closed his eyes. He was safe now. He could let go.

Ada could not move about the main room of the cabin without meeting reminders of Levi at every turn. He lay on the bed—her bed. His saddlebags rested near the door, his jacket hung off the back of a kitchen chair and the kit with bandages and herbs sat on the counter close at hand. Even his dog had curled up on the sofa next to Micah while he read a book she'd given him for Christmas the year before. She'd purchased another one for this Christmas, but it had been all she could afford. Their coffers had shrunk considerably over the past two years, and pride and guilt refused to allow her to go groveling to Harlan's mother, Marilla, begging for more.

The Widow Baxter had taken her in when she was fourteen years old. Had she not, Ada knew the fate that awaited a young girl, alone and unprotected. Had Marilla not saved her, she likely would not be here now. Marrying the woman's only son once she was grown had seemed a small price to pay. That she didn't love Harlan the way a woman should love the man she married didn't seem to matter. At least not until she had met Levi.

Then it mattered more than her next breath.

"Ma, is he ever gonna wake up?"

She stopped kneading the bread and glanced over her shoulder at Levi, who continued to sleep quietly and deeply. "Soon, Micah. Sleep helps a body heal."

Levi had barely moved since he'd passed out while she stitched him up last evening. A full twenty-four hours had come and gone. The storm the dark skies had promised hadn't materialized, petering out through the night. A fact that left Ada thankful. She needed to make a trip into town before Christmas Day to pick up Micah's gift at the mercantile and give him a chance to see his grandmother.

The wind had kicked up some drifts, blocking the pathways to the barn and chicken coop. She would need to shovel them clear after she fetched Micah breakfast and checked once again on her patient's wounds. She relished neither chore, but for entirely different reasons.

She walked to the window and looked outside. The bright morning sunshine glinted off the pristine snow and created a landscape pretty enough to make one weep with joy. But it wasn't joy Ada experienced that morning. Trepidation smothered her spirits and fear tightened around her heart like a hangman's noose.

Levi would not be going anywhere anytime soon.

The idea coiled around her and stoked emotions she preferred to keep buried. The feel of his skin beneath her hands had haunted her throughout the night, bringing forth memories of when she had touched him before, under far different circumstances. Memories that now lay shattered on the ground around her, broken into shards at her feet.

"You think the dog has a name?"

"He didn't say." What he had said, however, echoed in her mind. The judge had commuted his sentence. He was a free man. An innocent man. Not that she had ever doubted it. Despite his upbringing in his father's world, she'd seen the goodness in him, believed in it. Believed in him.

She'd been the only one.

After the robbery, the town had been set on their course and would not be moved from it. In the end, he'd been found guilty and, she was ashamed to say, when his conviction came down, hers wavered. Had she been wrong? Theirs had been a whirlwind romance. She'd known him only a few months, but she'd thrown herself into their affair with all her heart. Their relationship had burned hot and fast until giving in to their passion had seemed the most natural thing in the world.

She'd loved him completely and he'd claimed to feel the same. They had made promises, dreamed of their future together far away from Glennis Creek. She'd believed in him with all her heart.

But had that same heart blinded her to a truth she did not want to see?

She hadn't wanted to believe it. A man's goodness didn't come from his upbringing. Harlan was proof of that. An outlaw might have raised Levi and he might have done things he wasn't proud of, but he'd wanted to change. He'd wanted a new life.

Hadn't he?

She never had the chance to find out the truth. Levi had gone to jail, leaving her alone to fend for herself. Only by then the stakes were much higher than they had been when she was orphaned at fourteen. Then, she'd had the sympathy of the town, people who had cared. But she'd burned those bridges when she'd turned her back on the town's favored son. She was alone. Completely and utterly alone. If she wanted to survive, she'd had to let Levi go and rebuild the bridges she'd burned.

What other choice had she had? And so she'd let Levi go. Relegated him to a memory. One best left untouched, lost to the vagaries of time.

Something easier said than done with the same memory now taking up residence in her present and space in her bed, resurrecting all her old fears and doubts, putting in jeopardy the life she'd cobbled together in his absence.

"I haven't given the dog a name yet."

Levi's voice filled the silence, thick and tired. Ada's hand slipped off the dough she'd returned to and hit the wooden surface with a thud that reverberated up her arm. Her back stiffened and she locked her knees. She would not turn around. She wouldn't.

Behind her, the dog's feet hit the floor and its nails skittered across the wooden floor to the bed, Micah's softer footsteps not far behind.

"How come?"

"Guess I didn't have the time. He followed me from town and when the bear came upon us, he chased him off before he could make me his supper. Figure that means he deserves a proper name, don't you?"

The lure of his voice proved more than her body could withstand. Ada turned around and leaned her back against the work surface, twisting her hands in her apron. Levi looked a little worse for wear, but even from across the room she could see his color had improved and the easy smile she remembered far too well spread across his handsome face.

"Think you got the right of it," Micah said, lifting the small dog up onto the bed. It settled next to Levi's leg, staying near Micah, who scratched at the pup's ears.

"I'm not too good at naming things, I'm afraid. Never had a dog before. Maybe you could pick out a name for him?"

Ada stepped forward. "I don't think—" The words died in her throat as her gaze landed upon Micah, his expression lit up like a star-filled Colorado sky. She hadn't seen him this happy for longer than she cared to remember. For two years they'd existed, doing the best they could, but there had been more struggle than joy in their lives, stuck up here in this remote area with nothing but each other for company.

"How about Bruce?" Micah pulled himself up onto the side of the bed next to Levi and cupped the dog's face as it crawled into his lap.

Levi smiled. "Bruce?"

Micah shrugged and smiled back and the expression kicked Ada in the gut until she couldn't breathe.

"Bruce the Bear Chaser," Micah added.

Levi nodded gravely. "Bruce it is, then."

Micah's grin erupted across his face and Ada experienced an uncomfortable moment of envy that Levi had managed to do in one minute what she had failed at over the past two years. Yet, as much as she wanted to hate him for it, a part of her knew a sense of gratefulness. And understanding.

But the other part filled with fear. Levi would leave. He'd heal up and he'd head to Salvation Falls just as he'd planned before that bear had tried to make a meal out of him. He'd leave and take the dog and Micah's joy with him, and just like before, she'd be stuck dealing with the hurt and pain left in his wake.

Chapter Four

Levi watched the young boy play tug-of-war with Bruce, the two taking turns pulling each other with the braided rag rope he'd fashioned out of the clean parts of his shirt. The bloodied remains Ada had disposed of, and she'd brought him one of Harlan's to wear in its place. The soft flannel hung from his frame. Prison and nature had given him a leaner frame than Harlan, but while the man's shirt did not fit, his life suited Levi just fine.

For the past two days while his wound healed and his strength slowly returned, he'd soaked up the sense of home rife in the small cabin. Ada and Micah didn't have much, but they had what counted most. He could feel it. It bloomed in the small touches and soft looks Ada gave her son, and presented itself in the way Micah rolled his eyes with a devilish smirk at her commands or when she affectionately ruffled his hair. Numerous times Levi witnessed Micah stand next to her while Ada prepared their evening meal and simply lean against her arm, as if the boy understood they were in this together, that he appreciated everything she did even if he didn't have the words to say so.

It was the kind of thing Levi had spent his whole life wishing for, that sense of closeness and family.

He'd never shared that with his father. The closest he'd come to it was when he had found Ada. His gaze drifted to her now, unable to resist the lure of her. She stood staring out the window as if waiting for something to arrive. Or wishing something that had arrived would leave.

Except that he didn't want to leave. Not this bed, or this house. Not her life. Proof his brain remained addled. He never should have come here. He should have known one look would never have been enough. But his wanting didn't change any of that.

Ada had made her choice.

And it had not been him.

But like a fool, he wanted her. This. A little home filled with discreet touches like the scent of fir boughs hanging near the fireplace with sprigs of red berries poking out of it, reminding him Christmas fast approached. The worn quilt draped over the arm of the small sofa by the window. A small pile of dime novels stacked on a shelf next to a set of wooden blocks with the initials *A* and *M* carved into them.

Everywhere he looked, little hints of their life filled the cabin with love and laughter, making it a home. A place to belong.

It made his plans for starting over in Salvation Falls look downright pitiful. And lonely. And it made him wonder.

Could they have a second chance? Was such a thing possible? He was a free man now, and she was widowed. Did people like them get a chance to try again?

He shook his head. Likely not.

"You gettin' up soon?" Micah came over to the side of the bed with Bruce. The dog's back legs dragged across the floor as he growled and shook his head, his jaws gripped tight onto the knotted rope in the boy's hand.

"Think so." He wasn't sure if he had the strength, but truth of the matter was, the way his thoughts were running, he'd be better off getting up and getting out as soon as possible, because each passing minute made it easier to linger, to convince himself that they stood a chance. A crazy notion best left alone.

But there was another notion—a far more dangerous notion—that continued to plague him, and it had to do with the boy standing at his bedside.

He guessed Micah to be around eight, though, granted, judging the age of children was hardly an area he excelled at, given his limited interaction with them. But if his estimation was correct, the possibility existed that the boy could be his. The idea both thrilled and angered him. Even in the short time he'd been here he could see what a great kid he was. Smart and funny and with a charm that sure hadn't come from Harlan Baxter. Any man would be proud to call him son. But if Micah was his son, it meant Ada had kept the truth from him, turned her back on him and let another man raise his child.

"Are you staying for Christmas?"

Levi pushed the unsettling thoughts away and turned his attention to Micah. "Christmas?"

In the corner of his eye he saw Ada's back stiffen. Not an encouraging sign.

"It's a week from today."

"Can't say I've ever really celebrated Christmas."

Micah screwed up his face as if he'd never heard anything quite so ridiculous in his short life. "You've never celebrated Christmas?"

"Guess I never really had the kind of life that aligned itself well with partaking in that specific holiday."

"Huh." For a minute, Micah didn't say anything. Then he leaned a hip against the bed, his expression serious. "Well, don't you got a Christmas wish?"

"Have," Ada said, and Micah sighed in response and shook his head, then smiled at Levi as if they shared an understanding of women in general. He should likely warn Micah now that any understanding of women would be a rare event.

"Can't say I ever had a Christmas wish. And given I recently came nose to nose with a hungry bear and lived to tell the tale, I figure I've about used up all my wishes for one lifetime."

"That don't count," Micah informed him, obviously an expert on the subject of wishes. "That was luck. Wishes are different. Wishes are something you want just because you do and not because you have to."

"I see. And who do I make this wish to?"

His question received a stupefied look. "St. Nick. You make your wish, then, if you're really good, he'll make it come true."

"Ah." Well, that's where the idea fell apart. Levi hadn't been all that good for a good long time. He'd done things he was ashamed of, things he'd known better than to do.

"So, what's your wish?" Micah prodded.

Levi's gaze drifted over to Ada, to her straight

back and the easy curve of her hips beneath the homespun skirt she wore. One renegade curl had escaped the knot at her neck and snaked down her back, enticing a long-ago memory of how her blond locks looked cascading over bare skin, the silky feel of them wound around his fingers. He closed his eyes to block out the memory but ended up savoring it instead because he was too much of a fool not to.

"Maybe I do," he said.

"Think St. Nick will bring it?"

Levi let out a bitter laugh. "I think that might be a bit too much to hope for."

Micah shrugged and grinned. "Mama says hope can do a whole lotta things, you just gotta believe in it."

"Did she now?" She'd told him something similar once upon a time when he'd expressed a fear that he didn't know any other way of life but the one he'd grown up living. He'd hoped that he could be everything she deserved. She'd told him he just had to believe.

She glanced over her shoulder and for a moment their gazes locked and held, and something traveled between them. A memory of that moment, alive and heated and filled with possibility. It took his breath away even after she'd turned around and the embers of hope he'd tried to tamp down earlier flared to life once again.

So he closed his eyes and made his wish, because a man like him didn't get too many second chances. It seemed a foolish thing to pass on a wish, even if it would take a true Christmas miracle to make it come true.

Chapter Five

"I fed your horse. She's faring just fine," Ada said as she stomped the snow from her boots and looked up in time to see Levi out of bed and walking toward her on bare feet, shirt opened to reveal his bandaged ribs and bare abdomen. "What are you doing?"

He smiled at her as he reached down and took the split wood from her with his good arm. "Helping."

"I don't need your help." She hated how much she sounded like a petulant child.

"Didn't say you needed it." Levi crossed the room to the fireplace and dumped the wood in the empty bin, his lips tightening in a wince. "Just offerin' it."

"You need to rest. I don't want you pulling your stitches."

He turned and the muscles in his stomach shifted with the movement. She quickly shifted her gaze, but instead of away, it dipped lower, beyond the waistband of his worn denims, before quickly skittering away.

"Did you just look—"

"No!" Heat rushed up her neck and face until the roots of her hair tingled. "Most certainly not."

He approached her, fluid as a cat stalking a mouse. Though she doubted any cat could duplicate the playfulness that danced about Levi's sharp blue eyes and pulled at the corners of his mouth, reminding her of a time when laughter had come easily and often.

How long had it been since she'd experienced that? Since someone had teased her? Lightened her load? Harlan had never been the type for any of those things. She had missed them sorely, but she couldn't give in to them now. In a matter of days Levi would leave for Salvation Falls, for a new life. She refused to be pulled in by his easy charm and teasing manner. By his smiles that made his eyes dance and her body spark the way it did now as he loomed over her, leaving her staring at the edge of the bandage where it crossed just below his chest. Her fingers itched to reach up and touch it. Touch him.

She swallowed.

He moved closer and the warm tenor of his voice whispered around her. "If there's somethin' you wanted to see, I'd be happy to—"

She reached out and her hand landed square in the center of his chest to stop his approach and her wayward thoughts. The warmth of him spread up her arm, doing little to corral her growing desire. She took a deep breath. Even the air smelled of him, that intoxicating scent that had always reminded her of wood fires and fresh air.

"I don't want to see anything, thank you." Except that she did. Desperately. The effect this man had on her even after all this time was nothing short of sinful.

She'd avoided Levi as much as possible over the past several days, a near impossible task given their close proximity in the small cabin. His presence lingered in every corner until she'd had to escape to the outdoors, and even then reminders of him surrounded her. His mare chomping on oats and Bruce bounding about in the snowdrifts with Micah, laughter trailing wherever he went. The sound a constant reminder of all the things that had recently been in short supply.

She couldn't escape it. She couldn't escape him. In the short time he'd been here, he'd infiltrated every nook and cranny of her life, wormed his way back in until she found herself craving the sound of his voice, wishing for the feel of his hands upon her skin, the weight of his body covering hers, limbs and hearts entangled. The way it used to be. The way it should have been.

This was dangerous thinking. She couldn't let him draw her in. His charm and good looks had not diminished over the years despite his having spent them in prison. Granted, there were a few more lines, sharper angles, lean muscle over bones—

Levi's hand covered hers, holding it against his warm skin. "You're blushing."

She turned her head and stared at the wall over his shoulder, refusing to give in to the strange intimacy binding them together. "I am not."

"Liar." The smile in his voice made her insides swoop and dip and tears pricked at the corners of her eyes because a part of her wanted it so badly— wanted him. Wanted that feeling of lightness and hope his voice promised, as if something good waited just on the horizon and all she had to do was reach for it. But she had reached for it. Once upon a time she had thrown her whole heart at it. And it had dissolved, slipping through her fingers.

She yanked her hand away. He let it go but her legs refused to create a safer distance, the pull between them too strong to break and her will too weak to try. Levi reached into the pocket of his denims and pulled something out, holding it in the palm of his hand between them. She looked down. It was a piece of wood with the first hints of an animal carved into it. A bear.

"Figured since I had some time on my hands, I'd make Micah something for Christmas. It isn't much, but—" He shrugged.

"Oh—" Something in Ada's heart tore and the pain of it caught in her throat.

"What is it?" His fingers lifted her chin and dark eyebrows dipped before his expression was replaced by a teasing smile. His thumb brushed a gentle caress against the edge of her jaw. "Did you want one, too?"

She pulled away from his touch, wanting too much to lean into it, hating her weakness. "No, of course not."

"Then what? You think he won't like it? I was going to put Bruce down here." He pointed to a chunk of uncarved wood near where the bear's feet would go.

A modern-day version of David and Goliath, one of Micah's favorite stories. "He'll love it."

And he would. He looked to Levi as one of those daring adventurers from the dime novels he devoured, concocting a fantasy in his head about the unjustly imprisoned outlaw with a heart of gold. A good man who'd made bad choices, changed his ways and sought redemption.

She could hardly fault him. Hadn't she done the

same thing? Filled her head with any number of justifications to appease her conscience when she had thrown over staid and steady Harlan Baxter for the far handsomer and charismatic cowboy who rode into town one day and swept her off her feet, promising her the moon and stars?

"But you don't want me to give it to him. Why?"

"I have my reasons."

She forced herself to turn away and walked to the shelves above the kitchen surface. She needed space, room to escape the tension coiling inside of her, time to clear away the memories that threatened to tangle her up in their roots. She stood on her tiptoes and reached for the plates, but he'd moved behind her and reached beyond her, his height making it easy for him. His chest brushed against her back and she closed her eyes and gripped the edge of the wood, unable to do anything but stand there and absorb the sensation until he stepped away and set the plates down next to her.

He crossed his arms over his chest, winced and thought better of it, leaning his weight against the cupboards instead. "What are they? These reasons."

Ada opened her mouth. Then closed it. Then she pursed her lips to trap the truth behind them.

He arched one dark eyebrow. "Just so we're clear, I'm going to stand here until you tell me."

"Then I will go over there." She nodded to the sofa.

"And I will follow."

Oh, his stubborn hide! She'd forgotten about that part of him. "You can't arrive here out of the blue and demand answers that are none of your business."

He nodded, almost imperceptibly. "Fair enough. Then tell me this—how old is Micah?"

Fear gripped her hard, digging its sharp talons deep into her heart, the pain so deep she couldn't speak. But it wasn't enough to stop the frightening possibilities from running roughshod through her mind. Did he suspect? Had he taken one look at Micah and known? And if he did, what were his plans? Would he take her son away?

For years, Harlan had threatened her with that same scenario, holding the possibility over her head in order to keep her in line. He hadn't wanted Micah, but he had wanted to punish her for her defection, her betrayal. Would Levi do the same?

"He's seven," she said, adding one more lie to the pile. She forced her gaze to remain steady, hating herself as she willed him to believe her. "Why?"

"No reason. Just wondered."

She caught a flash of disappointment in Levi's blue eyes, and the realization that he'd suspected the truth carved another series of scars across her heart. He took a few steps away and looked around the cabin, though what he searched for she couldn't say. She opened her mouth, the truth on the tip of her tongue, but when he turned back to her, she closed it, swallowed it back, unable to trust him. Afraid to trust him. She had seen what the anger of betrayal could make a man do.

Levi shrugged, the broad width of his shoulders shifting beneath the too-large shirt he wore. "I don't have to give him the toy. I just thought..." He shook his head. "I don't know what I thought."

But she did. Guilt polluted her veins, bringing

with it a heavy dose of anger at how things might have been if their hopes and dreams hadn't been dashed and broken by the whims of fate. How different would their lives have been if they'd left town before the robbery had occurred? If she had told him the truth that day in the jailhouse instead of turning away from him? But the time for those questions had come and gone, the answers lost to the years that lay between the past and present.

"I just don't want—" She stopped. What? What didn't she want? She didn't want to fall again. Because it would be so easy. With each passing minute she spent with him, she could feel it happening all over again and she was helpless to stop it. And then what? Levi would leave; he'd go on with his life and the freedom he'd long been denied. And she would be left behind to wear the pain of his absence just as she had before. And so would Micah.

"What don't you want?" He turned and walked back to where she stood, filling her vision and lighting a fire beneath her skin that warmed her from the inside out.

"I don't want Micah to grow attached to you. I don't want him to think you're going to stay only to be left heartbroken when you leave."

"Sounds like you have some familiarity with that kind of thing." He came closer, his voice dropping until it thrummed through her. "Which is funny, don't you think?"

She pressed her back into the edge of the counter, trapped by his words and his closeness. "How is that funny?"

"Because it wasn't me that did the leaving last

time, was it?" His hand lifted and the tip of his finger traced the outline of her lower lip until she trembled. "That was you."

She closed her eyes and let the thrill of his touch and the painful truth of his words flow through her. She *had* been the one who had walked away. She'd had no other choice. None. And despite all the what-ifs that danced around her brain, if faced with the same situation all over again, she wouldn't do it any differently. Because it hadn't been about her. And it hadn't been about him.

She had done it all for the child growing in her belly.

His hand dropped away and he leaned in, one hand on either side of her, trapping her, enveloping her.

He leaned in closer until his breath brushed against her like a kiss. "Tell me what you *really* want."

She screwed her eyes even more tightly shut. She ached for his touch, every part of her pulling toward him as much as her head screamed for her to move. To leave. To get out of harm's way. To swallow back the answer to his question that rested on the tip of her tongue like a sour candy. Sweet and bitter.

She wanted him.

She wanted to go back in time and undo all that had been done. She wanted to leave Glennis Creek and the ugliness of their past behind and start anew somewhere else. She wanted a chance to live the life he'd promised her.

But she couldn't have any of those things. The secret she carried and the lies she was forced to tell made sure of that.

"I want you to get better and leave."

What other choice did she have?

Perhaps Levi should have taken the hint, packed up his saddlebags and ridden out that night, but he'd never been the type to give up easily. She had wanted him. He was certain of it. He could feel the connection they'd had all those years ago pulling them closer with each passing day. It wasn't just him. It wasn't his imagination.

That Mother Nature brought howling winds the following day only solidified his decision to wait things out. To stay and see if he could break through the barrier she'd erected between them and discover the reason behind it. There had to be one, though what it could be left him stumped. Did she resent him for being sent to prison? Did she think he didn't love her? That he hadn't suffered every day for the past eight years knowing she had married another man? Or was it guilt, because she had been the one to turn away? That seeing him now made her face the fact that she had gone on with her life while his had been taken from him?

He shook his head as he stared out the window. The woman had locked her thoughts up tight and hidden the key. But he'd find it. Come hell or high water, he'd figure out what was going on in that head of hers. He had a Christmas wish riding on it, after all.

"Can you see where the drift ends?" Levi glanced down his shoulder to where Micah bounced on the sofa next to him as they surveyed the winter wonderland beyond the glass. The clouds had cleared and the bright sun beating down on the pristine snow made it difficult to discern the peaks from the valleys.

"It ain't too bad. I seen worse." The kid sounded like a seasoned veteran and Levi didn't wonder that it was lonely for him up here with no one his own age to play with.

He'd experienced a similar kind of childhood. Pa and his gang had never stayed anywhere for too long, dragging him wherever they went. If they hadn't had old Doc Redding with them for most of his youth, likely Levi would never have learned how to read or write or do his numbers. But while the other men were drinking or carousing, the old man had ensured that Levi was learning those things. Doc had instilled in him the hope that a different kind of life might be out there. A regular life with a home and a family.

He hadn't really believed it, though—not until he'd met Ada.

"All right, then. Let's see about getting that snow cleared for your mother."

He wanted to surprise her by having the pathway to the barn and outhouse cleared for her before she awoke. Maybe if he made himself useful, she'd see the advantage in keeping him around a little longer.

The pair set to work. As much as Levi tried to minimize the movement on his injured side, the muscles on the left of his torso burned and ached. By the time they finished, he leaned his weight against the shovel and questioned the wisdom of his actions.

"You gonna stay for Christmas, Mr. MacAllistair?"

Levi wiped the sweat from his brow and looked over at Micah. The boy tossed snow into the air and

Bruce leaped up to capture it, with minimal success. Levi had already made peace with the fact that if Ada stuck to her guns and sent him on his way, he would leave the dog with Micah. A boy needed a dog, in his estimation. Especially a boy with no other companions to speak of.

"Can't quite say," Levi answered. "And I believe I asked you to call me Levi."

"You did, but Ma said I had to call you Mr. MacAllistair." Micah made a face. "It's kinda a mouthful."

Levi laughed. "I suppose you're right on that account." But he didn't contradict Ada, no matter that he thought the formality unnecessary. "C'mon. Let's go inside and get some of that warm cider simmering on the stove."

They tramped inside and stomped the snow from their boots. Levi shrugged out of his coat. Sweat had soaked the back of his shirt, and his legs wobbled as if he'd hiked up one of the mountains poking into the horizon. He undid the buttons of his shirt and pulled it off, setting it by the fire to dry out before struggling out of his undershirt. Getting dressed proved a far easier ordeal than getting undressed.

He managed to pull up the shirt far enough to cover his face before he heard Micah laugh. "You want some help?"

Levi grinned. "I'd be much obliged."

He bent down and let Micah pull the shirt over his head, then down his arms, finishing the task with a flourish that included a spin and a bow, much to the delight of Bruce, who barked his approval, then grabbed the shirt and started a tug-of-war competition. Micah's laughter filled the cabin and he promptly wrestled the shirt away from the pup and set it next to the other one by the fire.

"Them shirts are kinda big on you."

"They were your pa's shirts."

"Oh."

Something in the way he answered, the flatness of his tone and the lack of emotion that went with the one-word answer, caught Levi's attention. "You miss him?"

Micah shrugged and scooped Bruce up off the floor, hugging him close. "Suppose."

Levi hesitated. He wasn't in a position to take anyone to task for not feeling overly warm toward their pa, but Micah's comment surprised him. "You didn't get along?"

Another shrug. "I don't think he liked me much."

Levi straightened, his hands resting on his hips as he stared down at Micah, who maintained an oddly neutral expression despite the weight of his comment. Levi couldn't quite fathom it. The boy was downright likable, and while he hadn't spent a lot of time in the company of kids, he figured Micah was the kind of boy any man should be proud to call son. For a fleeting moment, he'd hoped—

Well, that was neither here nor there now.

"Well, I like you just fine."

Micah smiled and the twinkle returned to his dark blue eyes. Bruce leaned up and licked the underside of the boy's chin before falling back into his arms. Something ached deep inside Levi's chest. He rubbed at the spot, but the feeling remained.

"You know what this place needs," Levi said, turning the conversation in a lighter direction.

"What?"

"A tree. I hear people do that around Christmas, don't they? Put a tree up. Some decorations and such."

Levi had never had the opportunity to celebrate Christmas or to have a tree, unless you counted the branch Abbot Connolly had somehow smuggled into their cell one year after it had blown into the main yard. He'd propped it up in a corner and proclaimed it Christmas. It was February by then, but Levi hadn't been about to ruin the old man's joy. During those days, you learned to take joy where you could find it.

Micah's face brightened and he nodded. "We were gonna get one, but the snow's been too deep for me and Ma to get into the woods through the drifts."

"What do you say after breakfast we go out and find a proper Christmas tree?" He figured his side hurt like the devil already—what more damage could he do? Besides, seeing the kid's face light up as it did made the pain sting a little less.

"What are you doing?"

Levi spun on his heel to face Ada and his heart stopped. With her standing there with her hair tousled from sleep, her cheeks rosy and her body swathed in nothing more than a nightdress, warm knit slippers and a knitted wrap, he couldn't think of a time he'd thought her more beautiful. The truth of that realization hit him square in the chest and traveled downward with the speed of a wildfire on a dry plain.

"We was shoveling, Ma."

He was glad Micah answered, because all he could think of while staring at the disheveled blond waves pouring over her narrow shoulders and the sleepy expression stamped across her pretty face was how much he wanted to lift her into his arms and march them both into the bedroom and make up for all the years he'd missed with her.

She wrapped her arms across her chest as if she could read his unruly thoughts. "*Were* shoveling, Micah." Her gaze narrowed on Levi, fixated on his chest. "You're fit enough to shovel?"

The words she didn't say drifted between them. The suggestion that if he was able to shovel, he was well enough to get on his horse and ride on to Salvation Falls without delay. He considered his options, but given lying had never been a skill he'd adopted with much success, he opted for the truth.

"Seems so. Figured I'd give you a hand. Help out around—"

Her chin lifted to a militant angle. "I don't require your assistance, Levi. Micah and I can manage just fine, thank you."

She got her back up quicker than a bucking bronco with a burr under his saddle any time he suggested lending a hand. "I didn't say you couldn't manage. I just said, while I'm here, I might as well earn my keep."

"We're gonna get us a Christmas tree, Ma!"

Anger flared in Ada's eyes and as her gaze shot back to meet his, their conversation from the other day echoed in his mind.

I don't want Micah to grow attached to you.

But what about the attachment Levi felt for the boy?

"I figured with the deep snow it might be easier for me to get through the drifts. I can carry Micah on my back until we get past the worst of them."

Her gaze left Levi and rested on her son, where it softened, her love for him as clear as day. What it must be like to have that. To know a mother's love. He'd never known his own ma. She'd taken off when he was only five. His memories of her were like daydreams that drifted through his mind and disappeared.

"Fine, then," she acquiesced and Micah rewarded her by setting Bruce on the ground and throwing his arms around her waist. Her fingers threaded through her son's dark hair and she planted a swift kiss on top of the mussed-up locks. "But bundle up. I don't want any frozen fingers and toes coming back, do you hear me?"

"We will, Ma."

"And you'll eat a hearty breakfast before you go."

"Yes, ma'am," Levi answered, offering her his most charming smile.

For a brief moment, the hint of a smile tugged at the corners of her mouth and Levi had to check himself. He wanted to pull her to him and kiss her until that glimmer erupted into a full-fledged smile. Instead he stood there and soaked it in, accepting the small victory.

Her expression softened as she looked over the top of Micah's head. "Thank you for helping."

"You're welcome."

The sudden sense of inclusion in this small family

pulled deep inside of him, a strange combination of pain and pleasure. God help him, but he wanted to be a part of it. Part of this life she had made for herself and her son. Hang Salvation Falls. If she would let him, he'd stay right here in this little cabin with her and Micah.

Every hope and dream he'd harbored from the moment he'd met her crept out from the shadows and shook off the dust they'd collected, standing before him stark and unadorned. Ada Baxter had been the only real sense of family he'd ever known. In the short time they'd had together, he had felt loved. Had *been* loved. It hadn't been a lie or a lark. She had loved him, there was no mistaking it. If she hadn't, he'd have been shown the door long before now, injuries or none.

"I'll see to breakfast then," she said, quietly, breaking the spell between them, though not completely. It lingered in the air around them like the Christmas magic Micah talked about, filled with hopes and wishes and possibility. Victory, no matter how small, sang in his veins.

Levi smiled at Ada's retreating back as she made her way to the kitchen area.

Micah moved to stand next to him and nudged his arm. "I think she likes you," he whispered.

Levi didn't respond, but he couldn't stop the fool's grin that broke out across his face. Maybe he'd get that Christmas wish after all.

Chapter Six

Ada lost count of the number of excuses she gave for why she kept glancing out the window waiting for Levi and Micah's return from the thick copse of woods they'd disappeared into to find their tree. Bruce lifted his head from near the fire and whined, echoing her feelings.

"They'll be home soon, pup."

It frightened her how seamlessly Levi had eased into the fabric of their lives. Had a week passed already? His sense of warmth and laughter had infiltrated the shadowed corners of the small cabin and shone a bright light into them, illuminating everything that had been missing in their lives. Everything she had once thought her life would be.

But those days were past. She needed to stop hanging on to a dream. With a shake of her head, she returned to her rocking chair near the hearth and picked up her knitting. The fire warmed her legs and the smooth click-clack of the needles provided a small distraction. She thought to make Micah a warm pair of woolen socks for Christmas, but when she stopped to start the heel, it was clear her mind had wandered. The sizing did not match up and too late she realized it wasn't Micah she had been knitting for, but Levi. She moved to unravel the half-worked piece but stopped herself. It would be a parting gift, something to keep his feet warm against the Colorado winter as he rode off to his new life in Salvation Falls.

Her gaze shifted to the window once again. Sunlight shimmered against the white landscape.

What if we went with him?

She shook her head at the recalcitrant thought.

"Stop it," she admonished herself. "That is one tree you do not want to be barking up."

Besides, Levi hadn't made a single overture in that direction. Not really. Oh, he'd been charming— that man couldn't wake up in the morning without charming the sun out of its slumber. But he hadn't touched her. Well, that wasn't entirely true. Heat rushed through her at the memory of his chest brushing against her back as he'd reached for the plates. The tip of his finger brushing against her lip, whispering against her skin.

What do you really want?

Yearning raged through her, need and regret fast on its heels, unearthing desires she'd spent years denying. Desires that went beyond needing the comfort of a warm body. She'd had a warm body in her bed for nigh on five years, and not once during that time had she experienced an ounce of the passion she'd shared with Levi before his arrest. She hadn't been able to resist him. She still couldn't. He had her heart. He always had. For him, she had given up everything—propriety, common sense, Marilla's good opinion. For him, she had stepped away from promised safety and stability and had taken a chance. She had opened her heart. Loved.

And for her trouble, she'd been gifted with hurt, a broken heart and a baby growing inside of her.

Levi's baby.

How humiliated she had been, crawling back to Marilla and Harlan, pride in hand. She'd had nowhere else—*no one* else—to turn to. Marilla had agreed to take her in, but at a price. And for the entirety of their marriage, Harlan had held that price over her head. He had never let her forget that he'd saved her and her son. Never let her forget that she owed him.

The door flew open and Ada jumped to her feet, juggling the knitting in her hand and the ball of yarn in her lap. Bruce scrambled to his feet and ran past her. Levi came through the opening first, bent over and pulling the trunk of a Douglas fir with his good arm. Micah followed at the other end of the tree, a smile as expansive as the horizon spilling across his face.

"We got one, Ma! It's a beauty!" The dog barked and bounced as if to verify Micah's claim.

The scents of sap and fir filled the small space as they laid the tree in the middle of the floor. The snow that clung to its needles melted and dripped into a puddle beneath it as the fire's warmth reached out to encompass it. When it was upright, she guessed its top would sit level with Levi's eyes, but its substantial width made her glance around the cabin.

"Where exactly are we going to put this?"

Levi's gaze followed hers and when she met it, he laughed, his eyes bright. Humor carved itself into every plane and angle of his rugged face. He shook his head. "I have no idea."

She wanted to be angry. Wanted to grasp something—anything—that would keep her from falling for Levi's smile, to stop the warmth spreading through her center at the sound of his laughter. But it eluded her and before she could stop herself, she did something she could not remember doing in a very long time.

She laughed.

She laughed at the joy in her son's face. At the absurdly fat tree. And at the handsome, charming man who had tromped through drifts of snow to chop it down. Their laughter filled the room, so wonderful and welcome that she didn't ever want it to stop.

"Well," she said, catching her breath. "I suppose we should find a spot for it. Maybe we could move the sofa a bit and set it in the corner?"

Her suggestion was met with nods of agreement and they set about moving the necessary furniture. Levi nailed two thin planks of wood to the bottom of the tree to hold it upright and they nestled it into the corner.

"Smells like Christmas, doesn't it?" Micah stated, hands on his narrow hips as he looked from the tree to Levi.

An emotion Ada couldn't define flitted across Levi's features, causing his smile to waver slightly. "I will take your word for it."

The sad truth plowed through her conscience like a runaway train, whistles blowing, demanding her attention. Levi had grown up under horrible circumstances for a child, moving from place to place with a father who spent his life in pursuit of crime. When Levi had finally made a move to leave that life behind, he'd found himself in prison. Of course he had never had a proper Christmas. How could she send him on his way just days before and rob him of the chance to have one now?

"Then you're in for a treat," she said.

He glanced at her sharply, a question in his gaze she had no answer for. What would it cost her to allow him to stay?

Only her heart.

But he had that already, didn't he?

The rest of the afternoon passed with chores, and once their bellies were full and the dinner dishes washed and put away, she tucked Micah into bed with Bruce snuggled next to him and brushed back the thick, dark hair that was so much like his father's.

Her heart twisted.

She needed to tell Levi. The longer he stayed the more her conscience demanded to be heard. It was the right thing to do, but whenever she tried to find the words, fear hid them away and whispered into her heart—would he understand? Forgive her? Turn his back on her? Take Micah away to a better life than the one she could give him?

She didn't like the answer she came up with.

"It was a good day, wasn't it, Ma?"

She shook the thoughts away and pulled the quilt up higher to keep Micah warm until she joined him later. "It was a good day." She placed a kiss on her son's forehead. "Go to sleep, little man. Tomorrow we'll need to figure out how to decorate that behemoth you brought home."

He nodded, already beginning his descent into slumber. How she wished she could find such oblivion. But sleep had eluded her since Levi's arrival.

Each time she closed her eyes, the memories teased her and the truth taunted her and the fear tormented her. She wasn't sure how much longer she could go on like this before the dam broke and everything flooded out.

What would happen if it did?

She waited until Micah's breathing was deep and even, then gave him one more kiss and returned to the main area of the house. She stopped short.

Saints preserve her, was it too much to ask that the man keep his shirt on? "What are you doing?"

Levi glanced up from where he stood in front of the hearth. He had stripped down to his denims and his fingers probed at his bandaged wound, where a bright red dot soaked through the white strip of cotton. He gave her a regretful look.

"Think I might have popped a stitch or two when I was chopping the tree down."

Her mind refused to work properly and her mouth went dry. It was hardly the first time she'd seen Levi in a state of undress since his arrival, but the way the fire's light glinted off his skin, warmed it until she wanted to reach out and wrap herself around it—around him—

Stop it!

But it was too late. The thoughts were there. The memories were there. And so was the need. A desperate longing for him to hold her. Kiss her. Make her forget the past eight years she'd lived without all the things he'd promised her. Without him.

She fisted her hands until her nails cut into her palms. "Sit down. I'll get my kit and take a look at it."

She set her jaw and forced herself to think of the

task at hand, cutting away the bandage. His warm skin teased her fingertips as they skimmed over his wounds, looking for signs of infection. The gashes had healed well; there was no angry inflammation. The cause of the blood was exactly as Levi had suggested. Two pulled stitches, nothing more. No reason to sew them up again. Everything was healing as it should.

Relief flooded through her.

She dabbed a damp cloth over the wound to clean away the blood. Once it was dry, she wrapped a clean strip of bandage around his middle, and they had to stand toe-to-toe so she could reach around his solid frame. He held out his arms and she did her best not to imagine them folding around her, pulling her close, kissing that spot on her neck he always found, the one that made every nerve in her body jump to life.

She stopped, stilled. Tried to force the image away, but it refused to go. It refused to give her respite from the storm raging inside her. Her hands shook and the blood in her veins sang with awareness. Lower down, a deep ache grew stronger until she could barely stand it.

"Ada?"

His voice whispered around her and she bit back a whimper, because all she heard was the memory of it in her ear as his body had covered hers, warm and solid and comforting and real.

He lowered his arms and his hands covered hers where she had knotted the ends of the bandage in front of him. "What is it?"

She shook her head. She couldn't answer past the

lump in her throat. Not that it mattered, because she didn't have just one answer. She had a million different ones, though they all centered around a common theme. How much she wanted him to stay. To know the truth, to forgive her. How much she wanted to hope and how much she feared to at the same time, scared the dream would be ripped away again if she even dared.

His fingertips touched her brow and she closed her eyes as he drew a slow path down the bridge of her nose. He brushed the line of her jaw and it relaxed despite the tangle of emotions roiling inside of her. And then there was his touch on her lips, featherlight, teasing. She sucked in a breath and held it. Waiting.

He tilted her chin to his face. "Look at me."

She opened her eyes, unsure of what she'd see. What she found was a mirror of her own emotions, the feelings she feared the most. The things she wanted most of all.

And then he kissed her.

Levi's fingers slid deep into the thick mass of golden hair, knocking loose the knot she'd kept it in. The feel of those soft tresses falling over the back of his hand, the abandon of it, made him pull her closer. Hold her tighter. He was afraid that if he didn't, she would bolt. Come to her senses. Stop it. He couldn't stand the idea. Not now. Not yet.

Just give me this.

He'd waited eight long years, through his trial and long incarceration, to touch her again. To taste her and feel her body pressed against him. He'd counted the days, checked them off in his mind even though his sentence had stretched for years in front of him. Even though he had already lost her to someone else. He couldn't help it. The idea of losing her forever had been too much to bear. So he'd turned away from the idea of never getting another chance.

He'd told himself that if he could see her one last time, hear her voice. Touch her. Maybe it would be enough. Maybe then he could move on.

He'd been a fool.

He would never get enough of her.

One of her hands gripped his wrist, but she didn't pull away. If anything, she kissed him back just as hard. Tasted and teased until he teetered on the brink and didn't care if he fell over. He could die a happy man here in her arms, knowing his hopes had been rewarded. That fate had relented and given them a second chance.

Ada's hand slid around him and up his back, leaving his skin seared with heat, the bandage unable to protect him. His erection pressed against her and he wanted nothing more in that moment than to bury himself deep within her. To rediscover the beautiful curves and softness her body offered, to watch her react as he kissed and teased his way over every inch of her.

They had been barely more than kids the first time they'd given in to passion. Now they were older, wiser, hardened by the hand life had dealt them. But beneath it all, Levi still saw the woman he'd fallen in love with. The woman who had taken a chance, crawled out on a limb when good sense and propriety counseled her to climb back to safety. Age and circumstance had made her even fiercer, more beautiful, inside and out.

And he wanted her now more than ever before.

But he needed her to want the same thing.

He lifted his mouth from hers. "Should we stop?"

She shook her head and sought his mouth once more with a desperation that left him humbled, as if she sought to fill something inside of her that had gone too long ignored. He understood. He shared that feeling.

His hand found the long row of buttons at the front of her dress and released them from their moors, fumbling with urgency until the dress loosened around her and slipped from her shoulders. She straightened her arms long enough to let it fall and pool at her feet. Gooseflesh rose on her arms as she stood before him in nothing but her shift and underclothes.

Too many clothes!

Her hands left him and she pulled up her shift, bit by bit revealing lean thighs and rounded hips. Full breasts and flushed skin. She let the shift fall, then stepped out of the puddle of clothing and stared at him.

Her boldness amazed him. She was a sight to behold, and oh, how he wanted to hold her. To pull her against him and feel the softness of her breasts against his skin, run his hands over the slope of her waist. The fierce passion burning in her eyes fired through him. But the fear that pulled her skin taut tempered him.

"Ada, we don't have to—"

Her arm came up and covered her breasts and he

wished he'd bitten his tongue. Uncertainty filled her expression. "I thought you wanted—" Two red spots bloomed in her cheeks and her gaze fell away from his. "I—" She bent to retrieve her clothing, but he moved quickly and grabbed her wrist, pulling the shift from her hand.

"I have never wanted anyone more."

He hauled her into his arms and translated with a kiss all the things he didn't have the words to say. He lost himself in her and prayed it would be a long time before he was found.

He took a swift breath when her fingers fumbled at the buttons of his denims, her touch enough to make him lose the faint grip he still had on his control. The backs of her hands brushed against him and he swore she took far longer than necessary to get the job done, but he didn't complain. The pain of waiting was eased by the pleasure of anticipation.

He hauled down his denims and underdrawers and kicked them off, thankful he'd doffed his boots earlier. He pulled the ribbon on her drawers and slipped them over her hips. She gave a wriggle that was almost his undoing and they fell to the floor. His arms wrapped around her and lifted her against him, the heat and sweet sensation of her soft skin robbing him of breath. He carried her to the bed and gently laid her down, taking a moment to absorb the vision of her naked body.

"Levi." She reached for him and he joined her there, dragging the quilt from the bottom of the bed over them to cocoon them in their own private world. Neither of them spoke after that, as if words were an intrusion they could not endure. On the other side of the room, the fire crackled and popped, the logs tumbling in their cradle. The only other sound in the room was their breath, heavy, hurried.

His hands swept the length of her body and he reveled in the true bliss of her bare skin against his. Her breasts were fuller than he remembered, her curves more pronounced, as if she had come fully into womanhood while he'd been gone. He regretted he had not been there to see it. Hated that it was another man who'd been given that honor.

He pushed the thought away. None of that mattered now.

He explored her body with his hands, his mouth, his tongue. He found all of his favorite places, discovered new ones he'd not known before. Her breath caught as his hand slid between her thighs, stroking her. She was slick and warm. Inviting. His control ebbed. He couldn't hold on for much longer. Eight years was a long time, and though he wanted to prolong this magic for as long as possible, the moment she reached down and put her hand on him, waiting became impossible.

"Ada?" Her name was a question, a request.

She pressed her hips against him, and when she spoke her voice was urgent. "I want you, too."

Want. It was enough. For now. He settled between her legs and eased himself into her warmth, unable to breathe as she enveloped him. He stopped. If he died now, he would die in a state of perfect bliss.

She moved her hips to pull him farther into her, and he lifted himself onto his elbows and moved with her, in and out until every nerve in his body threatened to explode. He held on. Waited until her body stiffened and shuddered. A cry of ecstasy rent from her lips and was captured by his. Her kiss sent him over the edge to his own release, and for a few blissful minutes, the world became a wondrous place. The room—the bed—a safe haven where nothing could ever touch them.

He'd found home.

Chapter Seven

M adness.

It was the only explanation Ada had to explain what had happened between them. She'd been gripped by madness. They both had. She'd heard stories of people who lived too long in the wild, who slowly lost their minds with the isolation. But her madness had come from a different source. A source that had lived deep inside her since the day she'd turned her back on Levi in order to give his son a home and a future. A madness that had tormented her for the past eight years as she allowed another man to raise Micah as his own, yet not treat him as such.

A madness that haunted her as she'd continued to love a man who would never be coming home.

And yet here he was.

He had returned, and with one touch, one kiss, he'd illuminated everything in her heart she'd tried to deny. She loved him. Levi, for all his faults, had been kind and sweet. Loving and protective. Loyal. No matter how bad things became, he had remained steadfast. He'd fought for them, begged her to wait the sentence out, convinced that he would prove his innocence. He'd been strong, where she'd been weak. He'd had faith, where she had been filled with fear.

She'd loved him then and she loved him now. She didn't know how not to.

How many times had she wished she could go back? Do it over again. Find another way. But in the end, despite his faith and determination, Levi *had* gone to prison and the years had passed one on top of the other with no end in sight. She had made the right decision where Micah was concerned. Because of her marriage to Harlan, Micah never had to bear the shame of being labeled a bastard. The shame— of marrying a man she did not love—was hers to carry alone.

When Harlan had died suddenly two years ago and, out of spite, had left everything to Marilla, she'd left her shame over not loving her husband behind. He hadn't deserved it. She'd reluctantly agreed to continue keeping their secret regarding Micah's birth for her son's sake, torn between the truth and protecting her son.

No more. The time had come. She could deny it no longer. Levi and Micah both deserved the truth. But Marilla deserved to be told first, before the news broke. She owed the woman who had saved her that much at least.

"I thought in the morning we might hitch up the sled and go into town. We need a few supplies and Micah always likes to see his grandma before Christmas," Ada said. "We can make the trip alone. You needn't come."

Levi shifted behind her and nuzzled the back of her neck and a sigh of pleasure escaped her. She should leave the bed and seek refuge in the other room, but each time the thought entered her head, the warmth of his body, the sensation of being nestled against him kept her there.

His arm tightened around her middle and their bodies melded closer together.

"I'll go with you," he said. "I need to send a telegram to Salvation Falls. My cellmate I mentioned, Abbott Connolly? He told me when I got out, to contact the town sheriff. Said he was a good man and could help me out."

Ada didn't say anything for a long moment. He still planned to leave. Had this meant nothing? Did he plan on turning his back on her as she had him?

She swallowed past the pain. Perhaps it was no more than she deserved.

"You may not receive a very warm welcome," she warned him, forcing her voice not to waver, not to give in to the disappointment his intentions created.

"I'm not looking to make friends. I just need to send a telegram." His low voice rumbled against her and she shivered, wanting him all over again despite everything. "Are you afraid what people will think if they see us riding in together?"

"No." Not everyone. Just Marilla. If she told Levi the truth and he still kept to his plan and left for Salvation Falls, where would that leave her and Micah? Marilla Baxter was their only means of support, but that support came with one condition. A condition she was on the verge of breaking.

"Then it's settled. We'll leave directly after breakfast. As for now, I find I've got an appetite of a different kind." Levi brushed back her hair and kissed the nape of her neck, sending a ripple of pleasure down her spine. How wonderful it would be to turn around and lose herself in his arms once again. To forget what awaited her on the morrow. There were risks to be taken, truths to be told. Disappointments to be borne.

She knew she should stop this, but as his hand wandered over the curve of her hip and his mouth teased the tender skin of her neck, the idea of stopping drifted away and she turned toward him. She'd make one more memory to torment herself with after he left her behind.

They didn't speak for much of the trip into town. It was just as well, as Levi needed the time to figure out just what the devil he had done. What it meant, because it had meant *something* even if he couldn't pinpoint exactly what. They'd made love. Pure and simple. It hadn't been some rash action; it hadn't been two bodies sating physical needs. It had been much more than that. At least it had been to him, and given the way Ada had turned inward, insulating herself from him the moment she'd left the bed, he guessed it had affected her, as well. He hadn't forgotten how to read her, and something had her scared.

He understood the feeling.

One minute he'd been on his way to Salvation Falls with plans to pick up the tattered pieces of his life, put his past behind him and try to carve out a future. The next he was knocking on Ada's door, his side torn open and his hope laid bare.

Maybe—just maybe—his luck was finally turning around, making up for the nightmare he'd survived in order to get here. Maybe this was fate's way of giving him back all he'd lost. All they'd lost.

Another chance.

Did she want the same thing?

"Marilla will be at the church. The ladies' auxiliary is likely preparing for tonight's dance," Ada said, interrupting his thoughts. Micah wanted to see his grandmother and Ada said she had to speak to the woman about a few matters, none of which she felt compelled to tell him about.

Levi pulled on the reins and turned onto Main Street. Glennis Creek was a dying town, barely more than one road with a few intersecting streets branching out on either side. A couple of storefronts had boards across the windows where people had moved on to greener pastures. Only a few folks going about their business walked along the planked sidewalks. Higher up on a hill at the opposite end of the street sat Harlan's house, once a beacon of prosperity. Now even that building looked more tired and worn than Levi remembered. How long would it be before the town gasped its last breath?

"Not many people about."

Micah bounced in the seat between them, his excitement over coming to town—or going anywhere away from the mountain—palpable. "Ma said they all left on account of the railroad that passed us by and went to Salvation Falls instead."

Levi glanced over Micah's head to the boy's mother. "You ever think of leaving?"

Her lips tightened. "It takes more than thinking to make things happen."

Her cryptic answer left him no closer to determining her state of mind than before. Did she regret last night? Did she think he planned on riding away as if

it had meant nothing? Fact was, he wasn't going anywhere without her and Micah. He wished he could
tell her that, but with Micah sitting between them,
now was hardly the time.

He smiled to himself. Later. Tonight, after Micah
went to bed and they were alone, he'd tell her his
plan, and how she and Micah figured prominently
in it. "Guess you're right on that account."

He pulled up on the reins in front of the church.
Its white spire jutted into the azure sky like a spear,
reaching for the heavens. Once upon a time, Levi had
entertained the notion of walking down those front
steps with Ada on his arm, the two of them joined for
all eternity. It had been a nice dream, one he'd played
over and over in his mind while he'd sat in prison.
As far-fetched as the dream had become, it had still
been his favorite and he'd refused to give it up.

He stared at the steps now and realized that hadn't
changed. That he still could not let it go.

Levi set the brake and Micah and the dog jumped
down after him as he went round to the other side to
assist Ada. He held up his arms, feeling a pull in his
left side, although the pain had eased to mere dis-
comfort. She hesitated, then placed her hands on his
shoulders and allowed him to lift her down.

Once her feet touched the hard ground, he meant
to let her go, but his hands refused to budge from
her waist, as if they'd decided they were right where
they belonged and had no interest in going elsewhere.

"Levi?" Her fingers slid to his hands and he
wished they didn't have the barrier of leather gloves
keeping him from feeling the warmth of her skin.

"Do you regret last night?"

She shot a glance at Micah, but the boy had already bounded up the stairs to the church doors and disappeared inside, Bruce fast on his heels.

"Levi, I—"

"I'm not asking you for anything." Not yet, anyway. His hands tightened on her waist, but he resisted the urge to pull her closer. If he did, he would never let her go. "I just want to know. Do you regret it? The truth."

She shook her head. "No. Of course not. But—we need to talk."

"Agreed." He didn't like the way she said it, as if they were on different pages of a book. "About what?"

"I—" She stopped and captured her bottom lip with her teeth. When she looked up at him, he could see the fear and uncertainty in the depths of her green eyes. "Do you want me?"

Levi cupped her cheek, the warmth of her skin seeping through the leather, making him want her all over again. How funny that touching her could hold such power, but it always had. He had never forgotten it. Never forgotten her.

"Darlin', wanting you is buried deep into the marrow of my bones. It isn't going anywhere. Tell me you don't feel this thing between us every bit as strong as I do."

She let out a sharp laugh and she gazed up at the deep azure sky above. "I do," she whispered. A sweet smile played on her lips and he wanted to kiss her so thoroughly in that moment that what was left of the town would be scandalized if they knew. The only thing that stopped him was the *but* lingering at the end of that statement, unspoken but written in her eyes, in the uncertainty he saw there. But whatever it was that held her back, it hid in the shadows.

"Come with me to Salvation Falls." The words shot out of him before he could think. But what was there *to* think about? He loved her. Lived and breathed her. He'd always known it. As much as he told himself to forget her, he couldn't. Hadn't wanted to. She'd been home to him. The smell and touch and feel of her. All of it. None of that had changed.

"Levi—"

But he didn't let her continue. He couldn't. Her tone had the edge of rejection to it, and he'd had enough of that from her to last him a lifetime. This time it would be different. It had to be. "We could be a family, Ada. Glennis Creek is a dying town. Before long it's going to be nothing but empty structures and memories. Micah will have a better chance for a future in Salvation Falls. We all will. The future we always dreamed of. Don't you want that? Don't you want to spend the rest of our lives like last night?"

Color that had nothing to do with the cold air blossomed in her cheeks. She stared at a point on his chest and closed her eyes, her lashes fluttering lightly against her skin. He waited, his breath stuck in his throat, until finally she answered with a nod of her head.

He let the breath rush out of him and smiled, the future he'd been robbed of eight years earlier opening before him. "Well, all right, then."

"Levi, there's something I need to say."

"Ma!" The church door banged open and Micah's excited expression filled the doorway, something dark smeared at the corner of his mouth. "Grandma has chocolate squares. They're delicious!"

Levi laughed as Micah disappeared back inside. "You best get on in there before he gets his fill and has the bellyache to prove it. We'll talk more tonight, all right?"

"Okay." She smiled, but it looked forced. He leaned down and planted a kiss on the tip of her nose, then reluctantly let her go.

He waited until she disappeared inside the church before making his way down Main Street to the telegraph office, determined to make contact with Sheriff Donovan Hunter and begin preparing for the future he'd promised Ada all those years ago.

As Ada entered the church, the scents of pine and fir filled her senses and the quiet hum of women's voices lifted in song reached down and soothed her rattled nerves. Marilla stood in front of the choir, directing the ladies as they sang "What Child Is This?"

Once upon a time, she had stood among them. Now she stood on the periphery, no longer a part of the daily life of Glennis Creek. Most thought her exile was her own doing, a response to deep grief over the loss of her husband. Neither she nor Marilla had done anything to correct the misconception.

What would they think once they heard Levi was back in town and staying at the cabin with her?

Levi.

She took a deep breath. He wanted her. He wanted her and Micah to go with him to Salvation Falls. To have a life together. Her heart tried to soar at the news, but it remained too tethered to the past to take flight. She still had to tell him the truth and when she did, when he learned she had kept the truth from him, had allowed his son to be raised by another man—would he still want her then? Would the idea of starting a new life wither and die, killed by the secrets she had kept?

"Ma, come and try the cookies!"

Marilla turned and her arms stopped conducting; the singing petered out as if that was what held the ladies' voices aloft and without it, they could not go on.

"I believe you have had enough cookies, young man," Ada said, focusing on her son for a moment, a brief buffer before she faced the task at hand.

"Ada. It's lovely to see you. I didn't expect you and Micah until tomorrow." For the past two years, they had come down from the mountain and celebrated Christmas Eve with Marilla, returning that evening and spending the morning as just the two of them.

"There was a sudden change of plan."

"I see." She turned behind her to the choir. "Ladies, this might be a wonderful time to break for lunch. I've made arrangements with Linwood to prepare a lovely meal for you at the hotel. Please, enjoy yourselves while I have a visit with my grandson."

Micah grinned and eyed the plate of cookies again.

Ada gave him a warning look and then returned her attention to Marilla. "It's just to be a brief visit, I'm afraid. I hope it isn't too much of an inconvenience."

Her former mother-in-law pulled herself up to her full height, her stature made even more impressive by the fancy plumed hat she wore and the smart dress of silk taffeta, the underskirt sporting a red-and-green plaid reminiscent of the season. She was a large woman, built strong and sturdy and made to last. In the end, she had done just that—she'd outlived her husband and her son until only she remained of the family.

"My grandson is never an inconvenience."

Ada did not miss the emphasis on *grandson*. "Of course." She gave Marilla a tentative smile and received the same in return.

Their relationship had never fully mended after her return following Levi's arrest. The breach of her mother-in-law's trust had never completely healed. Micah provided a bridge between them, a link, even though they both knew not an ounce of Baxter blood flowed in his veins. Regardless, Marilla had embraced the boy and loved him all the same.

What would she say now when Ada told her Micah's real father had returned to town? Would it be the final crack in their relationship?

Once the other ladies had filed out of the church, Marilla turned to her. "And what has caused this change in plan?"

Micah wrapped his arms around his grandmother. "Grandma, we have a visitor. He got attacked by a bear but his dog saved him and he let me name his pup so I called him Bruce!"

He bent and picked up Bruce, who licked his face, then looked at Marilla expectantly. She took a step back, her attention transferring to Ada. Despite the smile she kept on her face, an underlying current of tension ran beneath her words. "My, my, but that is quite a bit of excitement. And what has happened to this man?"

Ada's heart pounded in her chest and she spoke up before Micah could. "He is staying with us until he is well enough to travel." *And take us with him.*

Marilla's gaze turned icy. "You have a strange man staying with you and my grandson in the cabin?"

"Oh, he ain't a stranger."

"Micah," Ada interrupted. This was not a conversation she wanted to have with him here. "Why don't you head down to the mercantile and see if Mr. Pickering can set aside the things on our list?" She reached into her pocket for the short list she had written out. "I'm sure there will be a peppermint stick awarded for your assistance."

Micah did not need to be asked twice. The boy had a sweet tooth that was insatiable. He took the list, kissed his grandmother and ran down the aisle in the wake of the choir. "C'mon, Bruce! Bye, Grandma! I'll see you later!"

His words echoed down the hallway, partially drowned out by Bruce's excited barking.

Ada waited until the church doors had closed behind him before turning back to Marilla.

"What does the boy mean, he isn't a stranger?"

Ada clasped her hands in front of her in an effort to keep them from shaking. It had been a long time since she'd stood up to anyone. She was well out of practice.

"It's Levi MacAllistair."

Marilla grasped the pearls at her throat and took a step back, one hand gripping the pew next to her for purchase. Ada stood still, waiting for the news to sink in before she continued. "New evidence proved his innocence and he was freed. On his way to Salvation Falls he had a run-in with a bear. He made his way to the cabin and we took him in."

"And you thought to bring him here? To flaunt him in front of the entire town?" Marilla spat out the words, her expression one of shock and anger. "You promised. We had an agreement!"

Ada let her gaze drop. She *had* promised. Years ago when fear had made her brain so addled she could think of nothing else to do. Levi's trial hadn't been going well, the guilty verdict a foregone conclusion. The town had been out for blood after losing one of their own. She would have been left alone and pregnant, both she and her child shunned and abandoned with no means of support. Save for Marilla and Harlan. All she'd had to do was promise to never breathe a word of Micah's parentage. To never allow the stench of scandal to taint the Baxter name.

"I kept my promise," she whispered. The cost had been great, but she'd endured it for Micah's sake.

"Do you think the people around here won't talk? Plenty still remain who remember what happened. It will take one look at Micah and *that man* together for them to start whispering and asking questions all over again. Harlan deserves better than that!"

"Harlan deserves nothing from me!" She clamped a hand over her mouth but it was too late—the harsh words were already out there, the damage done.

"He took you in after you deserted him to lie with another man."

Ada's hand dropped away and she acknowledged the truth of what Marilla said. But it wasn't the whole truth. "*You* took me in and convinced him to marry me. And every day after that, Harlan made sure he reminded me of the sacrifice he had made. The burden he'd taken on. He treated me with cold contempt and Micah as if he were an interloper. He never once showed my son the smallest amount of affection. Don't tell me you didn't see it."

Marilla pulled her mouth into a stern line. "What did you expect from him after what you had done?"

"I expected him to hate me. But not Micah. He had no say in what happened. He was just an innocent baby. He deserved better than what he got from your son. He deserved a father who loved him."

"And you think that's what you're going to get with that outlaw? A deserving father who will stick around and raise his boy properly? Does he know Micah is his?"

"No. I haven't told him. Or Micah."

"But you plan to, don't you? I can see it in your eyes. You think you can go back and recapture what you've lost. It's a fool's errand, Ada. You'll end up hurt and devastated just as you did the last time."

"Perhaps." She understood the risk. But she couldn't live with the secret rotting inside of her any longer. Not now, when Levi was free in the world, able to be a father to their child. "But he deserves to know. They both do."

"And then what? You expect it will be sunshine and rose petals forever after?"

Ada liked the idea of that. It had been a long time since she'd basked in the sun or allowed happiness to creep in and spread its light. So long she could no longer recall the feeling. But being near Levi made the memory a little stronger. Brought the possibility of feeling it a little closer.

"I want to be happy, Marilla. Is that such an awful thing?" There. She'd said it. Claimed the need she'd shoved into a dark corner for too many years, thinking she didn't deserve it for all the hurt she'd caused. Not just to Harlan and Marilla, but to Micah and Levi, as well. She'd thought she had been doing the right thing, but had she? Or had she simply done the easier thing? The necessary thing? She didn't know for certain any longer. But she couldn't change the past—she could only deal with the present and hope for a better future.

Marilla's expression softened and for a brief moment, Ada saw the woman who had first taken her in at fourteen. The woman who had soothed her fears and promised her everything would get better.

"It isn't an awful thing, Ada. But be careful what you wish for, my dear. Some say the truth will set you free, but from what I've seen, it only ties you down all the tighter. Don't expect absolution for your choices."

"I don't. I made my choices. And I've made this one. Levi has a right to the truth." The more time she spent with him, watching him with her son—their son—the harder it became to deny. Harder still to ignore the fact he'd be a wonderful father to Micah. The father the boy should have had instead of the one he'd ended up with. Now he had that chance. They all did. But at what cost?

"So be it. But know this, I will not pick up the pieces a second time. I wash my hands of it." Her voice quieted and sadness darkened her eyes. "I wash my hands of you."

Ada sucked in a breath as the word cut into her, softly delivered on sharp edges. She understood, but the understanding didn't make it hurt any less. "Fair enough."

"When will you do it?"

"I'm not certain. After Christmas Day." If things went badly, she did not want to ruin the day for Micah. He'd been so looking forward to it, even more so since Levi had arrived. "He's asked us to come with him when he leaves for Salvation Falls."

If he rejected her now, would he claim his rights as Micah's father and take her son with him regardless? The possibility frightened her more than she'd thought possible, resurrecting all the fears Harlan had embedded deep within her since the day she'd been forced to crawl back to him.

"And you've said yes?"

"Yes, though he may change his mind when he learns the truth." Fear of the unknown turned her stomach, and she placed a hand against her middle to try and contain the feeling before it spread through her.

"I won't wish you happy," Marilla said, stepping forward. She placed a hand over Ada's. "I can't. You understand?"

Ada nodded, words unable to break through the lump in her throat.

"Goodbye, dear." Marilla kissed her on the cheek and let go of her hands, walking down the center aisle without looking back. The finality of her words rang out like church bells and resonated deep within Ada.

She choked on a sob as the church door closed behind the woman who had been a second mother to her, leaving her alone with her fears.

But fearful or not, she had set upon this road, and she had to complete the journey.

Chapter Eight

"You've been quiet." Levi glanced over at Ada as they entered the cabin, their arms laden with supplies.

"Have I?" Even her response came as an afterthought, a few beats after he'd made his observation, as if it took a moment for her to pull herself out of wherever it was she had gone.

Her arms wrapped around the small package she'd purchased in town, holding it tightly against her chest as if to ward off the cold that had permeated the cabin during their absence. Her silence, the way she avoided his gaze, left him unnerved. Something had changed during her visit with Mrs. Baxter, something that had left an indelible impression on her. Something she appeared disinclined to share with him.

Micah came in after them with an armload of wood, Bruce trotting behind. Ada turned to her son as she set down her package. "Get washed up and ready for bed, sweetheart. I'll be in to tuck you in—"

"Ma!" He turned on her and the dog followed suit, plopping into a sitting position at the Micah's feet. "I'm not a child. I'm eight years old, practically a man! I can tuck myself in."

Something rippled across Ada's features at Micah's words but Levi failed to read it, his mind too stuck on the actual words to think about much beyond that.

I'm eight years old.

Except that he wasn't. He was seven. He had to be. Because if he wasn't then—

He looked to Ada. She did not gaze his way, but kept her eyes fixed on the boy. A muscle beneath her ear jumped and one hand fisted tightly at her side. When she spoke, her voice was wrong. Too high. Too lighthearted.

"I suppose you're right. You're growing up faster than I'd like, but I can't stop it. Very well, then. Off you go. Tuck yourself in, little man."

Levi stumbled backward, the world tilting and throwing him off balance. Ada kept talking in that voice that didn't fit, as if nothing had changed. Yet everything had.

Micah straightened. "Really?"

She nodded again. "Off you go."

Levi watched it all, each word and movement coming to him as if through a filter, the rosy glow of the day stripped away, leaving a raw image he'd been unprepared to see. Ada had put his earlier suspicions to rest and he'd let the idea go, accepting her words as truth, certain she wouldn't lie to him. Not after all they had meant to each other. The things they'd been through.

But she had. She had lied.

He's seven.

Except that he wasn't. He was eight.

The truth settled around him, its pieces too broken for him to fit them back together, and still she avoided his gaze.

"Can I take Bruce with me?" Micah asked.

"I'm sure that will be fine."

But Levi stopped him before he could go. "Micah, when's your birthday?"

Micah shrugged. "July twenty-ninth."

"And you'll be nine?"

"Yes, sir."

Levi nodded, did the sums in his head, felt the anger and shock in his chest burn hot and unforgiving.

Ada addressed her son; the high tone of her voice had dropped, becoming deeper, defeated. "Off to bed, Micah. We'll see you in the morning."

Micah stepped forward and kissed his mother on the cheek. "Good night, Mr. MacAllistair."

Mr. MacAllistair. As if he was a stranger. Not his father.

Once the door to the bedroom closed, Ada turned, fear embedded deep in the green of her eyes. He wasn't wrong. His first instinct had been the right one. Micah was his son. His chest grew painfully tight. He rubbed at it, but the feeling refused to abate, spreading to his throat, his lungs, his limbs.

It surprised him he hadn't recognized it earlier. And yet he had, on some level. In some moments, Micah's gestures or words or expressions had appeared so familiar, as if he'd seen them before but couldn't place where. And why would he have placed them? Ada had held her secret close to her heart, as if she was the only one who deserved to know. She'd denied his claim when he'd raised those suspicions.

I don't think he liked me much.

Micah's words resonated in his head and another

truth settled in, hateful and ugly. Harlan had known. And Harlan had resented the boy because of it. Why had she done it? Why hadn't she told him?

All those years he'd spent in prison thinking he had nothing waiting for him when or if he ever woke from that nightmare, and she had known all along. Ada, whom he had loved above all else, whom he had trusted, adored. She'd robbed him of his son.

Until he'd met her, he'd led a life forced upon him by his father and circumstance. He hadn't known any other way to survive, had never had a reason to try. A part of him had figured it hadn't mattered. One day he'd catch a bullet and that would be the end of it. That's how it was for men like him, living on the outside of the law. They'd put him in the ground and he'd be forgotten, barely more than a marker sticking out of the dirt to say he'd ever been there.

Until he'd stumbled into Ada on that fateful day and suddenly the sky had brightened and light invaded the dark. She'd given him hope. Purpose. He'd put her on a pedestal, thinking she was his salvation. And for a time she was. She'd loved him. At least he'd thought so. But when push came to shove, when darkness crept back in and brought their world crashing down around them, she'd abandoned him. She had gone back to a man who promised safety and security. And she'd let his son call Harlan Baxter father while he wasted away like a forgotten dream.

Ada bowed her head, her hands clasped in front of her tightly enough for him to see the whites of her knuckles. "You don't understand," she whispered.

"You're right, I don't," he said. The words scraped over his throat like shards of jagged glass and he wanted to drive the words into her. To hurt her as much as he was hurting. All this time, a piece of him had existed out in the world and he had never known. She'd lied to him with her silence.

Ada hugged her arms around herself. "I can explain."

"Doubtful." What explanation could she provide that would satisfy him?

He wasn't sure the words existed that could create a balm for the wound her lie had inflicted.

Ada stared at him, let her gaze roam over his handsome face, filled with pain and broken trust, and her heart boarded up its gates against the inevitable. Where did she begin? How did she say the words that would make him understand? What did it matter? He would not forgive her. She could see it in his face—beyond the shock and disbelief, she could see it. No words would be enough.

She reached out a hand to touch him, to anchor herself, but he pulled away, the muscles in his jaw tightening. He headed for the door and she rushed to it. As she was closer, she reached it first and pressed her back into it, barring his departure. He couldn't leave. Not now. Not like this.

"Micah is your son." The words rushed out of her in a whisper. Her gaze shot to Micah's bedroom door and then back to Levi.

He stepped back, away from her. The hope and promise she'd seen earlier in his eyes had turned to stone, crowding out everything else.

"Move." One word, filled with anger and purpose. She shook her head, her palms and back flat against the cold pine of the door. Levi reached out and banged his fist on the wood behind her, his face only inches from hers. "Open the door."

The words were strangled. Desperate. As if he couldn't breathe.

"Levi, please—"

But he didn't listen. Wouldn't listen. He reached behind her and grabbed the door handle, forcing it open, pulling her with it. Her lighter weight proved no competition to his superior strength and his determination to get out of the cabin, away from her.

She followed him out, the cold air hitting her sharp and hard as Levi stumbled into the evening, the deep snow that had drifted around the shoveled pathways pulling at his legs, slowing him down. Above them, the sky had darkened to a deep indigo punctuated with stars.

Ada grabbed Levi's sleeve before he could go too far. "At least let me explain."

He turned and pulled his arm from her grasp. "When did you find out you carried my son?"

She flinched at his words but held her ground. It was no more than she deserved.

"Shortly after your trial began."

By then, his fate had been all but sealed. The people in the town had wanted blood, and his father being sentenced to hang had not been enough. Though no real evidence had been given against him that wasn't lies and supposition, the townspeople had already made up their minds. He was guilty by association, if nothing else. Levi and Ada's entire world had crashed down around them. She'd been frantic, desperate to protect their baby growing in her belly.

"Why didn't you tell me?"

Thin strands of moonlight cast their glow across his features, bathing him in an ethereal light until he reminded her of an avenging angel.

"I was terrified. You were going to prison or— worse." She swallowed. Even now, all these years later, the tinny taste of fear filled her mouth. "All I wanted to do was protect our baby, but I didn't know how, so I turned to Marilla."

"And ran back to Harlan." The statement was laced with anger, barbed with sharp thorns and accusation.

She nodded. "I didn't want to, but Marilla said it was the only way to ensure the baby had a father and a home. I had no means of support, no chance of finding any because of—" She stopped, puffs of white dissipating in the air from her breath.

"Because of me."

Ada refused to meet his gaze. Refused to place the blame at his feet. He'd been an innocent victim in all of this, sent away for a crime he hadn't committed, years of his life stolen from him, their future together ripped away. "I made the decision to do what I did."

"She knew you carried my son? And Harlan knew?"

Ada met his hard gaze without flinching. "Yes. Marilla said if I married Harlan quickly enough, we could pass the baby off as coming early. That no one would question whether Micah was his."

"So you sold yourself for a better life."

The underlying meaning in his words pounded into her like fists and left her reeling. She reached out and grabbed the one thing she could find. Anger. Justification. The sense of desperation she'd experienced over eight years ago when she faced bringing a baby into the world on her own in a town that had turned against her because she'd chosen the wrong man.

"You were all but convicted. At worst, you would hang. At best, you'd be incarcerated. I was on my own. You couldn't help me. You couldn't even save yourself!" He recoiled, but she kept going, needing him to understand. Needing to know she hadn't wanted to hurt him, only to save their son. "What kind of life would Micah have had? How would the townsfolk have treated him—the bastard child of a convicted murderer? I would have been run out of Glennis Creek without a cent to my name and no way to care for our baby. So you tell me—what other choice did I have?"

"You had the choice to at least tell me!" His voice roared between the space dividing them, across the past to the present, bringing with it all the anger and hurt her betrayal had wrought. She didn't fight it. He had a right to it.

Fate had dealt them a hard hand, and she'd played it as best she could.

"What would you have done? What would you have had me do differently?"

He said nothing and the truth settled between them into an uncomfortable silence. In the end she had set aside her own needs and put her son's first, ensuring he would not suffer for her weaknesses, that he would be safe and cared for.

"You could have told me—after Harlan died."

"I wanted to." Every day that passed, the guilt of her silence weighed heavy in her heart. But Harlan had tied her hands. "Harlan left everything to Marilla. She agreed to support us provided I kept my silence. She wanted to protect her son's memory. It was all she had left."

Levi turned away from her. After a moment, he tilted his head back to address the stars. His voice had calmed, anger now replaced by raw pain. "For over eight years I thought of this day. Dreamed about it. It was crazy." He laughed and the sound was as bitter as the cold air around them. "You were married and I had years left on my sentence. But when I heard Harlan had died, I thought maybe...I was such a fool."

"No!" She took a quick step forward, then stopped, his stark posture not inviting intimacy, especially not from her. "It wasn't foolish."

Hadn't she thought the same thing? Hadn't she dreamed of it every night, too? Sometimes those dreams were the only thing that got her through the next day. That, and watching Micah grow, so much like his father in so many ways. Levi had been gone from her life, but he'd left a piece of himself behind, and she would do whatever was necessary to protect the amazing boy they had created.

"I can't stay here tonight."

"There is nowhere else to go." She took another step toward him, needing him to understand even if he couldn't forgive her, but his warning glare stopped her in her tracks, the cold from the ground beneath her seeping into her feet and traveling upward. "It is far too cold and you're still healing."

"I'll be fine."

"No. If you're leaving, at least give Micah a proper

goodbye." He didn't answer, so she pushed on. "Take the bed. I'll sleep in Micah's room tonight. We can talk more in the morning."

He looked at her and what she saw in his gaze frightened her. "You think a night's sleep is going to change anything?"

She wished she could tell him yes. But she'd told enough lies.

She turned and tromped through the snow back into the house. For a while, she stood next to the woodstove, letting its warmth permeate the ice that filled her bones. In the corner, the Christmas tree stood in the shadows, decorated with strings of berries and bows made from scraps of leftover material. The sight of it pained her. Once upon a time she had loved Christmas, believed in the sense of hope it always brought her.

She shook her head. Whatever hope she'd harbored for her and Levi lay in tatters outside in the snow next to the man she loved—had always loved. She waited for Levi to come inside, but as the wood burned down and she fed another log into the stove, she realized her wait was in vain.

With a sad and heavy heart, she took off her coat and placed it on the hook by the door, then went into Micah's room.

The cold hit her full force, as if she'd taken a wrong turn and walked back outside. Her breath came out in a visible puff of white vapor, and directly across from her the curtains billowed softly against the window, revealing an opening about two feet in height.

Her gaze shot to the bed, where moonlight cut

a swath across its middle. A lump filled its center, but there was no sign of the dog sleeping next to it.

"Micah?" She rushed to the bed and threw back the covers.

The bed was empty.

Micah was gone.

Chapter Nine

Levi stood in the snow, unable to move. Out of the corner of his eye, he could see the Christmas tree inside with its strings of berries and homemade decorations hanging from the branches. Something about the tree calmed him. His first real Christmas tree. His first real Christmas. Just the sight of it had given him faith that everything would work out.

A strangled laugh cut the air around him and he turned away from the sight, from the image of her standing on the other side of the door, worried and upset. He didn't want to see her side of things. Didn't want to give her his pity or his understanding for the choice she'd faced. None of that erased her lie.

Why?

What had she thought he would do? Run into town and scream the news from the top of his lungs for all to hear? He wanted to. In the short time he'd been here, Micah had squirmed beneath his skin, and his fondness for the boy went beyond just thinking he was a great kid. Had a part of him known for certain all along? Seen a part of himself in his son? Maybe.

His son.

Funny thing was, the boy had been right. He'd made a Christmas wish and it had come true. He'd wished for a family of his own. And tonight Ada had presented it to him, but it came wrapped up in lies and betrayal.

"Be careful what you wish for," he muttered and another bitter laugh escaped him. He shouldn't be laughing, but it beat crying in this kind of cold, freezing the tears to his face and burning them into his skin.

"Levi!"

Ada's voice startled him, shattering his reverie like thin ice, leaving it crumbled on the ground at his feet. He heard something desperate in her voice and didn't even have the word for it, but he reached the door before he was even conscious of moving at all. She met him there, throwing the door open. The expression on her face stopped him in his tracks.

"What is it?" *Micah.* The name whispered through him and dragged with it a fear he'd never thought possible.

"He's gone."

He shook his head, refusing to acknowledge the words. "What do you mean gone?"

She gulped air in short breaths. "His window is open and he's just…gone. He's run away. I can see tracks by his window, but it's too dark to tell where they go. I—do you think he heard us?"

Guilt bled through Levi's veins. He hadn't been quiet when voicing his anger. On a still night, the sound could easily have carried. Why hadn't he thought of that?

Why did Micah run? It was dark and cold and he had nowhere to go.

But hadn't he been about to do the same thing? Because Ada had told him Micah was his son. Somewhere in the miasma of emotions attacking him from all sides, he knew running made no sense, but it had been instinct. It had been what he'd always done when trouble brewed or things got tough. It was what his father had taught him.

He kept his voice calm for no other reason than it seemed she needed it and despite everything, he had to give it to her. "He couldn't have gotten far. Stay inside, I'll find him."

"No! I'm going with you!"

She tried to move past him but he caught her, feeling the pull against his injuries as she fought him. He held her tight, her desperation to see her son—their son—safe making her strong, feeding a beast inside of her he was only beginning to understand. To share.

Nothing else mattered now. Only Micah.

His hand cupped her face and forced her to look at him. "He might come to his senses and return home before he gets too far. He'll need you here if he does."

Slowly his words reached her and she nodded, but the terror did not leave her, indelibly carved into the fine bones that made her so beautiful. He pressed her back inside with him, grabbed his rifle and a lamp from the kitchen table, and made to leave.

"Levi—"

He stopped and turned to her, and in that moment, the years peeled away and there in the middle of the room stood the girl he'd fallen in love with, the girl who had been riddled with fear the last day he'd seen her. The day she'd come to say goodbye. The day she had known she carried their child.

A sliver of understanding wound around him and he had the sudden need to comfort her. How crazy was that? Very. But it didn't change the facts. So he set his rifle and lamp down and walked straight up to her, wrapped her in his arms and kissed her hard.

"I will bring him back. I promise."

It was a stupid promise to make. The woods were dark and, as he'd discovered the hard way, filled with hungry animals fighting to find their next meal. He didn't care.

Nothing was going to stop him from protecting his son.

He had forgotten how absolute the dark of the woods could be. Prison had its own kind of darkness, but it wasn't like this. The lamp barely illuminated anything beyond the end of his mare's nose and the thick trees blocked out any assistance from the moon and stars. All he had to go by was the trail of footsteps left behind. Two sets—one straight, the other crisscrossing over them. Bruce. At least the boy had the dog with him. It gave Levi some small modicum of comfort.

Though not much. Fear kept sliding through him, hissing and taunting him with its frightful ideas of every horrible thing that could happen to a young boy stumbling through the woods at night.

"Micah!" He called the name repeatedly until his throat ached and his voice grew reedy. He willed it to hold out. "C'mon out, son. Your mother's worried and I'm freezing my particulars off. Can't imagine you aren't feeling a little of both those things."

Silence answered back.

His son had obviously inherited his mother's stubborn streak.

He urged his horse on, following the footsteps and holding the lamp high in front of him. His horse's ears flickered and the mare snorted. Levi pulled up on the reins and held still, listening. Trying to see through the darkness. There was nothing.

Disappointment flooded him. He shook it off. He didn't have time for that. He didn't have time for anything that wouldn't bring Micah home to his mother. Nothing else mattered.

He continued, each step bringing him closer to understanding, if not to his son. *Their son.* Had Ada experienced the same single-mindedness when she'd realized she carried their baby? Their circumstances had been dire. Looking back now, knowing how things had played out, her question haunted him.

What would you have had me do differently?

Nothing. As much as he hated to admit it. What other option *had* she had? None that he could think of. He'd been selfish. He'd been too angry to see past his own hurt to the truth of the situation. She had set aside her own wants and needs to ensure Micah had the best life possible. A life Levi couldn't have given him.

She had done what she'd had to.

Just as he had to carry on now.

No matter the cost.

A bark echoed through the darkness and his mare snorted in response. He turned toward the sound. "Micah?"

More barking.

Levi kicked his heels against the horse and they headed as swiftly as the deep snow would allow toward the sound. When he reached it, he found Micah huddled against the cold near an old gnarled tree, a lamp bouncing in his hand as he tried to quiet the dog, sending tendrils of light flitting across the white snow.

"Bruce, hush!"

"Too late, son. The jig's up."

Micah turned to him, his face set in a stern expression, his ears, nose and cheeks bright red from the cold. "I'm not going home."

Levi cocked his head to one side. "You plan on sleeping out here tonight?"

He received a militant stare as his answer. Micah was definitely his mother's son.

"All right, then. You got a bedroll?"

The stare faltered.

"No? Food, then?"

Micah's mouth turned downward.

"Hmm. Well, sure hope that bear doesn't come back. You stay safe now." Levi pulled at the reins and turned his horse around.

"Wait!" Levi smiled but checked it before turning back to face Micah. "Maybe I could come back. I guess. Bruce is kinda cold."

"Sounds like a smart idea. Sure would hate to find you and Bruce frozen solid by morning. I'd have some explaining to do to your mother if that was the case."

He held his arms out to take Bruce from Micah, then lifted the boy up to sit in front of him, settling the dog in his lap.

"You ain't even gonna be there in the morning. I heard you fighting. What she said about you being my real pa." Micah sniffed and from his vantage point Levi saw his bottom lip wobble. "Is that true? Are you my pa?"

Levi nodded, unsure of how best to answer him. How could he explain? He was well out of his depth and wondered what Ada would do. What she'd say. "I am, Micah. I'm proud as hell about that, too. And I'm not going anywhere." The truth of the words rang through him. "We're going to be a family."

"But you were so angry."

He gave a little laugh and shook his head. "I expect I was. It was a bit of a surprise, finding out I was your pa. But a good surprise."

"Why didn't Ma tell us?"

"Well, that's a long story and I guess you got a right to hear it, but I think right now the important thing is to get you home out of this cold and let your ma know you're all right. She's frightfully worried about you."

Micah sniffed and nuzzled his face into Bruce's neck. "Yes, sir." Then he said, "I'm glad you're my pa, too."

Levi smiled and something unfamiliar filled the empty spaces inside him with a warmth he hadn't thought possible. He pulled Micah tighter against his chest.

"Let's go home, son."

Chapter Ten

Ada had never experienced such relief as when she saw the horse come out of the trees and realized there were two riders and not one. She threw open the door and ran outside, heedless of the cold or the fat, fluffy flakes falling from the sky.

"Micah!"

"He's fine," Levi called out. He slid from his horse and reached for the boy to help him down. The moment Micah's feet hit the ground, the boy ran to her. She fell to her knees and wrapped her arms around him and the dog, offering a silent thank-you to the heavens for his safe return. She didn't even want to imagine what she would have done had Levi not succeeded.

She looked past Micah to the man standing by his horse. "Thank you," she whispered, but the words seemed inadequate. Despite the trouble between them, he hadn't hesitated. He'd headed out and brought their son home safely.

He tipped his hat toward her. "I best get this ole mare to the barn. Better take Micah inside and warm him up. I'll be along shortly."

Ada directed Micah to the warm fire she'd kept going, needing something to keep her busy while she waited for their return. The cider simmering on the woodstove filled the warm and cozy cabin with a spicy aroma. She poured Micah a mugful.

"Here you go, sweetheart." She pulled the quilt from the sofa and wrapped it around his shoulders as he sat cross-legged on the braided rug in front of the flames.

"Mmm." He closed his eyes and took a sip.

She watched her son and wondered where to start. "I suppose I have some explaining to do."

Micah looked over at her. "It's all right, Ma. I guess I was a bit mad, but I'm happy, too. Besides, I already knew Harlan wasn't my pa."

Her heart stopped. "You did?"

He nodded. "I heard him say it once. Figured that was why he didn't like me as much as you did. But Levi seems to like me fine, so guess it makes sense he's my pa, right?"

"I guess so." Ada couldn't help smile at the logic of children, how quick they were to accept, unburdened by the judgments and expectations the years hung on you.

Micah took another sip of cider, a thoughtful look spreading across his features. "I think he'll make a good pa."

She smiled. "I think so, too." She always had thought so. It had pained her to watch Harlan's indifference, knowing that if it had been Levi in his place, it would have been a different story.

The door opened and Levi walked inside, stomping his feet to knock the snow from his boots.

Micah glanced over his shoulder. "Can I call you Pa now?"

Emotion rippled over Levi's face as he swept the

hat from his head and placed it on the hook next to the door. "I think I'd like that."

Micah nodded, the matter settled. "Good." He lay down in front of the fire and opened the quilt, motioning for Bruce to crawl inside. The pup eagerly accepted the invitation.

Levi looked at her then, hesitantly, as if unsure whether he should approach or not. She patted the spot on the sofa next to her. "Please." She wanted him near her. Even now, with Micah home safe, she needed to lean on his strength.

He joined her, sitting close enough for her to feel the cool air that still clung to his body. "Thank you, Levi. I know we have plenty to—"

He reached out and covered her hands with his, shifting slightly to face her. She held her breath, afraid to hope. Something had changed, she could sense it, but what it meant, she had no idea.

"I understand," he said. "What you did. I get it now. When I was out there looking for Micah, I knew there wasn't anything I wouldn't do to bring him home safe and sound. I'd sell my soul to the devil if I had to. Anything."

His confession seeped through her, traveling through her body until it filled her, wrapped around her heart and squeezed. "Levi."

She didn't know where to start. There was so much to say. Too much. She wanted to tell him what she had gone through when she turned away from him. How every day since she'd wished it could have been different. That she had missed him and loved him, craved his smile and laughter and light.

She glanced at Micah, but her son's—*their*

son's—eyes were closed. The day's events had left him spent. She knew the feeling.

Levi followed her gaze, then squeezed her hand. "Here's how I see it. At the end of the day, I don't want to live without you. Or Micah. And I figure if we've survived everything else, then we can survive this, too."

Tears choked her so that she couldn't speak, only nod.

"Besides, I told Micah we were going to be a family and I'd hate to go back on a promise to my son."

The words, and the love with which he said them, left her staggered. How she loved this man, how she had always loved him. And *would* always love him. "I'd like that."

Levi smiled and lines creased the corners of his eyes that shone in the firelight. "Well, all right then. Guess we should kiss on it, seal it proper. Then maybe tomorrow we can ride back into town and see if the preacher can't make this union proper, too."

Marry Levi? Her heart soared. "But tomorrow's Christmas Eve."

He nodded. "I know, but you see, I made a Christmas wish, and if I'm going to make sure it comes true, we're going to need to be married."

"What was your wish?"

"This." He smiled and kissed her. His lips were warm and the heat of his touch reached everywhere inside of her, chasing away the darkness and shadows.

"Your wish was a kiss?" She wasn't complaining. It was a good wish and she'd be happy to make it come true every day for the rest of the days they had together.

He laughed. "My wish was you. And Micah. Being a family."

She smiled back and touched his face, tracing its lines and angles with the tips of her fingers. How could she be so lucky as to be given this second chance?

"I love you, Levi MacAllistair. Merry Christmas."

He gathered her in his arms, pulling her close and kissing her again, deeper this time, filling the action with all the promises he'd given once upon a time. It had taken a while, but he'd made good on them in the end. And she intended to do everything in her power to ensure he never regretted his choice, to let him know he was loved truly and completely.

Micah groaned and rolled onto his back, not quite as asleep as Ada had estimated. "Are you guys going to be doing a lot of that kissing stuff?"

Levi smiled, broke their kiss and looked, first at Micah and then at Ada, and the love that gleamed in his eyes gave her his answer. "I sure hope so, son. I sure hope so."

"I know so," Ada said, the Christmas wish she'd made every year since the day she'd left Levi to save their son coming true before her very eyes.

This year, it would be a very merry Christmas, indeed. As would all the Christmases to come.

* * * * *

SNOWBOUND
WITH THE COWBOY

Carol Arens

Author Note

It's that time of year to make our lists, check them twice, put on our shopping shoes and head to the mall. To wrap the presents and tie up the bows, send out the cards and bake the treats. It's my Christmas wish that you'll find a few peaceful moments to relax in a cosy chair with a warm drink and a Christmas story.

Best wishes—and may visions of sugarplums dance in your head.

Chapter One

Wind, cold and piercing, blew up Mary Blair's skirt. She was mightily tempted to curse the icy nip biting her thighs, but she didn't hold with cursing... moreover, she was temporarily living at the parsonage.

Staring at the woodpile under the eaves of the stable, she reckoned that if she did give in to the urge to cuss, it would be directed at the absent Reverend Peter Brownstone more than the weather.

As early as this morning it had been clear that a storm was blowing in, and he hadn't had the foresight to bring the wood to the house and stack it under the covered porch.

Truly, the only thing the man had noticed this morning was his new bride blinking gooey eyes at him.

Looming honeymoon or not, he did have an obligation to the orphans in his care.

And to her, as far as that went, since he had hired her to tend them during the prewedding hoopla and then during his absence.

Well, she'd best be quick about this splintery business. The moon had long since been obscured by heavy clouds and the temperature was dropping as fast as a stone tossed into the well.

And thinking of the well, the besotted Mr. Brownstone had also neglected to haul extra water into the house. What did he think four children were going to drink, ice?

Mary tucked five logs into her apron then crossed the yard. Bent over from the weight, she kept her head up, her gaze focused through the window beside the front door. A great snapping fire danced in the hearth and she yearned for its warmth.

Maybe if she filled her vision with flames, her teeth would quit chattering.

After half an hour's hard labor, she had managed to tuck a nice pile of wood under the porch roof and cover it with a tarp. Next, she hauled a heavy bucket up the back steps and dumped water into the big kitchen barrel setting beside the stove.

The exertion of trip after trip to the well warmed her some, but not enough to dispel the shiver.

The first snowflake brushed her cheek at the same time as she shoved the lid over the mouth of the well and latched it into place.

A secure covering over the well was the one thing she had insisted upon before taking this job. One could not be too cautious when dealing with little ones.

By the time she reached the porch steps, the ground was dusted in white. By and large, she enjoyed snow, especially this close to Christmas, but it concerned her that old-timers had predicted this to be a great blizzard.

Even though the parsonage was a bare mile outside of town, snowed in was snowed in, no matter the distance.

Swiping the flakes from her coat and the sting of cold from her fingers, she went back into the house.

Warmth wrapped her in a hug and she sighed. A cup of tea would be a nice reward for her work. She would sit by the fire, gaze out the window and watch the snow blow by, feeling content in a rare quiet moment with the children upstairs asleep.

She crossed the parlor, then paused at the kitchen door, looking back at the room. The rectory was a lovely, cozy home. Plenty large enough for the family that the newlyweds had in mind.

Decorated in warm hues of gold, brown and red, it was a place that she had only imagined in her dreams. She was fortunate to be able to live here until the New Year, when the reverend and his wife would return.

On her way to the pantry, she ran her fingers over the long, polished wood table. Maybe someday...one never knew what path life might take.

She drew the pantry door open and reached for the tea. At least the reverend had made sure there was plenty of food for the children, and that the milch cow in the stable had enough feed.

Fifteen minutes later she had changed into her sleeping gown, tied her red plaid robe snug at her waist and was reclining on the big stuffed sofa with her toes toasting in the warmth of the flames.

She waited for the anticipated contentment to flood her, for the peaceful yet exhilarating spirit of Christmas, which was only ten days away, to wrap her in its joy...but then she spotted the letters to Santa on the table beside her.

Knowing what was in those letters kept contentment at bay. She was certain that the reverend had not given the missives a glance. It was up to her to fulfill those wishes, and they were quite beyond her.

Four-year-old Brody wanted a dog. He was certain that Santa had one just for him. Well, strays did wander by on occasion. But if a blizzard was coming, that slim hope would be dashed.

Brody's twin brother, Caleb, wanted a pa. Even if there were such a thing as a stray father, the blizzard would keep him away, as well. All she could do for little Caleb was pray that he would thrive without one.

Seven-year-old Maudie wanted a mother. After spending a week with the child, Mary would be happy to take that role. But she wasn't married and had no home of her own and therefore nothing to offer…except affection. That she would give in abundance for as long as she was here.

Then there was Dan, with a big wish. At ten years old, he wanted a horse. The boy was certain that life would be forever wonderful if he got an equine friend for Christmas.

Sadly, she had only ten dollars to her name. Not nearly enough to purchase a horse and maintain it.

It broke her heart to think of Christmas morning coming, the children clambering down the stairs, their faces glowing with wonder, only to find handknit socks instead of a ma, a pa, a dog or a horse.

Or a baby…that was Mary's Christmas wish. As long as impossible wishes abounded, she might as well add her own, although she'd never write it down.

Her parents had been told by three doctors not to

expect that blessing for her. There had been an accident when she was young—she didn't remember much of it except that there had been a lot of blood and her mother had cried for a long time.

It had been her father, though, who had prepared her to accept her fate. He'd said he knew what it meant to love a child of one's own. No man should ever be denied that right. He had done his best to make sure she understood, even before she was of an age to know what he was talking about.

Even dolls had been forbidden to her because he feared that they would nurture the desire for a family.

All her life she'd known she would not be a mother, but that did not keep her from wanting to be. Knowledge did not keep the longing away when she saw a pregnant belly or the heartache when she sat beside a woman nursing her infant…heard the baby's contented coos.

A gust of wind shook the windowpane and roused her from her self-pity.

Here she sat, hale and hearty, which was more than could be said of many folks. Moreover, she enjoyed her job as a nanny. As a substitute mother, she was able to pour her love into many children instead of just her own two or six.

Partings were hard, though. But usually after a good cry, she would be off to nurture another friendless child with her heart nearly intact.

Most of her assignments involved caring for the little ones who needed love the most. And truth be told, she needed to give them love as much as they needed to receive it.

At this very moment, though, it was time to put

her secret longing for a baby aside and study the problem at hand. That being, how was she to play Santa when it was impossible?

Naturally, no solution presented itself.

Better if she relaxed in her chair, sipped her tea and listened to the sweet song of the blowing wind.

If she didn't, the thought that she avoided like one would avoid a hot wax burn would creep into her mind.

In addition to never being a mother, she would never be a wife.

Men wanted offspring. Her father had tried to prepare her for that fact, but still, it broke her heart when the few suitors she'd had sought other brides as soon as they discovered her dysfunction.

She would never have a child…she would never have a husband. Life was what it was—she had come to terms with that. Most of the time, at least.

In all, she was blessed. She'd been given a sound, healthy body and a heart that cared for others.

This was enough for her. Sharing herself with children who didn't have a parent made her feel aglow inside.

Feeling the love they gave back made her feel like a mother…just of a different sort.

Something bounded toward him in the snow. Joe Landon stood tall in the saddle, squinting his eyes and trying to make out what it might be. Flakes, tossed about on an erratic wind, blurred the image, but he could make out that it was coming and coming fast.

Whatever the brown critter was, it wasn't alarming his horse.

From a hundred feet away, he heard it yip. A dog was all it was. From fifty feet away Joe could tell that the animal was distressed. Scared of being caught alone in the storm was his guess.

"Best we see to it, Charlie," he said to the horse, then urged him forward with a click of his tongue.

Having gotten Joe's attention, the dog spun about and ran back the way it had come.

"What do you reckon it's doing?" Joe said. "Where'd it even come from?"

The dog spun back about to bark at him. Apparently he wasn't approaching the dog as fast as it wanted him to. It dashed back, ran two circles about Charlie, then bounded away.

The temperature was falling and falling hard. He needed to get to Willow Bank, not play games with a dog.

But a sense of something being wrong told him that this was no game. In spite of the blizzard sweeping in, he couldn't just leave the confounded pup to freeze.

Besides, dogs didn't usually act this way without there being trouble.

Even Charlie must feel the wrongness in the air, because he quickened his gait.

Two animals having a sense of wrongness made him feel ill at ease. He leaned forward in the saddle to scan the horizon. The land didn't reveal a thing, being increasingly smothered with snow.

He followed the dog for a quarter of a mile before he spotted a wagon wheel, wrong end up, half-buried in white.

Leaping from Charlie's back, he struggled through shin-deep snow, his heart thudding against his ribs.

It was too quiet…unnaturally still. Even the dog had quit barking.

He walked the perimeter of the wagon and spotted the body of a man. He knelt beside him. That's when he noticed the woman. It appeared that they had both been killed when the wagon flipped. From the way things looked, he didn't believe they had suffered.

With the snow falling thicker and faster, there was no time to attend to the bodies. There was nothing to be done now but to take the dog, continue on his way to Willow Bank and report the tragedy to the marshal.

He whistled to the dog, but it had curled up in the snow, lying there as though it didn't want to leave its folks.

"Come on, fella." He didn't know if it was a male—the dog was too shaggy to tell. "I've got a big old ranch for you to run on…if you stay here you'll freeze."

The dog whined.

"You'll like the place. You can chase cows all day long."

The dog seemed unimpressed, but at this point it didn't matter what the critter wanted. Joe wouldn't have its death on his conscience. Walking a short distance from the wagon, he knelt and scooped the hairy beast up.

From a divot in the snow a pair of blue eyes blinked at him. A tiny fist, curled up tight, waved about.

Stunned, he set the dog aside and lifted the baby.

Her cheeks were as pink as the bow tied in her hair. She didn't feel overly cold...thank the good Lord. The dog must have been keeping her warm.

The baby wrapped her fingers about his thumb and smiled. He guessed that she must be only a few months old.

"Don't worry about a thing, little lady. I've got you."

He tucked her inside his buffalo hide coat, then mounted Charlie. The dog trotted alongside, glancing up every now and again.

Reaching inside his coat pocket, he withdrew his harmonica and pressed it to his mouth.

He played "O Holy Night." The music drifting serenely among the snowflakes sounded like a prayer.

That was what he intended. A prayer of safekeeping for the souls who had gone home today, but also a prayer of thanks for the life that had been spared.

Emotion constricted his throat, but looking down, he saw the dog's tail wagging.

Chapter Two

In her dream, someone was pounding on a drum.

Pounding, pounding, pounding, with no sense of rhythm.

She sat up suddenly in the chair. Not a drum or a dream—someone was hammering on the door with a great deal of urgency.

It had to be midnight or later; the logs in the fire had burned to embers.

A gust of wind whirled under the eaves with a moan.

She scrambled out of the chair and hurried for the door, her heart thundering from being awakened so suddenly.

What on earth could have brought someone out in what had clearly become the blizzard that the old folks had predicted?

She opened the door to see a man standing on the porch. Truly, he looked more like a snowman, with the brim of his Stetson filled with snow, his coat embedded with it and his boots caked in ice.

A dog rushed inside, shaking itself and flinging snow far and wide.

The shaggy animal could get the whole room damp and she'd still want to fall on her knees and welcome it with a grateful hug.

Would the man part with it for five dollars? That would be half of all she had, but for Brody's sake, it would be well worth the price.

"Please," she said, tugging on the man's coat sleeve because he seemed to be frozen to the porch, "come inside."

"I'm obliged, ma'am." Frost dusted his lashes. That had to be what made his eyes look so incredibly blue. "Is this the parsonage? Couldn't tell for sure with snow hiding the landmarks."

"Yes, and welcome."

In spite of the fact that she was indicating he should come in out of the cold, he stayed put on the porch.

"Have you got room in the stable for my horse?"

He had a dog...and a horse?

Next she would find out he was here to adopt twin boys.

For all she knew, beneath all the snow he really was Santa Claus.

"There's room and plenty of feed, if the horse doesn't mind rooming with a cow."

"Wouldn't feel at home without one." He smiled, his teeth straight and white.

If she wasn't mistaken, his eyes flashed briefly in playfulness in spite of the fact that, at this late hour, he had been traveling in a blizzard.

She suspected that beneath the hat, coat, scarf and layer of snow, he was a sight more handsome than Santa.

"Room for you, as well...here in the house, of course."

"Greatly obliged."

"I'll fix you something warm to drink while you tend to your horse. Later, you can tell me what brings you out in the middle of the night, and in this weather, no less."

Please, dear Lord, let him be looking for orphans.

"It's...well, something I found."

He opened his coat and handed her an infant.

The world tilted. Her mind whirled, then went white.

The next thing she was aware of was warmth on her face. A velvety-smooth tongue licked her from chin to temple. The dog!

The stranger's very solid and muscular thigh shifted behind her back as he knelt on the floor, supporting her.

Cracking open her eyes, she watched him shove the dog back. He gazed down at her. A lock of black hair curled across his forehead. His brows slanted down, showing concern.

In one arm, he cradled the baby.

She'd never fainted in her life and could not be sure that she had done it now, but in her defense, it was not every day that Santa came knocking at the door.

Joe pressed his hand on the woman's shoulder when she tried to stand up.

"Whoa there, ma'am. Best take a minute until your balance is steady."

"It is," she sputtered. "I can't imagine what happened. Honestly, I've never fainted before."

When it seemed that she was going to get up in

spite of his good-sense advice, he slipped his arm about her back and eased her up.

Blushing, she glanced at him, held his gaze. He wondered if she was embarrassed about the faint, or because he, a stranger, had his fingers curled about her ribs.

Whatever the case, he'd been raised better than to let a woman lie on the floor unaided.

Add to that, she had looked like an angel in that Christmas-red robe, her blond hair loose and fanned about her on the rug.

A man would have a heart as black as the ace of spades not to offer assistance.

"I reckon you were asleep when I knocked on your door," he said. She shifted her gaze from him to the baby. "I can only imagine we were a shock."

"More than you know." She stepped beyond his reach, but he closed the gap in case she went down again. He couldn't be sure what was wrong with her.

"You found her, you said?"

He nodded, didn't want to have to tell the story of how, but this was the orphanage and the baby a recent orphan.

"Soon as I get the animals settled, I'll make a pot of tea and tell you what I know."

"I'll make the tea."

He thought she might be up to it, but might not.

"I know how. Pretty darn good at it, in fact," he assured her while touching her elbow to lead her to the chair beside the fire. "I make it for my ma before bed every night. Besides, the baby needs warming. We've been riding for hours, and it's cold as a glacier out there."

He set the child in her arms and was relieved to see that she went into the parlor and sat without protest. He hadn't made it up about the baby being cold. For a time the little one had been as cozy as a moth in a cocoon beneath his coat. But a blizzard was a damn cold thing, and a deep chill had begun to set in.

The weather had especially taken a toll on the animals, being exposed to the elements as they had.

"I won't be long."

He added a log to the embers in the hearth, then gave them a stir before he walked toward the door. He motioned for the dog to follow. It must've been well trained, because it trotted after him, wagging its fuzzy tail.

"Your dog is welcome to stay in the house."

When he turned to smile his thanks, she was gazing at the baby, a look of utter longing on her face.

He had a story to tell, but he wondered what hers was.

The baby girl snuggling in her arms was not hers, she knew that…in her mind she was well aware of it.

She touched the pink ribbon tied in the mass of dark hair, let her fingers slide through loops so soft she barely felt them under her fingertips.

"What happened to you, sweetheart?"

Clearly, the child had been well cared for. She was plump in all the right places and wearing a pretty gown that appeared to have been stitched by loving hands.

That was what Mary would do if she were blessed with a baby like this. Make her the finest wardrobe that caring fingers could sew.

She stroked one pink cheek and the baby turned her mouth toward her finger. The man who brought her had said that they had been riding for hours. No doubt she was getting hungry.

Footsteps pounded on the porch. Having returned from the stable, her guest must be stomping the ice from his boots. When he opened the door, a blast of frigid wind fought him for control.

She'd give him credit for shoving the door closed without spilling a drop from the pail full of milk that he carried.

"The poor little mite will be getting hungry," he said, then turned toward the kitchen.

She ought to get up and help, but it had been an age since an infant slept in her arms. Moreover, he had said that he could make tea. It only followed that he could warm milk.

What he would not know was where the reverend kept baby bottles. The parsonage, having served as the orphanage for some years, was well stocked.

She sat for a moment more, then kissed the baby's cheek. She laid her on the couch, where the warmth of the fire would easily reach. Padding across the room, the dog sniffed the child, then followed his tail in a circle and settled on the floor below her.

Coming into the kitchen, she found a pair of mugs on the kitchen table. Fragrant steam from the tea curled into the air.

Her visitor stood with his back toward her, stirring the milk in a pot. It was a little surprising to see a man so comfortable in the kitchen.

He turned, flashed her a grin. There was something about the crinkle at the corners of his eyes and the lift of his lips that made her feel an affinity to him.

How odd. She was certain that they had never met.

She would not forget a man as appealing as he was. Chances were this sensation of connectedness was simply due to the common goal of caring for the child.

Clearly, it could have nothing to do with him alone, since she had barely spoken more than a few sentences to him.

"Will she be safe in there, alone with your dog?" It seemed so but one could not be too careful.

"He isn't mine, but I've reason to believe that he would give his life for her."

That was a relief…and the dog did not belong to him? Perhaps she could acquire a Christmas gift for Brody and keep her money at the same time.

"I'm Mary," she said. "Mary Blair."

"Joe Landon." He nodded his head. "Many thanks for letting us in. Where's the reverend, by the way?"

"In Chicago, on his honeymoon."

Joe Landon's brows arched. "Now, that's a surprise. I figured him to be a lifelong bachelor."

"Well, one never knows. So you and the reverend are friends?"

"Acquainted, more like it. I try and catch his sermons when I'm in town." He removed the pan with the milk from the stove and set it on the side table she used for food preparation.

Mary went into the pantry, stood on a stool and reached for the basket on the top shelf where the reverend kept items for infant care. It was just beyond her reach, but if she went up on her toes…

"Careful." Suddenly Joe Landon was standing beside her, his hands poised as if ready to catch her.

"I'm steadier than I look." She could not help but be embarrassed that he thought otherwise.

"Here, let me help you down."

He took her hand and didn't let go until both her feet were firmly on the floor.

That odd feeling of connection hit her again. She'd be a fool to deny that she liked the sensation, and she had never considered herself a fool.

"I'll get it." He didn't need the stool to reach the basket.

He'd taken off his outer coat when he came inside. The one he kept on was of well-worn leather having a greenish hue.

Standing close to him because of the tight space in the pantry, she caught the scent of cowhide…also a whiff of fresh straw that clung to him from having been in the stable.

He smelled quite manly. She started to sigh, then caught herself. Sometimes, though, it was hard not to wonder what it would be like to have a man of her own…a man like this one.

From what she had seen of him so far, he was both kind and handsome…heroic as well, she figured. Chances were he had taken some risk riding through the storm to get to the parsonage.

He handed her the box.

Since it would be inappropriate to remain in the close confines of the pantry when the task of retrieving the infant items was finished, she hurried out and set the box on the table.

Opening it, she found a pretty porcelain bottle painted with red flowers.

"It looks like Christmas." She took it out, then washed it with soap and water.

"Give her something cheerful to look at while she's feeding," Joe said, then plucked the bottle from her hand and dried it with a dishrag.

"I've yet to hear her story, but I imagine her mother would want her to have pretty things," she said, surprised at the little giddy-up that her heart took when his fingers had brushed hers in taking the bottle.

"What do you say we sit in here to talk so as not to wake her? I'll tell you what happened…or as near as I can figure what did."

Since the view into the parlor was wide-open, Mary sat on the long wood bench at the table. Joe sat opposite her.

It went through her mind that she ought to run upstairs and change out of her nightclothes. But it seemed a silly thing to do in the middle of the night, and moreover, it was shallow when the story he had to tell would no doubt be life shattering to the baby.

Folks didn't ordinarily bring children who had parents to the parsonage…especially at this hour and in a blizzard.

A hankie was what she ought to go running upstairs for.

Joe drummed his fingers on his mug, his eyes downcast.

He looked up suddenly, his expression somber.

"I was on my way to town on ranch business. My family owns a spread about twenty miles north of here. It had already been snowing for some time when I came upon the dog. Well, it wasn't that I came upon it so much as it hunted me down. It was raising a ruckus, so I followed it to an overturned wagon. The baby's ma and pa were dead. Looked like they didn't suffer. As near as I can tell, one of them must have tossed the baby from the wagon when it was going over. She was only a few feet away. My guess is that the dog had been watching over her, keeping her warm."

"Poor little Amelia."

"Amelia?"

"Her name is embroidered on the hem of her gown."

He nodded. "She's got her name. That's something of them, then."

They sat in silence for a moment, the only sound being the wind battering the north side of the house. Was it her uneasy imagination that the house actually shook?

The blizzard was more intense than it had been even moments ago.

"Angels must have guided you here. I hate to think of what might have happened had you been delayed."

"An angel opened the door, and that's a fact."

Maybe he shouldn't have said that out loud. The lady was a stranger…a blushing stranger, now.

He had no way of knowing if she would be offended or take his comment with the appreciation he had intended.

"I didn't mean to be forward, ma'am. But the plain truth is that in this weather we might not have made it the extra mile to town. Our survival depended upon you opening the door. For me and little Amelia, you were an angel."

The flattery, however sincere and well-intended, seemed not to sit well with her. She shook her head, waved her hand in negation. "If it hadn't been me, it would have been someone else."

"Still, it was you. I'm just sorry the shock of us made you faint."

"Oh, that…it wasn't shock. Certainly not a faint," she said, looking defensive. "I simply got up from the chair too fast and was light-headed."

"All the same, I'm grateful." He knew full well that she was not being completely truthful. She had been fine until he'd handed Amelia to her.

"No need to be. The parsonage exists as a place of refuge, after all." She took a sip of tea, gazing silently at him for a moment. She did have beautiful eyes, the expression soft, doe-like. "At least until the reverend gets back from his honeymoon. I reckon, since you brought Amelia here, you have a right to know about the changes that are coming."

"I can guess. The new wife wants to make this a home for herself and her husband?"

"It's understandable…and they want a big family."

"Are there other orphans living here?"

"Four of them. Until last week there were ten but the town held an adoption social. Six found homes. Amelia would have gone first had she been here. Folks do want babies."

That's something he knew all too well. It had been twenty years since he'd done his time in an orphanage. To this day he broke out in a nervous sweat remembering how it had felt to stand quietly in a row with the other children, wondering which of them the potential parents would choose.

The babies always went first, then the little ones.

He had been nine the first time he had stood in that lineup. For two years he'd faced those inspections with his shoulders straight and his knees clacking.

Then one Christmas Eve, Cornelia Landon had offered him a home.

Before taking him to the ranch, she'd made a stop at the mercantile and purchased him a warm coat, new clothes and two peppermint sticks, one for each fist. While he sat by the stove enjoying the unexpected treat, she did a lot of shopping.

The next morning, he woke to find that Santa had visited for the first time since he'd lost his ma and pa.

"The ones who are left," he said, his heart beating past the remembered ache of rejection. "How old are they?"

Mary ran her fingertip around the lip of her mug. "Dan is ten. Maudie is seven…then there's the twins. Brody and Caleb are four."

He nodded. "It won't be easy for Dan, given his age. And the twins, unless they're split up…but the girl…"

Mary shook her head, a frown dipped her brows. "There was a farmer who wanted her because he'd lost his wife. The reverend and I thought it would not be a good placement for her. The man was slovenly and we feared that he wanted a housekeeper more than a daughter."

"I've seen that happen." Not all the potential par-

ents he'd witnessed coming into the orphanage had
had the children's well-being at heart.

"Have you?"

He nodded. His reasons were not something he felt
like discussing at this moment. This talk was about
the children who lived here.

"He would not have been kind to her," Mary said,
returning to the subject of Maudie. "And truly, there
was something about him…his eagerness to have her
that set us on edge. Especially after he offered to…
well, to buy her. Fifty dollars."

"Whatever Maudie's future holds, it's got to be
better than belonging to the farmer." Even if the poor
child spent the rest of her childhood without a family, it would be better than that.

For the millionth time, he sent up a silent prayer
of thanks for his adoptive mother. Life with his birth
parents had been a sparkling dream, but life with
Cornelia had been a miracle.

"I reckon I'll get to meet them. From the looks of
the weather, I'll be here for some time."

Footsteps pounded down the stairway. The boy—
Dan, he reckoned—dashed into the kitchen gripping
a fireplace poker in his fist.

"I heard a man's voice, Miss Mary," he gasped,
his small chest heaving. "I came on the run."

Chapter Three

"It's all right, Dan. This is Mr. Landon." Mary moved over on the bench and patted it, inviting Dan to join them. "He'll be staying with us until the storm passes."

Hesitant, Dan hugged to the doorjamb. While he didn't come into the kitchen, he did put the poker down beside his bare feet. He nodded his head.

"It's a pleasure, Dan." Joe Landon smiled at him, then he winked. "I hope you don't mind sharing the house with a dog for a while."

"Dog?" Dan spun about. His gaze, which would be obscured by the sleep-tumbled hair hanging in his face, scanned the parlor.

"There it is," she told him. "Keeping watch over the baby."

She heard Dan gasp, then he approached the dog. It looked like a mound of brown fur more than a canine.

The furry creature lifted its head, sniffing the air.

"Will it be aggressive, do you think…because of Amelia?" she asked.

"Let him smell your hand, son," Joe called after him. "Then you can squat down and get acquainted."

The dog licked Dan's hand. When he knelt down, it laved his face, thumped a rhythm with its tail.

"Brody's gonna pee his pants! Can I go wake him up?"

"Don't you dare, young man." Peace was a rare thing in this house, mostly occurring only in the wee hours, as long as no one was sick or having a nightmare.

"You like horses, Dan?" Joe asked.

Standing slowly, Dan pivoted, the dog forgotten, the baby not even noticed. His mouth fell open.

"There's a pinto in the stable who is partial to boys. You go on back to bed real quiet-like, and I'll let you meet him tomorrow."

To Mary's very great surprise, Dan rushed into the kitchen and extended his hand to Joe.

"Welcome to the parsonage, sir."

After Joe returned the greeting with a handshake, Dan rushed back toward the stairway.

Halfway up, she heard a muffled "Yee-haw!"

She stirred the tea in her mug with a spoon. Staring at the swirling liquid, she swallowed the emotion that cramped her throat and threatened to make her weep.

For the month that she had known Dan, this was the first time she had seen him genuinely happy.

It was the horse that made him smile, just as the dog would make Brody smile. More than smile, she reckoned. Dan had not been far off in his declaration that the four-year-old would pee his pants.

When she glanced up at her guest, she half expected to see him sporting a long white beard, his cheeks rosy red and smiling.

"Thank you, Mr. Landon." What she wished she could do was lean across the table and give him a hug of gratitude. What she gave him was a ladylike smile. "You can't know what that means to him."

"I'd be pleased if you called me Joe."

It felt as if she ought to have been calling him that all along. She'd never had this feeling of kinship with anyone so quickly before.

Odd as it was, she felt that when the storm passed and he went on his way, she would miss him.

How could that be? Many people had come and gone in her life. Rarely did her thoughts linger overlong on them.

There were Ma and Pa, naturally. She did miss them. Come summer, she would plan a nice long visit to Virginia.

"If you'll call me Mary."

"Be pleased to, ma'am... Mary."

A quick smile animated his handsome face. Didn't it even shine from his eyes? Her heart beat a little faster.

What kind of fool was she? She knew nothing about him other than that he had business in town and served his mother tea. He could be married with a brood of babies, for all she knew.

Certainly a man as appealing as he was would be spoken for.

"There seems to be room for a ride inside the stable. I'll take Dan with me when I do the feeding in the morning."

"I'm grateful. Dan hasn't had an easy time since he lost his ma and pa."

"What will happen when the reverend comes back?"

Heartache is what.

The expression on her face must have reflected that thought because Joe's smile faded.

"Unless someone in town changes their mind and wants to adopt him—or any of them—they'll be put on the orphan train that's coming into Railhead Springs next week."

"I thought the trains brought children from the east out here?"

"That's right…but the reverend made arrangements with the folks from the Children's Aid Society to pick them up."

"Could be they'll find fine homes." Joe stirred his tea, stared at it the way she had done a moment ago. "Could be they won't. There's no one here in Willow Bank willing?"

"We did try, but given Dan's age…and to tell you the truth, he's been through hard times. Folks don't take to a sullen child. Then there's Maudie. Like I said, Mr. Blankford wants her…but that won't do. And even she's older than folks want."

"The twins are young. That should be in their favor…but they might have to be split up."

"There was a couple from town who took them, but they didn't understand the energy required in wrangling a pair of lively four-year-olds."

The memory of the boys being returned after only a few days still rankled. But it did have to be said that they were a handful, and their would-be mother had looked completely exhausted. The couple might be right for Amelia, but then again, babies were also tiring.

A suddenly urgent wail came from the parlor. She

started to rise but Joe reached across the table and caught her hand.

"Don't trouble yourself. I'll see to her."

His palm felt warm…callused. Maybe it was because of the wild weather punching the house, and his grip was so solid and safe feeling…but she didn't want him to let go.

There was something special about Mary's hand, the way it felt so small and delicate in his.

Made him feel like protecting her. Not that she would likely welcome being protected. She seemed to be a capable woman, what with having the care of four…now five orphans.

For some reason that made him want to champion her all the more. If his ma could get inside his head right now, she'd tell him it was because of his past… that he had a need to make things right.

This was different, though. And, howdy-do, it was a good thing his mother was not in his mind, because he didn't want her to be privy to his suddenly carnal thoughts.

Not only did he not want to let go of Mary's hand, he wanted to lean across the table and kiss her, long and hard. Her lips had been calling to him ever since she had slipped against him when she fainted.

"Joe," she murmured. It was not his imagination that she sounded as suddenly breathless as he was. "The baby."

While he had been lost in a sudden yearning for Mary, Amelia's cry had upped in urgency.

"You look done in, Mary, and I reckon the children will be up in a few hours wanting breakfast. Get some sleep. I'll tend the baby."

He snatched up the bottle, then walked into the parlor. Feminine footsteps padded behind him.

Settling onto the couch, he picked Amelia up. The poor little mite pushed the nipple of the bottle around with her tongue for a moment. Probably wasn't used to feeding from cold rubber.

"Try this," Mary said. Settling beside him on the couch, she covered his hand as he held the bottle, guiding and turning until the baby latched on. "Oh, my goodness, you are a hungry little thing."

"Appreciate the help, Mary. I've bottle-fed calves, but they're not so particular about what they suckle from." He missed the smooth heat of her fingers when she plucked them away. "I can handle it from here. Go on up to bed."

"I'll sit a spell if you don't mind. Babies just grow so fast. A body's got to look her fill while she can."

The last thing he minded was to have Mary sitting on the couch beside him. Seemed as though he couldn't get enough of the warmth radiating from her body, how it mingled with his.

The pair of them weren't touching, but they might as well have been, for all the—what he could only describe as—anticipation arcing between them. He wondered if she felt it, too.

It didn't take long for Amelia to finish the bottle and drift into a contented doze.

"You'll need to burp her." Mary lifted the baby from his arms, then settled her on his shoulder. "Just pat her back until…oh, my…until she does that."

"She ought to be content for a while now," he said.

"A few hours, at least."

Mary stood up. So did he.

"Well, then," she said, her gaze lingering on Amelia for a moment, then shifting to him.

Something inside him danced a dizzy jig. He had the oddest sensation about her...that he and Mary were bound somehow.

The idea was unsettling. Fate...predestination? It made his head swim that he felt this way toward a woman he'd only just met. It made no logical sense.

"I guess I'll go up to bed," Mary said.

Briefly, she stroked Amelia's hair, then she turned and walked toward the stairway. He watched her go while he rocked the infant to and fro, more than a little distracted.

By Mary's lithe form and her graceful movements...by that mysterious something tugging at his heart.

He supposed it wasn't proper to take notice of how her hips swayed under her nightclothes, how her backside seemed sweet and round, but he was only a man and therefore bound by the laws of nature to notice.

"Joe." She spun about on the third stair, her robe flaring about her ankles and revealing pretty pink toes. "I was just wondering if...that is, I thought maybe..."

"What is it?" She had something to say but seemed shy in voicing it. He figured he knew what it was. "If you're worried about having a stranger in the house, I can sleep in the barn."

If he could find his way there in this blizzard.

Even in the dim light of the fading fire, he saw

her blush. That high coloring sure did make her look pretty.

"It's not that. The parsonage is open to all." She curled her fingers in the fabric of her robe. "I was just thinking that if you are married, your wife must be worried."

"I'm not married…are you?"

She shook her head, turned and dashed up the stairs, those lovely round hips churning.

Yes, sir, it was a damn good thing that his mother could not get into his mind.

Mary closed the door to her bedroom and, leaning against it, tried to catch her breath.

Heat rolled off her in waves. She had never said anything more embarrassing in her life. She had tried to be subtle about asking, but her roundabout way had been so very obvious. Just because she desperately wanted to know something, that didn't mean that she had to ask.

She ought to have let it come up naturally in conversation, not just let her heart come blurting out of her mouth.

How would she ever face Joe over breakfast? He would correctly assume that there was only one reason she would ask that question, and that was because she was interested in him in a special way.

Which she was.

That, however, did not mean she could follow that interest. No, indeed. She had nothing to offer a man. Especially a man like Joe, who, it seemed, had everything to offer some lucky woman.

Mary threw herself belly first onto her bed, then pounded the mattress with her fists.

What had made her give in to imagining a life that could never be hers? A husband? His babies?

Silly, silly fool. Pa had tried to warn her.

Flopping over on her back, she stared at the ceiling and listened to her bedroom window rattle perilously in the wind.

It was the baby…that had to be it. Amelia had stirred up motherly yearnings in her, which in turn led to dreams of—

She shook her head, frustrated at her inability to tuck her emotions neatly into place.

Once the child found a home, Mary's turmoil would settle. Raising other folks' children for however brief periods of time would once again fulfill her needs.

She would have sighed, relieved at settling that issue in her mind, but it was Joe's face, not Amelia's, that filled her dreams as she drifted off to sleep.

Joe added enough logs to the fire to give several hours of burn. When Mary and the children woke there would be at least one warm room.

He gazed at the leap of the flames, listened to the comforting crackle of the burning wood. After a moment, he turned to look down at Amelia sleeping on the couch.

Poor little mite. She looked content, having just been fed, but if the wagon hadn't overturned, she would be in her mama's arms now.

"How would you feel about having a rough ole cowpoke hold you for a while?" He picked her up, then sat down on the couch. "I won't be as soft as your ma…won't smell as good, either, I reckon, but maybe I'll do for tonight."

He thought about his own mother. She'd fare all right in the blizzard. The hands at Landon Ranch could be counted on to watch out for her and Clay.

Part of the reason he concentrated his attention on the woman he loved above all others was to keep his mind off the one upstairs.

It didn't take long to lose that battle. No matter what he tried to occupy his mind with, his thoughts returned to Mary.

Did she sleep in a sheer gown or a heavy warm one? Did her fair hair splay about her pillow or did she confine it to a braid? Did she keep her hands tucked under her chin or did she recline them on either side of her head with those slender fingers maybe tangled in her hair?

What a fine howdy-do. This line of thinking was bound to keep him from getting a wink of sleep.

Of course, Ma would be delighted to know this.

If there was one thing his mother wanted, it was for the ranch house to be overrun by grandbabies.

It was not likely that his brother, Clay, would provide them.

Clay was simple. Sweet and loving, yes, but his special mind would keep him Ma's little boy for the rest of his life.

Not that Ma minded that. She had picked him because he was special. When he had been three years old, Clay's natural parents had been ready to assign him to bedlam.

When Ma heard of it she had cried and prayed... prayed and cried.

He'd gotten a brother that year for Christmas, the best gift he'd ever received. That was even truer for Pa. Clay had made the last years of his life joyful.

Knowing that Clay was there to love Ma made it easier to leave the ranch for extended periods of time, as he was required to do.

And Ma deserved love. He wished he could expand her family...but a man couldn't marry willy-nilly to achieve that goal.

He had wooed two lovely women, but when the time came for a proposal, he'd back out. Regrettably, with Veronica and Adele, he'd felt no sense of spirit harmony. Hadn't felt it even after months of courtship.

He feared that the disappointments had left him cautious, a bit tarnished, maybe.

Odd that he'd felt an affinity for Mary, a woman he'd only just met.

It was all too perplexing to think about after the long day he'd had, and he was bone weary.

If only he could put images of Mary to bed... hell, to rest, was what he meant...he might be able to sleep. But try as he might, her smile and her gentle expression filled his mind.

In the morning he'd get to know her better. Over breakfast he'd discover who the woman was under those feminine nightclothes.

No...that's not what he meant, either. But it was, in fact, true.

Physically, Mary was lovely, and he believed that

at heart, where true beauty lived, she was exceptional.

The baby stirred. He rocked her, crooned some nonsense baby words. When he did, he noticed a stack of well-worn sheets of paper on the small table beside the couch.

The handwriting on the top one appeared childish. Curious, he picked it up.

It was a letter to Santa from Dan. He wanted a horse. On its own, a letter to the jolly man was special, but a letter from an orphan…

Something twisted in his gut.

The next letter was begun in a barely legible hand. He would not have been able to read it if it had not been finished by an adult. Judging by the pretty swirls and flourishes, it had been Mary.

"'Dear Santa Claus,'" he read out loud. "'Please bring me a ma to love me and fix my hair up pretty. Dan says you can't bring that, but I believe. Love from Maudie. P.S. I have not been naughty, not even once. P.P.S. Just once, but only a little bit.'"

If his heart had twisted for Dan, it downright wrenched for Maudie.

The next two letters Mary had written on behalf of the twins. Brody wanted a dog. Luckily, there was a dog needing a boy.

Caleb wanted a pa.

"Hell," he whispered.

They could have the dog, and Joe had horses to spare at the ranch. The problem was, a horse required care and feeding. Couldn't expect an orphan bound for the train to provide that.

Even given the problems, Dan's wish was easier

filled than Maudie's and Caleb's. A ma and a pa…
that was a bit too much to ask, even of Santa.

"What do you reckon Mary wants?" he asked
Amelia. "What is it that—"

Suddenly, he knew… Mary wanted a baby.

Remembering the way she had looked so longingly at the child, he should have guessed it right off.

There must be something keeping her from having one…or maybe she'd had one and lost it.

Sad that some folks needed children and didn't
have them. Equally sad that innocent children needed
parents and lived in orphanages.

Praise the good Lord that there were women like
his mother and Mary who were willing to love them.

It couldn't be easy for Mary, knowing what was
in the children's letters to Santa and being helpless
to do anything about it.

She must have been relieved when he'd knocked
at the door and in sauntered a dog. No wonder she
hadn't minded the mess the hairy thing had made.

He could only imagine how she'd felt when she'd
spotted the horse. Her heart must have tripped over.

Must have seemed more than chance…a dog and
a horse.

But it wasn't until he placed Amelia in her arms
that she had swooned.

Thinking on it, the dog and the horse would have
been a dream come to life.

But the baby! She must have seemed a miracle.

He didn't want to think how hard he had made
things for Mary—by handing her the thing she
wanted most.

Any number of families would be given an infant before a woman on her own would.

"Hell again," he sighed.

Trying to settle on the couch, he stretched out full length with the baby on his chest and his arms cradled about her.

Just as well give up any idea of getting some shut-eye. Mary had walked straight into his heart and damned if he could get her out…and damned if he wanted to.

Chapter Four

Dozing on the couch, Joe half roused to the puff of warm breath on his face.

Too sweet to be the dog's. Not the baby's—she continued to sleep soundly on his chest. He wasn't lucky enough for it to be Mary's.

Was it even dawn? He didn't think so, but the intensity of the blizzard made it difficult to tell.

Coming fully awake, he peered into the face hovering over him.

"Maudie?" It could only be.

The little girl nodded, her brown eyes somber yet wide with curiosity.

"Is anyone else awake?"

She started to say something, but shook her head instead. Blond curls shivered about her face.

Careful not to jostle Amelia, he sat up.

"A pleasure to meet you, Miss Maudie."

Once again she nodded her head. He suspected she wanted to smile—her lips twitched ever so slightly—but she held it back.

After regarding him silently for a moment, she turned her attention to the baby, touched the small fist. Amelia woke up.

The baby flashed a great smile. Maudie smiled back.

"This is Amelia," he said. "Would you like to hold her?"

Vigorous nodding indicated that she would.

Odd that Mary had not indicated that the little girl could not speak.

Maudie climbed onto the couch and he settled the baby in her arms.

"Just keep your arm behind her neck, give her some support."

Maudie followed his instructions with an ease that told him she had handled an infant before.

"Would you like to tell the baby your name?" he asked, testing to see if she was actually mute.

"Hello, Amelia," she said. "I'm Maudie. Are you an orphan, like me?"

"She is."

"Don't worry, baby, you're so cute and little, somebody will want you."

"You're doing a good job, Maudie. I think you've held a baby before."

She glanced up at him with a grin. Odd that she would speak to Amelia, but answer him with only nods and smiles.

"Is there some reason that you won't speak to me?" he said, sitting down beside her.

"The reverend says not to speak to strangers unless they're looking to adopt you."

"I'm Joe Landon. I got here last night after you were in bed."

"I'd best not keep talking, Joe Landon, unless you came to adopt me. You are a stranger, even if I know your name."

"You're a fine little girl, Maudie, but the reason I'm here is because I brought Amelia."

Maudie nodded, then leaned down to kiss Amelia's cheek.

"I'm an orphan, just like you," he told her. "So I reckon I'm not such a stranger after all."

"Did your mama and papa get sick and die, too?"

"They did."

Apparently she no longer considered him a stranger, because she leaned against him and rested her head on his arm.

"I had a baby sister…she died with Mama and Papa, so I came to live with the reverend."

"When I was adopted by my new mother, I was older than you."

"You were?" Her eyes grew round, hopeful looking. "Maybe someone besides Mr. Blankford will want me. I'm not so very old."

It was hard to imagine who wouldn't want her. Miss Maudie was an exceptionally charming child.

"Is that your dog?"

"It came with Amelia. I reckon it's an orphan like the rest of us," he said.

"He'll need a name, then."

"Maybe you can name it, once we find out if it's a he or a she."

"He's a boy for sure. When I came down I caught him peeing on the firewood. His leg was lifted."

"We'll have to excuse him this once—what with all the bad weather, he wouldn't want to go outside." Joe looked at the woodpile beside the hearth. Sure enough, there was a dark stain dribbling down the logs. "Poor fella's probably confused, missing his folks."

"Do you think Brody can have him? He wants a dog more than he wants a new ma and pa." She glanced up at him, her eyes clouding suddenly. "It must be because he can't remember the old ones. He and Caleb were only one year old when somebody left them and ran away."

He'd have cussed a blue line at the cruelty of it had it not been for Maudie and Amelia sitting beside him.

He was saved from the lingering temptation by the sound of small footsteps pounding down the stairs.

"Santa comed! Look! He bringed me a dog!"

Mary was not certain that Brody wasn't correct. She hurried after him and Caleb, stuffing her hair into a bun as she trailed them down the stairs.

Only last night, she had been near tears wondering what to do about the letters to Santa. This morning there was a dog spreading brown fur all over the house. There was a horse waiting to be ridden about the stable as soon as the weather cleared.

For Dan's sake it had better be soon. She had heard his restless tossing in the wee hours and doubted that he had slept a wink.

"And I got a pa!" Caleb shouted then tore across the parlor to leap onto Joe's lap.

To her relief, Joe opened his arms to welcome the boy.

In a moment Caleb would have to be told that this was not a papa brought by Santa, but for this one instant, she couldn't find the heart to say so.

"It's not Christmas yet, Caleb," Maudie informed

him. "He's not your papa…but we can talk to him because he's not a stranger."

"Is so my pa!" Caleb snuggled his head against Joe's shoulder.

Joe glanced at Mary, his expression stricken.

"This is Joe Landon," Maudie explained. "Santa didn't bring him, because he's an orphan, just like us."

Mary nearly missed the bottom step. No wonder he looked so pained. He had walked in these children's shoes.

"Caleb," she said, trying to figure a way to rescue Joe from his predicament. "Did you see the dog? Wouldn't you like to pet it?"

"Him," Joe said with a sudden grin and a nod at the firewood.

"Yep. I'll be right back, Pa." Caleb hugged Joe tight around the neck, then dashed off to join his brother in squeezing the dog's big, hairy middle.

He looked like a patient animal. She was plenty grateful for that. A stain or two would be a small price to pay to see the boys happy.

"He'll need a name," Joe said, getting up from the couch to squat down beside the twins.

"Santa would want Brody to choose," Caleb said.

"Santa didn't come yet!" Maudie called, a frown creasing her brow.

Poor baby. She would not believe that Santa had already come, because that would mean that he had failed to bring her a mother.

It couldn't be that Caleb and Brody would get their wishes and she would not get hers.

All of a sudden Mary's head pounded. Christmas was coming down upon her like a hammer on a nail.

What was she to do?

Prepare breakfast, that's what. Flapjacks were predictable. Mix the batter, pour dollops of it onto a skillet and you got what you wanted.

"Let's name the dog Rover, Pa!" she heard Caleb exclaim.

"You don't get to choose!" Brody cried. "He's my dog. Hey, Pa, how 'bout we call him Bounder?"

"You don't get to call my pa Pa!"

"Do so! Your pa is my pa too 'cause we're brothers."

"Then that's my dog as much as yours."

At that, Maudie began to cry.

Since Joe was the one who had brought the blessings and the troubles, she left him to sort things out.

A task with a predictable outcome awaited her in the kitchen.

It had been nearly twenty-four hours since the blizzard began and still, sheets of white blew past the parlor window. Mary smeared the moisture that had formed on the inside of the glass with her fingertips.

The children must have gotten used to the constant noise that battered the house, because they slept peacefully in their beds, from youngest to oldest.

She couldn't help but wonder if it had to do with there being a "pa" in the house. Perhaps it was his presence that made them feel secure.

There was no denying that she would sleep more soundly knowing Joe would be downstairs.

Funny, the reverend had never made her feel that

way. Of course, there was a huge difference between the men.

The reverend's round eyes had a tendency to blink, giving him the appearance of an owl. Occasionally, this made him seem wise, but most of the time he just looked nervous.

The reverend was slight of build, his demeanor typically serious.

Joe Landon looked as though he might break out in laughter at any given moment, yet there was that in him that seemed deeply sensitive. Even though she'd known him only a short time, she had seen evidence that he was a man of great compassion.

Moreover, he was far from slight of frame. Indeed, he was very well put together, with a muscular build and a confident stance. Add to that his dark curly hair, those sparkling blue eyes…well, he quite turned a woman's head.

Boot steps clicked across the floor behind her.

She turned from the window to see Joe reach for his big coat where it hung on the rack.

"I'm going to see to the animals," he said, sliding his capable-looking arms into the sleeves.

"It's late." She hated to have him go out in the weather even though the task needed doing.

The children had kept their "pa" busy all day and well into the evening. In truth, Joe had seemed to be having as much fun as the children, giving piggyback rides, tossing the little ones into the air and playing hide-and-seek.

In her opinion, he would be an excellent father, one who would delight in the job. It was a shame that he was not married so that he could adopt one or two of the children, as they clearly doted on him.

"I'll come and help." It wasn't right that he should have to do the chores alone, and to be quite truthful, she wanted to spend time with him.

"You've done enough today. Put your feet up by the fire. Besides, it's awfully cold out there. I'll see to things."

She shook her head. "I need to get out of the house. And it's only a short distance to the stable. How cold can it be?"

Cold enough that, four steps onto the porch, she found that she could not breathe.

"You've got to walk backward." He took her by the shoulders and spun her about to face him. Wrapping the edges of his coat about her, he buttoned it, tucking her neatly inside. "Wrap your arms around me and hold on."

With one hand on the rope that he had strung from the porch rail to the stable door, and the other about her back, he pulled them against the wind, inch by freezing inch.

"Easy now, slow and steady breaths."

Easier said than done. While the icy air no longer robbed her breath, Joe did. With each step she took backward, her chest rubbed against his. His breath, fogging the air, hit her face in warm puffs.

There was a furrow in the snow beside the rope that had been formed by repeated trips to the stable to let the children ride the horse.

Her foot caught a divot and she slipped.

"Got you." Joe supported her with his arm bracing her back.

She placed her hands on his shoulders and all of a sudden Joe led them in a quick step-hop-step.

All they needed was music.

Or maybe not. Joe began to hum a toe-tapping tune.

Then he whisked her inside the stable door.

With a long, lingering gaze at her mouth, he un-buttoned the coat behind her. His lips passed within inches of hers when he peered over her shoulder in order to see what he was doing.

She inhaled the scent of his breath, then as quick as that, he stepped away.

"I'll milk the cow," she said because she needed to do something other than stare at his lips and imagine the kiss that might have happened with the two of them standing bow to button.

That kiss, she guessed, would have changed her life.

Some things happened that way. On the surface commonplace, but once experienced they would take a lifetime to forget.

"Better warm your hands by the stove first so you don't make the poor critter bolt."

Joe opened the stove door, added two logs. Once again, she was grateful for him being here. Left on her own, she didn't know what she would have done. The poor beasts would have been cold and hungry... the cow in misery for want of milking.

With her hands warmed, she took the milking stool from the wall, set it beside the cow, then sat down.

Joe mucked out the horse's stall.

"I'm sorry you lost your folks, Joe." She was not

truly prying into his private business since Maudie had blurted out that he was an orphan. She could hardly ignore the fact.

He nodded. "I was nine when a fever took them both. Luckily, Cornelia Landon found me. As fiercely as I missed my own ma, there were only a couple years of my life that I lacked a mother's care. Cornelia was everything my own mother would have been, and I love her all the more for it."

"I only hope the children find someone like her."

Joe worked around her, raking the cow's stall. In a few moments the stable smelled of fresh hay and straw.

"I'll need to get to town as soon as the weather allows…report the wagon accident to the sheriff."

"I think there's some snowshoes behind all that rubble in the corner."

A selfish part of her wished that the snow would last for a long time and that he would be forced to spend Christmas with them.

Mentally, she shook herself for wanting to play house with Joe. The storm would end and he would go home to his ranch. Daydreams would not do her or the children a lick of good.

She realized music was filling the barn. Joe was playing a harmonica…a decent rendition of "Here We Go A-Wassailing."

The tune was lively. Sitting on the stool, she could not help but tap her toe…to pull on the cow's udders in time with the music.

With each note, she timed a stream of milk into the pail.

Behind the harmonica, she saw Joe's lips curve in a grin.

"Here we go a-wassailing…" she sang, because it was nearly Christmas and she had yet to sing out in the spirit of the season.

One should not become so caught up in worry that one forgot to live the joy each day brought. And since Joe arrived, there had been an abundance of joy.

Without missing a note, Joe reached one hand toward her.

This was one moment that she would celebrate the joy.

She rose from the stool and touched his hand. His palm felt rough, warm as it curled around her fingers.

He twirled her about, making her skirt swirl wide around her ankles. She dipped to a curtsy, then rose when he slid his hand about her waist and drew her back up.

She sang and he played. If she had spent a happier interlude, she could not recall it.

Twirl, two-step, prance from one end of the stable to the other, laugh, then pick up her song. Before she knew it, she was breathless and her hair had come undone. It bounced merrily down her back and over her chest.

She noticed Joe looking at it. Maybe she ought to tuck it back up, but truthfully, it gave her a delicious shiver knowing that he was looking.

His steps slowed, then stopped. He tucked the harmonica into his shirt pocket.

He touched a wave at her temple, followed the curve of the strand with the backs of his fingers, over her collarbone to the upper curve of her breast.

He stopped there, but let his hand linger, sifting her hair between his thumb and finger.

The pressure of his knuckles against her chest riveted her attention in a way it had never been riveted.

"I like you, Mary."

"I like you, too, Joe."

The glimmer in his eyes kept the tune going in her mind even though she had quit singing.

"May I kiss you?" he asked.

That would be a mistake. She shook her head. No, most definitely not... "Yes."

His lips came down upon hers, sweet...tender. For some reason her mind brought up an image of a snowflake settling on a red rose.

She lifted up on her toes, wrapped her arms around his neck, answering his kiss. The snowflake in her mind melted, dripped down the rose petal with a sizzle.

Chapter Five

The clock downstairs chimed midnight. Ready for bed but unable to sleep, Mary sat at her vanity while she brushed her hair one hundred strokes, then, absently, one hundred more.

She'd gone and done it now. Tasted forbidden fruit.

The memory of Joe's kiss would follow her about like a ghost for a very long time, maybe even forever. No doubt, she would be going about her life, mending a sock or hanging out laundry, then, *boo*! There he would be haunting her…making her wish for a life that could never be.

Some pages were better left unturned, she had always believed, and now she knew why she believed it.

From now until her dying day she would be feeding off a memory.

"But it can't be denied," she said to the confused-looking woman staring back at her. "That if one must feed off a memory, better a sweet one than a bitter one."

In the mirror's reflection, she saw her bedroom door open.

"Miss Mary." Maudie stood in the doorway

clutching her rag doll tight to her chest. "I'm scared of the wind."

And who would not be? The snow had quit an hour ago, but the wind screamed about the house like a banshee gone berserk.

It was reassuring to know that Joe slept on the couch with Amelia beside him in the cradle.

She opened her arms. Maudie rushed forward and she scooped the child up. Standing, she twirled about then toppled with her onto the bed.

"Would you like to sleep with me tonight?"

"I could pretend you are my ma."

Snuggling Maudie close, she drew the blankets about them.

Mary's heart ached for them both. If she had a future to offer the child, she would do more than pretend. "Yes, my princess. For tonight I'll be your ma and you'll be my little girl. But only for tonight. You know I can never really be. You need both a ma and a pa."

"Mr. Joe could be my pa and you could be my ma."

Wind shook the window in its frame. Maudie shivered so Mary hugged her tighter.

"Close your eyes, sweetheart," she said, kissing the soft hair that tickled her nose. "I've got you."

But for how long? Until the next Blankford came along?

If Mary, a woman grown, felt the haunting need for a simple kiss, how much more must this little girl feel the need for the love of a family?

It only took a moment for Maudie's breathing to change to the slow, even pace of slumber.

Mary prayed herself to sleep, asking for a Christmas miracle that would give Maudie and the other children families to love them.

Strapping on the snowshoes, Joe wasn't sure what was more challenging, the blinding snow of yesterday or the piercing wind that blew this morning.

In the end, it didn't matter. His business with the sheriff could not be put off another hour.

He squared his shoulders, then set off toward town, but even his buffalo hide coat didn't keep him from shivering.

Still, all he had to do was remember Mary tucked inside his coat...the slide of her appealingly round body against him...relive her kiss and, howdy-do, that would at least keep his mind warm for the trek to town.

There was something about her...sweetness, a quick sense of humor and yet deep concern for the welfare of needy children. Miss Mary Blair was a woman of uncommon inner beauty. And she had shown all this to him in that kiss. He'd tasted the very spirit of her.

He had to admit that she had shaken him, left him sleepless all night long. No kiss had ever moved him that way.

That had to mean something...to his life...for his future.

Couldn't figure why that should be so, since he'd only known her a few days.

He nearly stumbled over the snowshoes when it occurred to him that his mother hadn't known him at all when she'd brought him home, and yet they had loved each other from the very first hour.

He'd always been so cautious with his feelings, his commitments. Even with the women he had courted, he'd stopped short of fully giving away his heart.

Scarred by grief at a young age was what his mother feared. She had cautioned him on more than one occasion that he might be so determined to avoid loss that he would never have anything to lose.

He reckoned she might be right, but then again, maybe it came down to neither Veronica nor Adele being the right woman for him.

Their kisses had been pleasant, but they'd never left him sleepless.

As much as he wanted to keep warm by dwelling on Mary's lips, the reason for his trip to town pressed upon him.

Once in town proper, he was surprised to see folks out and about. Life in Willow Bend went on in spite of the weather.

It was with some relief that he found the sheriff sitting in his office, a fire blazing in the stove and a pot of coffee on the boil.

"Landon," he said, rising from his chair behind the desk. "What brings you into town in this weather? How's your ma and your brother?"

"I'm here on ranch business, and the family is doing well."

The sheriff poured him a cup of coffee, then they sat across the desk from each other.

Joe told him what he had found in the snow and about Amelia.

"I know the family," Sheriff Burtrand said, his

bushy brows drawn. "Newcomers. Woman was real nice. Her husband wasn't a bad sort, but headstrong as a goat. When he took a notion into his head, no amount of arguing good sense could keep him from acting on it. Must be why he took his family and headed out with a blizzard coming on. It was a lucky thing for that baby that you also lacked the common sense to stay at home."

Hell, ranch business was ranch business, and it needed doing, but he sure as shootin' would not have taken a wife and baby along.

"Do you know if Amelia has other kin who might want her?" he asked.

"Poor mite…not that they ever spoke of. Won't take long to get her placed, though, being a baby and with Christmas upon us."

All of a sudden Joe's coffee turned on him. He had spent a good amount of time caring for Amelia and the thought of handing her over to some stranger didn't set well.

Damned if he didn't want her for himself…to bring her home to Ma and Clay!

As far as that thinking went, he couldn't help but imagine Ma's joy if he were to bring home all the orphans.

But they weren't stray puppies or kittens to be brought home willy-nilly. Orphans deserved two parents.

"How have things been at the parsonage?" Burtrand refreshed Joe's coffee, then his own. "No trouble with Blankford?"

"Would there be?"

"Depends on whether he's sober or not. I got a

lot of complaints about him riding out the blizzard at the saloon."

"But why would he cause trouble?"

"He wants little Maudie. Says she reminds him of the girl he lost. Now, with his wife gone, he wants the child bad. To my mind, what he really wants is someone to do for him. He'd work that little girl to the bone. He was hopping mad when the reverend turned him down for adoption. Between the two of us, Joe, I don't think he's right in the head."

Joe turned hot and cold all at once. The papa bear inside him rose up on hind legs, fur bristling and teeth bared.

"I'd better get back."

"How long are you planning to stay around?"

"I was going home tomorrow, but it looks like I ought to stay until Reverend Brownstone gets back."

"I'm not saying Blankford would cause trouble, but I will sleep better knowing you're there."

"The sooner I take care of my business at the bank, the quicker I can get back to the parsonage."

He turned to walk toward the door, jittery nerves making him want to run. On the way back, those snowshoes were going to feel like fifty-pound weights.

"Hold up a minute," the sheriff said. "There's a bag of toys and such that the townsfolk collected for the orphans. It'll save me a trip if you take them with you."

Burtrand went into a back room, then returned with a bulging gunnysack and handed it to him.

Joe slung it over his shoulder and nodded his thanks.

The playthings inside would keep the children busy on Christmas morning. Unfortunately, he knew from experience that once the fun wore off, they would still be longing for homes of their own.

Mary was falling in love. Sitting in the chair by the fire, she rocked Amelia and watched her nap. Her heart swelled. It also ached.

Her love for this baby could only be temporary. She stroked Amelia's plump pink cheek and hummed "Silent Night."

The irony hit her all of a sudden and she had to laugh. There was nothing silent going on in this house.

With Christmas a few days away, Joe had decreed that it was time to bring home a tree, and it had been bedlam ever since.

Lovely bedlam, though, with the boys hopping about, running up and down the stairs, whooping and knocking over the coat rack in their eagerness to get out the door.

Finally, with the last male rushing out of the house, things grew suddenly quiet.

Maudie, domestic to the bone, had decided to stay and bake Christmas treats for the boys when they returned.

What a lovely life this would be if it were real.

She shook herself, adjusting her thoughts.

This was real—just real for the moment. Moreover, many people did not even have this.

"You are blessed beyond belief," she whispered.

For a barren woman to have the opportunity to love and tend children was a wonderful thing.

"Maudie?" she called. "Let's get to making those treats so the boys can have something to warm them when they get back with the tree."

Maudie spun away from the window, where she had been watching Joe and the boys walk toward the woods.

"You could have gone with them," Mary said, wondering if Maudie might regret her decision to stay.

She shook her head, curls bouncing about her face. "I used to watch Mama make Christmas treats. She liked to sing when she did it."

"Let's go into the kitchen, Miss Maudie, and have a fine time." She reached out her hand and the little girl ran to her.

She could only hope that Maudie's mother was looking down and that she was happy to see her daughter smiling.

In the kitchen she set Amelia in the cradle near the stove. She gathered flour, eggs and the rest of what they would need.

A cloud must have passed across the sun, for the light in the room suddenly dimmed.

Odd, it had been a perfectly clear day. She turned to look out the window.

The sky was bright blue. Evidently the cloud had sailed harmlessly on and they could count on good weather for the rest of the day.

"What shall we sing, Miss Maudie?"

"Angels we have heard on high," she began in a fresh youthful voice.

"Sweetly singing o'er the plains," Mary joined in.
The back door opened with a crash.
"I come for my girl."

Chapter Six

Joe and the boys had cut down a tall, beautifully limbed tree. Truth to tell, he'd had as much fun in the picking as they had…and it couldn't be denied that he had been the one to want the ten-foot-tall fir.

Looking at it now, being towed home by his horse, he only hoped it would fit in the house without too much trimming.

A finger of guilt poked his gut, because he ought to be back at the ranch hunting up a Christmas tree with his brother, Clay. But he couldn't ignore the duty he had here to watch over the children and Mary.

Everything else came second to that.

And he'd had a spitting good time with the boys… more fun than he could recall having in a very long time.

"Somebody left the kitchen door open," Dan remarked.

"Maybe Mary burneded our cookies, Pa," Caleb whined in distress.

Apparently, it wasn't burned cookies that distressed the dog. All of a sudden he growled, bolted, then tore across the snow toward the house.

"Wait here, boys!" Joe called out behind him while he sprinted after the dog.

At the kitchen door he saw the wet tracks that the

dog's paws left on the floor, along with those from a pair of big boots.

"Back up," he heard Mary order from the parlor, her voice low, firm. "I don't want to hurt a drunk, but I'll run you through and don't think I won't."

"I've flattened heftier women than you...better armed ones, too."

Barreling out of the kitchen, Joe took in the scene at a glance—Mary halfway up the stairway with a bread knife gripped in her fist, the blade reflecting a bolt of sunshine streaking through the parlor window. Behind her, Maudie holding Amelia, both of them crying. Bounder-Rover in front of them all, teeth bared and snarling.

Joe launched at Blankford's back, tackled him around the hips and yanked. In a commotion of flailing limbs they rolled down the stairs.

Blankford was bigger than he was, but older and drunk. It only took a shift and a thump to get the fellow belly down with his arms pinned up behind his back.

Glancing up, he noticed Dan standing nearby holding a long dishcloth.

"My pa's a hero," he heard Caleb say.

"No more'n Bounder-Rover is," Brody exclaimed, rushing toward his dog.

Ripping the towel down the middle, Joe bound Blankford's wrists, his feet, then tied them to the solid leg of the heavy dining table.

He knelt beside Blankford, speaking quietly so that children would not hear. "You might be drunker than a fly floating in rum, but that doesn't mean you won't dance toe-to-toe with the law."

Glancing up, he saw Mary sitting halfway up the stairs, holding the girls and looking pale. She had set the knife out of sight—possibly under her skirt.

Caleb and Brody were wrong about who the hero was. There was no doubt in his mind that it was Mary.

She had been like a mama bear, ready to battle to the death to protect her young ones. Of course, she had been a sight prettier doing it than a bear.

It would be a good long while before he forgot the fire of authority blazing in her eyes. Something shifted inside him, because all of a sudden he recognized the same devoted quality in her that his mother had.

Lucky was the man who married this woman.

"Did my cookies burneded up?" Caleb asked.

Mary laughed suddenly. She reached one arm toward the boy. He and the dog raced toward her at the same time. She ruffled his hair and the dog's fur.

"I believe they are burning as we speak, but don't worry, I'll make double to replace them…and something for you, too, you wonderful hairy dog."

"If you'll be all right for a few minutes, I'll haul Blankford to the sheriff."

He saw it in a flash, a shadow dimming her eyes that revealed how frightened she had really been, and that she did not want him to go.

"Go ahead," she said with a smile that he knew was for the children's benefit. "By the time you get back, Maudie will have decorated a special cookie just for you."

"You'd do that for me, Maudie?" he asked.

She hiccuped, nodded her head then wiped her nose on her sleeve.

What he needed at this moment was to wrap them all up in his arms, reassure himself that they were all right.

But he could see that they were, at least on the outside.

He untied Blankford, yanked him up from the floor. Whew! He wrinkled his nose at the scent of stale alcohol mingled with fresh.

"I'll be back before that cookie cools off, Maudie," he said. He winced at her tremulous smile, then dragged his captive out of the house.

In Mary's opinion, decorating the Christmas tree was the very thing to help the children get over the fear that the intruder had left in his wake. Stringing popcorn garlands and hanging candy canes was the medicine to return the smiles to young faces.

While the children adorned the pretty fir as far up as they could reach that is, Joe played his harmonica.

One could nearly forget the unpleasant business of this afternoon. Nearly, but for her, not altogether.

When that wicked man had threatened Maudie, she had been ready to run him through with the knife...she who had never purposefully harmed a living creature.

Would she have? Looking at Maudie now, her expression sweet and untroubled while she sat on the blanket trying to make Amelia smile, she knew she would have.

It would have changed her to the core, but—

"Sometimes life gives us hard choices. Once

we've made them we can never really be the same."
All of a sudden, Joe was standing close to her while
she gazed out the window.

Moonlight glittered on the snow, making the night
view of the yard look like something out of a fairy
tale. The world was certainly full of beauty...and
ugliness.

"How did you know that I was thinking of that
very thing?"

"Your expression. There's a little crease between
your brows. It starts here, then goes off this way."
He smoothed it with his thumb, then he fingered the
hair at her temple. "You were wondering if you could
have used the knife. It's only natural that you would
be troubled about it."

"I was...I believe that I could have." She sighed
and leaned her head into his touch, because there
was something about Joe that made her feel safe,
and right now she needed safe.

"I'm just glad you were here," she said.

He nodded, looked out the window, his thoughts
seeming far away. She wondered if at this moment,
he saw the earlier ugliness rather than the beauty of
this night.

"Me, too," he said at last. "Here's the truth, pure
and simple. If you'd been forced to take that action,
it would have been his own fault, not yours."

"I know that, in my mind I do. But in my heart
I feel so—"

"Brave, Mary. What you were was brave." He
gathered her up in a hug and she let him. His chest
rumbled when he spoke and she sank into it. "Besides, the dog would have attacked before you got

the chance. I don't reckon you'd hold it against him, think that he was a bad dog."

"He was courageous and wonderful."

"As were you."

He looked into her eyes. It was as though she could read his heart. He wanted to kiss her.

There was no denying that she wanted him to. She lifted up on her toes, ready to meet him halfway.

"Mr. Joe!" Dan called. "How we going to get the star way up there?"

The children! She had all but forgotten they were in the room. She must be blushing brighter than the red stripes on the candy canes.

"I'll lift Maudie up," he said, quickly backing away from her. "It's only fitting that an angel should set the star on top."

He glanced back at Mary with a wink. He could not have made it any clearer that he was remembering calling her an angel that first night.

Joe Landon certainly had a way of making her feel topsy-turvy.

Hours later the house was still and silent, everyone settled in slumber.

Luckily, the children, being children, appeared to have recovered from the day's ordeal shortly after the hot chocolate and cookies hit their bellies.

An hour ago, Joe had checked on each one of them.

Watching them dream securely under their blankets with the parsonage walls holding at bay the uncertainties of life...it did something to him. Made him feel grateful in a way that many folks would not understand.

As glad as he was for the peaceful slumber of the house, it did leave him alone with the silence.

A silence that had the worries in his head nearly shouting out loud.

The clock chimed midnight and reminded him that Christmas was one day closer.

A day closer to Maudie's and Caleb's dreams being dashed. No ma for Maudie, no pa for Caleb.

A day closer to the time when he would have to leave them all behind and go home to the ranch.

It worried him to the bone. The farmer wouldn't be in jail all that long.

Somehow, the children had grabbed him by the heart.

As had Mary. He knew he ought to be cautious where she was concerned, just like he'd always been. Sure didn't want to end up with another broken heart.

Sure didn't want to end up a lonely old man, either.

All of a sudden it was hard to imagine a future without Mary and the children in it.

Since he wasn't going to get any sleep, he got up from the couch, put on his boots and coat, then went outside.

Might as well worry standing up. Hopefully pacing would keep his stomach from spinning like a whirligig.

First he went to the stable to check on the animals and add a log to the stove. Then he walked back to the front porch, all the while gnawing on the fact that the orphans' time at the parsonage was running out.

Everyone knew about orphan trains. Many of the children went to decent homes…but others—

The idea of any one of these precious little ones ending up like some he'd known…hell, it wasn't the frigid weather turning his bones cold at the moment.

He stared up at the moon to rid himself of the pictures that charged unbidden into his mind— Maudie being treated like a servant instead of a beloved daughter, the twins desperately crying at being separated and Dan's self-esteem crushed at being passed over time and time again.

Try as he might to separate his own past from the fear of the children's future, he could not.

Turning back toward the stable, he quickened his steps in an attempt to outrun the worry. Too bad it caught up with him before he ever drew the door open.

He glanced back at the house when the glow of lamplight spilled across the snow. He turned and saw Mary's shadow cross the curtain. Maybe she was wakeful, too.

It couldn't be easy for her, growing to care for the children she nurtured, then having to give them up.

Chances were, one day she would marry and have a passel of little ones of her own, ones she would never have to say farewell to.

Mary with a newborn at her breast—it was a lovely image that ought to make him happy for her. Why was it that all he felt was an uncharitable lump in his gut?

Because he—

All at once her bedroom window slid open. She leaned out, gazing down at him. A mass of wavy hair tumbled about her shoulders, caught a dusting of moonlight. She tipped her head sideways, gazing at him with a question in her eyes.

Because he…wanted her for himself!

The thought flashed upon him quicker than a thunderbolt, but now that the revelation had embedded in his heart, he knew it was never going away.

He wanted Mary…he wanted all of them.

If Mary wanted him, too, they could save the children from the orphan train, give them a wonderful life.

"What are you doing, Joe?" She crossed her arms over her chest and shivered. "It's freezing cold out there."

"Will you marry me, Mary?" he blurted because the thought was so momentous, so exciting, that he could do nothing but express it.

Mary was the woman who was meant to be his. No long courtship would convince him otherwise. What he had seen in that mental flash was his soul's companion.

"Will I? No, of course I won't. You'd better get back inside before what's left of your brain freezes."

"That was sudden… I'm sorry. Meet me in the parlor and I'll propose the way a man ought to."

She shook her head, then slammed the window. Her lamp went out.

At least he'd gotten her attention. Certainly once he asked in the proper way, explained how it would help the children, she would accept.

It was a disappointment when he came inside and discovered that she was not there to greet him at the door. In fact, he didn't even hear footsteps to indicate that she intended to come down at all.

Maybe all she needed was some time to let the idea settle in. In that case it would be better if he didn't go knocking on her bedroom door.

He lay down on the couch to try and sleep, but now that he knew he wanted to be a husband to Mary and a father to the children, a dozen sleeping potions would fail to make him drowsy.

The clock chimed one, then two before he heard footsteps tapping down the stairs.

Chapter Seven

Coming down the stairs, Mary yanked the collar of her quite respectable robe about her neck, then knotted the belt at her waist.

Her houseguest had apparently lost his mind and at the same time robbed her of a good night's sleep.

Crossing the room in the dim light of the dying fire, she approached the couch and bent over him.

Perhaps he was not insane but ill…feverish, no doubt.

Gently, so as not to awaken him, she drew the backs of her fingers across his forehead, then down his cheek.

Humph, he was as cool as she was.

Without warning, his eyes popped open and he sat up. She squeaked in surprise and jumped backward.

"Since you aren't sick, you must have fallen and hit your head." She studied the shape of his skull, looking for a lump under the mess of lovely dark curls.

Nothing was obvious. The only way to know for sure would be to run her fingers through his hair. That did not seem appropriate.

"Something like that." He grinned, then got up to add a log to the fire. "I expect I have got some explaining to do."

"That might help determine whether the doctor can wait until morning."

"I don't need a doctor, Mary. I need you." He scooped up her hand, led her back to the couch, tugged her down and then sat facing her. "It hit me all of a sudden."

"Something certainly did…you asked me to marry you."

"Not with much elegance, but I meant it." He touched her cheek, then leaned forward. She felt the delicious warmth of his breath huffing against her lips. "I won't quit asking until you say yes."

"I won't say yes, Joe." How could she?

She turned her face away because the sincerity in his expression was making her forget how rash his offer really was.

"I'll give you and the children a good life."

"The children?" She snapped her gaze back at him.

"We would adopt them…all five. And more after that." He rubbed his thumb across her bottom lip. "You'd like that, wouldn't you? These last few days have given us a taste of how good things could be. Marry me and we'll have this for the rest of our lives…and I won't have to sleep on the couch."

The man tempted her. He was handsome, affectionate and brave. Everything a woman could dream of. And dream she had, but sadly, the secret visions she indulged in during the wee hours were fantasy, blown away by the realities of daybreak.

She could marry no man—it didn't matter how wonderful he was, how she felt about him.

"I know you love the children. They could be yours and mine, all wrapped up and legal."

She wanted to run upstairs and weep, because he was offering her a miracle, one that she was honor bound to refuse.

"I can't marry you, Joe." She set her spine to firm her resolution and lock away the tears that threatened.

"But you want to. I see it in your eyes… Mary, why do you look so sad?"

He drew her up in a hug, cupped the back of her head in his hand.

Say yes, yes, yes, her heart screamed, but stubborn common sense screamed back just as loudly. She clung to him, fighting to keep those words unsaid. If she did, though…just said that one little word… she would have everything she'd ever dreamed of.

And Joe would not. If she cared for him enough to marry him, could she then deprive him of life's most precious reward?

"I've seen how you are with Amelia. You want a baby of your own. I'll try morning and night to give you one…just say you will be my wife."

Poor Joe…no matter how eagerly he tried, his efforts would be futile.

She wriggled out of his hold, then stood up and backed away.

"No, Joe. I'm not the woman for you…or for any man."

"I reckon I have some say in that."

"You don't."

"The only way I'll quit asking for your hand is if you tell me you don't, at least, like me."

Sorrow sliced her heart in two because she more than liked him.

"It doesn't matter how I feel...'m barren."

That revelation seemed to set him back some. He sat silently, staring at the floor for a long time, chafing his hands.

At last he glanced up, moisture welling in his eyes.

As she had suspected, the news had been a blow and it hit him hard. It proved to her, once again, that she was correct in her position to remain unmarried.

"Mary, there's all kinds of barren. Not being able to give birth to a child is only one of them. You've a fertile heart. I would never see you as barren."

"And I'd never see you holding a child of your own."

"You'll see it in a couple of days. I aim to adopt our orphans even if you turn me down."

"But you are a single man. The judge might deny you."

"He might, but I've got the ranch to offer...give them security. And Ma, she'll give them as much love as any child could ever want, but..."

He looked away from her, silently studying the wool flowers woven on the rug.

"But what, Joe?"

"It's you they already love, it's you I—"

"I wonder if the judge really would refuse you," she said quickly, because if he had been about to declare his affection for her, no amount of willpower would keep her from dissolving into a weeping mass.

This man, whom she cared for deeply, had just

offered to make her secret dreams come true, and she'd turned him down.

"I hope not, especially since Blankford has gotten a lawyer to try and take Maudie."

That was shocking! She hadn't known.

Blankford was obsessive. And simply because he'd had a daughter before did not make him a fit parent.

"The judge would never give custody of that sweet child to a crazy man."

"Not if she's mine first."

Joe would be able to keep her safe, of that she had no doubt. Poor Maudie—all she wanted was what most children took for granted…loving parents.

Setting aside the issue of her inadequacies as a wife, perhaps she was incredibly selfish to turn him down. Moreover, it appeared that her desire to spare one kind of pain was only going to create another.

She had been ready to flee to the sanctuary of her bedroom. Instead, she returned to the couch and sat next to Joe, feeling as if she was about to hurl herself over a cliff with no swimming hole beneath.

She might have sat at the far end of the couch to say what she intended, but here she was, indulging in that safe yet itchy feeling whenever she was close to him.

"You ought to have the children, Joe. You love them and they love you…but I, well, I can never be the woman you need."

"You'll always be the woman I—" She covered his lips with her fingertips because she could not endure hearing him say that he cared for her.

"I accept your offer of marriage. But with one condition."

"Whatever it is, I accept." His grin was broad. His eyes glistened. How was she to tell him the rest?

"Our marriage will be temporary, for the sake of the adoption. Once the children are settled at the ranch, I'll be on my way."

He looked deflated, but it couldn't be helped. "Will you at least stay for Christmas?"

"Until the day after, but no longer…and no matter what, you cannot try to hold me by saying things like…well, things."

"Things like there's that pull between us that says we were meant for each other. I can't think I'm the only one to have felt it."

All she could do was stare silently at him, because she did feel that pull. If she denied it, it would only ring of a lie.

"Things like 'I love you'?"

"Don't say that, Joe."

"And what if I accidentally blurt it out?"

"It would make it so much harder for me to go… and clearly I have to."

"Looks clear as mud to me, but for the sake of the children, I accept your terms."

She nodded, stood up, then with a shrug that could mean anything from *I've done my duty* to *please make me change my mind*—she had no idea which— she turned toward the staircase.

Joe's hand caught hers from behind, and none too gently. He whirled her about so that she fell against him. Then with his hands cupping her face, he kissed her…made a meal of her, more like. One hand slipped behind her head, then the other curled around her back to draw her tight to his chest.

She was not going to respond to this seduction, she couldn't…except for one tiny moment so she could memorize the taste and the scent of her temporary husband.

After a long moment, he let go of her and set her at arm's length.

"We had an agreement," she sputtered.

"You told me not to say anything." The humor in his grin matched the mischievous twinkle in his eyes. "I didn't."

"Humph!" She twirled about and headed for the staircase.

Halfway up, she heard him.

"Mary, there's more to a marriage than procreation."

By noon the next day, Mary had become Mrs. Joe Landon. So said the marriage certificate that she had signed with her own shaking fingers.

The adoption process had been started and an hour later the Christmas tree tied behind the big sleigh that Joe had rented.

They were going home—at least, the children were.

For all her misgivings about what she had done, she could not help but be infected by the high, joyful spirits.

Five children now had a father when they had not even had the hope of one the day before…and not just any father. They had Joe, a man who had put them first. When he might have gone on with his life, untroubled by attachments, he had loved them, had chosen them to be his own.

She was married to a rare and wonderful person… until the day after Christmas. As much as she regretted it, her father was right. Watching Joe with the children only proved that. Someday he would hold an infant of his own and he would know that she had done what was for the best.

"Pa," Dan said, his voice cracking on the word. "Can you show me how to drive the team?"

"Come on up here, son. Take hold of the reins."

Dan clambered over the seat back. In the past, he hadn't smiled easily, but the grin on his face at the moment gave her a glimpse of the boy he must have been before his parents became the victims of bank robbers.

"I have a pa and a sister…lots of brothers, too," Maudie said, snuggled under a blanket with her and Amelia. "So I reckon Santa's going to leave a real special ma under the tree for me on Christmas morning, don't you?"

"I…well…I—" she mumbled, having no idea of how to respond.

Joe turned about to shoot her a glance, then saved her from having to reply by plucking his harmonica from his coat pocket and asking Maudie to sing along.

A lump the size of an apple clogged her throat because if her body was like a normal woman's, she would dive into marriage with Joe headfirst. Without a second thought she would sit under the tree on Christmas morning and open her arms wide, claim Maudie as her daughter.

But she did not have a normal woman's body…
only a normal woman's heart.

"Look there in the distance, children." Joe pointed
to a large two-story house that would have been in-
distinguishable from the snow had it not been for
the smoke curling out of four tall chimneys. "We're
almost home."

A single tear slipped down Mary's cheek because
she was happy for them all…certainly, that was why.

"Good thing, Pa," Dan said. Clearly he was fond
of using the title. "Looks like it might snow."

Mary wiped her cheek on the blanket so that no
one would see the dampness.

Chapter Eight

$\mathcal{A}$s soon as the sleigh glided into the yard, his mother flung open the front door and rushed onto the porch, hands on her hips and a welcoming smile rounding her flushed cheeks.

The spicy scents of cinnamon and cloves drifted from the house.

"You making gingerbread men, Ma?"

"I am if you're bringing company for Christmas."

Joe leaped from the wagon and bounded up the stairs two at a time. He gave his mother a great hug, feeling the warmth of home fill him up.

This woman had given him so much over the years. He was grateful to finally be able to give her something in return...something he knew she had dreamed of for a long time.

"Not visitors, Ma...grandchildren." Naturally, she looked properly stunned. "I've adopted them. Three boys and two girls."

"Oh, my lands," she whispered, waving her white apron to express her joy. "And the young lady?"

"That's Mary... I'll need to talk to you about her later."

"You're sweet on the little gal! I see it in your eyes."

"More than sweet on her, I reckon... Ma, she's my wife."

It was a lucky thing that his mother was a strong woman, full of faith. The news of an instant family might send one with less backbone to the floor in a fit of vapors.

Still might send Ma there when she discovered that Mary was leaving him the day after Christmas.

"Maudie, Dan, Brody, Caleb…this is your grandma Cornelia."

Mary mounted the steps and handed the baby to his mother. Not everyone would have noticed, but he did and it broke his heart…the ever so slight hesitation as she gave the baby over.

"This is Amelia," Mary said with a smile that he knew was given with the greatest effort. "Your son saved her life."

With her free arm, Cornelia folded Mary up in a hug.

"That's my boy. He's been fetching home baby this and thats for as long as he's been mine." With her arm still about Mary, she lifted up on her toes and kissed Joe's cheek. "Grandchildren this time? I could not be happier, son, or more proud of you. Now, take your children upstairs and find who belongs to what room while I take my daughter-in-law on a tour of her new home."

The sooner he spoke to his mother about Mary the better, but for now he figured it couldn't hurt to have them get acquainted.

Could be Ma might convince Mary to stay.

There had been a time, early in her marriage, when his mother had grieved over not being able to bear children of her own, but that didn't keep her from becoming the most loving mother on God's good earth.

"Dan, boy," he said. "How'd you like a room that overlooks the paddock and the barn?"

The grin on his freckled face answered for him.

"Pa?" Brody yanked on his pant leg. "Can Rover stay in the house?"

"That's up to Grandma Cornelia."

"He's a real good dog, Granny," Caleb explained. "He only piddles on the woodpile."

"The dog's the one who really saved the baby's life," Joe explained because his mother had never allowed a dog in the house before. "He's a protector."

With a long glance at each anxious face, his mother nodded.

"I reckon he can stay as long as he cleans up the crumbs from under the kitchen table."

"Thanks, Granny! He's real good at crumbs." Brody whooped.

The twins hugged her skirt, one on each side.

"How will I tell the two of you apart?" his mother asked with a pat to each wavy-haired head.

"I'm Caleb."

"And I'm Brody."

Unless he missed his bet, his mother would know who was who among the flying feathers of a pillow fight.

Over by the doorway, Joe's brother, Clay, stood shyly, hanging back as was his way among strangers. As big as he was, blending in wasn't easy.

"Clay, baby, come over here and meet some special people," his mother said.

"People for me?" Clay always asked this question

upon meeting strangers. Ma did not always answer yes, but when she did, it meant that she trusted them not to be unkind to her special boy. Joe reckoned his brother must recognize this distinction, because whenever Ma said they were his, he gave them his heart…a very special gift, in Joe's opinion.

"Yes, my love." Ma smiled at Clay with the warmth that she always had for him. "Maudie, dear, wouldn't you like to go into the kitchen with your new brother and help him put eyes on the gingerbread men?"

Even though Clay was actually the children's uncle, and quite a bit older in age, with Clay the way he was, Joe reckoned his mother figured brother was the more appropriate relationship.

With a bright smile, Maudie skipped to Clay and took his hand.

"Yesterday," she said, tipping her head back to peer up at Clay, "I didn't have any brothers. This morning I got three and now I have four."

"Me, too," answered Clay.

"On Christmas morning Santa is going to bring me a ma. I'm going to wait all night by the tree."

"Can I wait, too?"

"I'd be grateful, Clay," she said, then she disappeared into the kitchen hand in hand with her newest brother.

He dared a glance at Mary. Just like he figured, she seemed distressed.

"Let's get you all settled upstairs," he said, then herded his brood of boys toward the big stairway in the parlor.

He glanced back once more to see his mother

with Amelia cradled in one arm and her other about Mary's waist.

Gray head bent to golden one, his mother carried on a quiet conversation with his wife.

Tonight, he ought to write a letter to Santa and ask for a special favor…that Ma would be able to succeed in luring Mary to make her home here at the ranch.

He sure hoped so since, thus far, he had not even come close to being able to.

The very last thing he wanted was to send his wife away the day after Christmas with a friendly fare-thee-well…as though she did not mean everything to him.

It had been Mary's intention to remain in her bedroom, to hide out and ignore the pull that this home had on her heart.

Cornelia, clearly not realizing that Mary was only a temporary member of the household, had lovingly presented every corner and crevice of the house as though she were sharing a precious gift. And so she would have been, had circumstances been different.

With the home's lovely wide stairway, big fireplaces and picturesque windows, it was the stuff of her dreams. And it was not only the walls and polished floors that enticed her. It was the loving spirit of the place. For all that she tried to hide from it, Landon Ranch called her to stay and make it home.

She would have remained shut away in the room, safe from the temptation to give in to selfishness and live here forever, had Joe not been standing outside her door playing "Jingle Bells" on his harmonica.

But he was, and with December 23 only hours

away from slipping into Christmas Eve, she could not resist his invitation to a starry sleigh ride any more than she could a kiss in the moonlight if he were to offer one.

She ought to know better than to flirt with temptation, but her toe had been tapping to his tune. She let him help her into the sleigh, enjoying the joyful yet oddly melancholy feeling that being around him caused.

How puzzling that as time with Joe grew shorter, the stronger both the joy and her melancholy became.

"You warm enough, love?"

He shouldn't call her that. It would only make the parting harder.

"I'm bundled in furs with warm bricks at my feet." And because his endearment warmed her insides, she couldn't find the backbone to protest it. "How about you?"

"Warm…real warm with my wife beside me."

She started to remind him of the brevity of their marriage…their arrangement, but he lifted the harmonica to his lips and began to play "Jingle Bells" again.

And after that he played "O Holy Night."

And maybe it was.

With Christmas Eve so near and the full moon casting long shadows on the snow, with an icy breeze scratching through the bare branches of the trees, the night was both peaceful and expectant.

She looked up at the stars and sang along. Next, Joe played a tune about Christmas trees and she let her voice ring out to that one, as well.

After a time, Joe quit playing and pulled the team

to a halt at the top of the ridge that overlooked the valley where the house was built. Smoke curled from each of the chimneys, then whisked away into the dark. A few of the windows glowed soft amber.

She and Joe looked at each other and laughed, because she figured that while he had a talent for his instrument, her singing voice left something to be desired.

He put his arm about her shoulder, drawing her close to his side.

He smelled warm, so very male. She glanced sideways at him, watched his breath puff white in the icy air. She sighed, feeling the tug to her heart that only happened when she was close to him. Against her better instincts, she rested her head on his shoulder...couldn't help it.

Yesterday it had seemed that bad weather was coming, then the wind had risen and blown it away. But just now a cloud snuffed out the moonlight that had been reflecting on the snow. In a few moments it drifted on, but a gathering of storm clouds mounded on the horizon.

"What will you do? After Christmas, I mean?" Joe asked.

"Spend some time with my parents in Virginia, I suppose." It had been too long since she had seen them. "Until I find another position."

With two gloved fingers, he touched her chin, tipped her face toward him.

"Don't go, Mary."

"I have to, I—"

Lowering his lips to hers, he silenced her with

a long, tender kiss that made her forget how cold it was beyond his embrace.

"No...you don't. Stay here...let me be a real husband to you. Let me love you."

She buried her face into the warmth of his neck. He was everything to her.

Because she loved him, that made her decision to leave all the more valid.

"That would so be easy, Joe." When she spoke, her lips brushed the bit of warm skin exposed beneath his ear. "You are offering me everything I ever dreamed of. A home...a family."

What could she say to make him understand?

"Tell me," she said after a long, confidence-gathering breath. "What kind of person would I be to repay your affection with selfishness? And...and I do care for you, Joe. But you need a woman who can give you children."

"First of all, I don't have affection for you. I love you. And second, you've given me five and we've only been married a couple of days."

And she would be forever grateful for what he had done for them, but that didn't change what she had to do.

"Can you honestly tell me—" she looked him hard in the eye to make sure he understood "—that you wouldn't miss having the experience of lying with your wife and hoping that your seed would bear life...that you don't want to feel the bump of the little one under your hand? Being there to hear its first cries...I can't give you that and I won't deny you having it."

He set her at arm's length but kept his hands on her shoulders while he held her gaze.

"Hell, Mary…I would like that. So would you… but there are more important things."

"What could possibly be?"

"Loving. It's all that remains in the end." He touched her cheek, then her bottom lip. "Any pair of fools can give birth to a child. Not everyone can give them what you can. Every day I see how you give of yourself."

Yes, she did love the children. When she was gone she would think of them every day. Pray for them every night before she fell asleep.

"That doesn't change the fact that I'm not a whole woman."

"A whole woman? Do you think that my mother is not? That my father felt cheated in any way? I can tell you he didn't, not one single day. He loved me and Clay as if we had been born to him…more, maybe, because he didn't expect to ever be a father."

What could she say to that? Clearly, Cornelia was not lacking in any way.

"I'm sure he was a rare and special man."

And Joe was not? Her argument fell apart like a snowflake hitting hot water.

Still, she wasn't wrong in her determination to leave him and let him find a woman who could give him a more fulfilling life.

No matter how Joe denied it, men wanted fertile women. Her father and her past had taught her that.

"I've had suitors in my life." She glanced down at her glove-bound hands, folded in a knot on her lap. "To a man, they walked away once I told them."

"I'm not a suitor. I'm your husband." He drew her close again, folding her up in a great hug. "Those men were fools. I loved you before I knew, and now that I do, I love you all the more."

"How could you possibly?"

"What if I were sterile? Would you abandon me?" His chest rumbled against her when he spoke. The warmth of his breath brushed her ear. "I don't believe you would."

"I'm not abandoning you." She shoved away from him, because she would never leave him for that reason. Confusion hit her from every which way. "We had a bargain. It's not the same thing."

Clearly, he was hurt. It was her fault. She turned her face from him. If she had to look at the pain in his expression for one more moment she would burst out sobbing.

"Take me home," she said, then realized with a stab to her heart what she had said.

In spite of the fact that she would carry the name of Mrs. Joe Landon for a while, this lovely ranch would never be her home.

And just because she believed he was sincere in what he said tonight, that didn't mean he would feel the same way three years from now.

Even though it broke her heart in a dozen ways, Joe would never truly be her husband.

Chapter Nine

$\sim\!\!\infty\!\!\sim$

She was leaving him and there was not a single damned thing he could do to prevent it.

It shouldn't be a surprise. He'd agreed to her terms. Sure hadn't been sincere in doing it, though. His hope had been that she would see his home, meet his family and then decide this was where she ought to be.

Hell, this *was* where she ought to be. It felt like corralling a cat getting her to see it that way, though.

Joe brushed a snowflake from his nose. The storm was coming in fast. They'd be lucky to make it back to the house before the snow was too dense to see through.

"What's that down there on the path?" Mary asked. She'd slid over to the far side of the bench and it felt as though she'd already gone to Virginia. "It looks like a lantern."

"It is." It shouldn't be, but there it was, bobbing up and down as though someone were carrying it past the barn toward the pasture. "Hold on tight."

He snapped the whip over the horses' ears. The sleigh jolted forward, the blades half slipping on the ice.

Within moments, the dependable team had delivered them to the paddock.

"Ma!" He tossed the reins to Mary, then leaped

from the wagon before it had come to a full stop. "What's wrong?"

Something had to be, to bring her out into the cold in the middle of the night.

"Oh, Joe!" She lifted her skirt and hurried toward him through the deepening curtain of white. "Maudie has gone to look for Santa!"

"How long ago?"

"I don't know. It must have been some time ago, though. Clay woke me. Seems he wanted to go, too, but she told him she needed to go alone. I guess he stewed for a while before he came in to have me dress him proper so that he could follow her."

"Why would she do such a thing?" Mary asked, scrambling down from the sled.

Joe knew why and he guessed Mary did, as well.

"According to Clay, she wants a mother sitting under the tree on Christmas morning."

The stricken look on Mary's face sliced his heart open. Still, there was no time for comforting.

"Send out the dog!" he called behind him on the run back to the sleigh.

How long had his little girl been gone? How long could she last in the storm?

He'd give his life to feel her warm little body in his arms right now, to see her smile...to hear her giggle.

In this awful moment, the ripping of his gut reaffirmed the one thing he knew to be true.

He would not love Maudie more had he implanted her seed, had he felt her move in her mother's womb and heard her first cries.

Maudie was his daughter no matter how she had come to him.

* * *

Standing on the front porch, Mary shivered. She gazed past the snowfall and into the darkness beyond the barn until her eyes hurt. Where could a small child possibly go to keep warm?

No place, was where.

The front door hinges squeaked, sounding loud in the silent, aching night.

"Come inside, dear." Cornelia slipped an arm about her waist and urged her back toward the warmth of the parlor.

"This is all my fault," she admitted.

"It's no more your fault than it is Santa Claus's. Come now, before you catch your death."

Like poor sweet Maudie? And like her Joe?

She knew him well enough to believe that he would not return until he found the child.

Once inside, the heat wrapped around her, but the comfort of it made her feel guilty. She ought to be out there looking along with Joe.

She went to the parlor window and, once again, began her vigil.

All of a sudden Cornelia was standing next to her, pressing a comforting cup of tea into her hand.

"Have faith, dear. Joe will find her. Now tell me, why do you think this is your fault?"

"Maudie wants a mother."

"And don't I see one standing here?"

Mary shook her head. How did she tell Cornelia, who was clearly a far better woman than she was, the truth?

"No...not really." She set the tea aside and wrapped her arms about her middle. "The truth is, I married

Joe so that he could adopt the children. The day after tomorrow...well, I'm leaving."

"And yet you love my boy." Tipping her head to one side, Joe's mother considered her.

There was no way to answer that, so she stared hopelessly, silently, at the whirling snow.

"Mary." She heard the clink when Cornelia set her cup down, felt the strength when the woman placed her hands on her shoulders and turned her. "Daughter, tell me why you feel that you need to leave a man who you obviously love?"

"Because I'm barren." For a moment, she surprised herself, blurting that out, but as she thought about it, Cornelia might be the one person to understand.

"Of course you aren't!" Joe's mother's expression softened, a wealth of compassion warming her eyes. "You've as fertile a heart as any I've seen. Surely you've noticed how the children look at you...and my son, well, he's gone quite barmy." Cornelia touched her cheek in the same way that Mary's own mother would. "Oh, my dear, it takes more than the inability to carry a child to make one barren."

"I believe that of you. It's just that I do love Joe. I want better for him than an infertile wife."

"Maybe it would be best to leave that decision up to him. But I understand how you feel."

"I thought you might."

"There was a time...oh, six years into my marriage, it had to have been, when I actually left my husband because I thought the same thing as you do now. He found me, of course, and set me straight. It was later that I came upon Joe..."

Cornelia was silent for a moment, her gaze distant while she smiled. No doubt she was reliving the moment she'd found him, the same as a woman might do when reliving the moment of giving birth to her infant.

"It was the best moment of my life," she said at last. "Remember what the Good Book says, Mary? 'And now abide faith, hope, love, these three; but the greatest of these is love.' Hear me, child, it's not giving birth…it's giving love that counts."

"I think I see something!" Mary went up on her toes, squinting her eyes as though it would make the objects moving toward the house more clear. "It's Joe and the dog!"

She began to run for the door, but Cornelia constrained her.

"He'll bring Maudie in just as quickly if you stay inside. Gather up those blankets and warm them by the fire while I get our girl something hot to drink."

She dashed for the blankets while Cornelia rushed toward the kitchen.

"One more thing, Mary." Cornelia paused in the kitchen doorway. "If you don't mind an old woman's preaching. I believe that with your barrenness, the good Lord gave you a gift…please think about what it might be before you leave us."

With that, the front door burst open and Joe rushed in with Maudie in his arms, her lips pale and her skin blanched.

Chapter Ten

Mary spent all day, then into the evening, at Maudie's bedside, warming and then replacing blankets. Even though the child's temperature had been stable for a while now, she could not stop tucking freshly heated covers over the small mound in the bed.

She did this for her own sake, she reckoned, more than Maudie's. Somehow she could not get the picture out of her head of Joe carrying the child inside, limp, unconscious.

She had been so still and cold, Mary hadn't known if Maudie was even alive.

If it hadn't been for Joe's dogged determination to find her, she would not have been.

After such a long time outside, frost had turned his eyebrows white and stiffened the dark curls poking out from under his hat. It had taken a long time for him to quit shivering.

After all these hours, Maudie still had not regained consciousness. But at least her cheeks were pink. After changing the blanket one last time, Mary decided it might be safe to sit down on the chair beside the bed. The room was warm enough, with all the wood Joe had been feeding the fire.

How did other mothers get through this sort of thing? How did they—

Mary froze with her hand reaching toward Maudie's cheek.

Other mothers? What had made her think that? She was not a mother, she was a temporary caregiver...she was only passing through Maudie's life...

She was...hopelessly in love with the child.

She glanced at the chair beside the fireplace where Joe had fallen asleep, his legs stretched long and his arms crossed over his chest.

She was hopelessly in love with him, too.

Crossing the room, she stood beside his chair and watched him sleep. Poor man, he could only be exhausted.

If she didn't think she would wake him, she would smooth the weary shadows under his eyes. She would bend over and kiss him, then curl up on his lap, rest her head on his chest and stay there forever.

Cornelia had told her to think about something...a gift that God had given her along with her affliction. She'd been so worried and so busy that she hadn't given it a thought.

Now that she took a moment to reflect on things, she realized that the past several hours had revealed to her what the gift was. She didn't need to think any further on it.

The greatest gift one could give a man was to love his children, whether they be of his body or of his heart...this was everything.

"I saw him," Maudie said, her voice low, as though she might be talking in her sleep.

"Maudie." Mary spun about, then rushed to the bedside. Kneeling on the floor, she stroked the small forehead and brushed the curls away from her face.

Apparently Joe sensed her movement. He rose from the chair with a lurch. It scraped backward across the wood floor.

He knelt down on the other side of the bed, placed his hand on Maudie's head. When he did, his fingers covered Mary's.

"We were so worried, sweeting. Why would you go out into the snow?" Joe asked.

"I needed to find Santa Claus."

"He expects little girls to write letters to him," Joe murmured.

"But I had to tell him I needed a ma." Joe squeezed Mary's hand. Clearly, he didn't want her to feel that Maudie's misadventure was her fault. It was, though. No display of absolution on Joe's part would change that. "The boys already got what they wanted…and now I'm getting a ma."

Maudie smiled, her expression showing complete confidence that what she said was fact.

"Santa can't bring everything we ask for," Joe said, his voice tight. No doubt he would give his daughter the world if he could.

"That's what he said, too. But he did tell me he's bringing me a ma. She'll be sitting under the tree in the morning. There's another surprise, too, but I'm not supposed to tell what it is even though he showed it to me."

"I didn't see Santa when I found you, love."

"Well, Pa, he is magic. He just didn't want you to see him 'cause you're a grown-up."

Mary looked at Joe and returned his smile, because who dared to argue with that?

* * *

The very moment that Christmas Eve turned into Christmas Day, the snow clouds gave way to the moon. From his bedroom window, Joe watched the stars glittering like ice crystals.

Only six hours until Maudie's faith would be crushed…until his own heart would be broken.

There would be no mother under the tree for his child. No lifelong love waiting for him with open arms.

He began to pace his room and kept at it for three hours, gathering the fortitude to face the situation with the courage that a father needed.

Come morning it would not be his broken heart that would be comforted, but his daughter's.

Tomorrow, after he escorted Mary to the train, then he'd grieve.

Weary with pacing, with daybreak still hours away, he slumped into his fireside chair. He wondered if his mother was awake. Sometimes the excitement of Christmas left her wakeful. He ought to speak with her about Mary's plans to leave. In all that had happened, he hadn't had the opportunity.

Coming out of his bedroom, he tiptoed down the hall toward his mother's room.

He paused at the head of the stairs. A lamp glowed dimly below. He'd been certain that he'd snuffed them all out when he'd come up.

It popped into his mind that perhaps Santa was below leaving Maudie's mother under the tree. In spite of his melancholy, he laughed silently at the picture it presented in his head.

He wasn't laughing a moment later, when from

the bottom of the stairs, he saw Mary asleep, tucked halfway under the branches of the big pine.

Approaching slowly, he touched his chest to make sure his heart remained inside, because it felt as though it wanted to beat right past his ribs.

Did this mean...it had to, didn't it? Why else would she be lying there wrapped in her red robe and looking like the gift he had been praying for?

He squatted beside her, noticing the tracks of tears on her cheeks. If she regretted making the decision to stay, if it didn't make her happy, he wasn't sure he could take it.

As much as he loved her and wanted her love in return, he couldn't keep her here because she felt guilty over breaking a child's heart.

For a long time he watched her breathe, the rise and fall of her chest, the way her hand curled under her cheek.

"Mary," he whispered, not meaning to wake her, but only to feel the shape of her name on his lips... hold the sound, the feel of it close to his heart.

Her eyes blinked open, foggy with confusion.

Then she smiled, reached her hand up to him. He wrapped his fingers about hers, pressed their joined hands to his heart.

"Look Joe, Santa came."

"For Maudie...or for me?" He had to know even though the answer might slay him.

She tugged him down, cupped his face in her hands.

"For Maudie for as long as she needs me...for you...forever. I love you, Joe. Merry Christmas."

He rolled on top of her, feeling the lush shape of her beneath him.

"You sure, Mary?" He felt her sigh, but she was smiling, so hope soared. Still, he had to say the rest. "I don't want you to make a decision you'll regret. Your staying—is it only for them?"

Her arms looped about his neck and she drew him down for a kiss, but stopped short of their lips meeting. "It's only for you."

Then she kissed him and it was like being kissed for the first time. In a sense it was, since this was the first time it ever meant happily-ever-after.

"I love the children…you know I do," she said while she nibbled at his lips. "But Joe, it's you I want a future with. One day the little ones will be grown, gone to live lives of their own… I'll still be here loving you."

"Well, then, Merry Christmas to us."

The children were sound asleep—he'd checked. His mother was probably dreaming of sugarplums. Not even a mouse was stirring.

"As a rule, I don't peek at gifts." He wondered if she noticed that his hand trembled when he tugged on the belt of her robe. "But you are the prettiest package I've ever been given."

"And only held together by this one little bow," she said, stroking his fingers as he untied the belt at her waist.

The tie unraveled. The robe was the only garment she had on. Merry Christmas indeed.

There ought to be something said in this moment of ultimate commitment. The next hour would be as binding as the legal vows had been…more so, even.

*Bone of my bone, flesh of my flesh…*he ought to say something of that nature, but at the sight of Mary's naked body, words failed. Must be because the blood had drained from his brain and settled elsewhere.

He dipped his head, tasted the ambrosia of breast, then nipple. While he might not be able to use his mouth to speak, he could still use it to communicate.

He tasted the hollow of her throat, nibbled up her neck, felt the beat of life pulsing under his lips.

Finding her mouth, he took her lips. They tasted sweet, even salty as she arched up and pressed herself to him.

He drew back, looked into her eyes.

"Why were you crying, love?" His voice returned but his heart constricted. "You and I, we've found a miracle."

"That's exactly why. I never expected—" Her voice wavered. He flicked away a fresh tear with his thumb. "To be touched in this way."

"Like this, you mean?"

To demonstrate, he traced a slow line down her belly with his finger. The hot, moist core of her femininity closed about his thumb. Her hips lifted to his stroke, shyly, but true to nature's urging.

"Not in a million years," she gasped.

"Expect it for a lifetime." With a slow stroke and circle of his finger, he drew a throaty moan from her.

"I never expected to see a man naked, either," she whispered, half-breathless. "Take off your clothes, husband."

He couldn't remember the motions of doing it, but all of a sudden his pants, shirt and everything else were gone. He only hoped that come morning, they wouldn't find his red underwear at the top of the Christmas tree.

Cool air washed over his back. Mary smoothed her hands along his spine, over his backside, then his thighs where they braced on either side of her hips. The heat of her palms vanquished the goose pimples pebbling his flesh.

He dipped his head, taking her breast in his mouth, suckling and pulling as he entered her.

When she clenched about him, when he spilled within her, it was him who had tears in his eyes.

Lying on top of her, moisture dripped onto her chest.

"Did I do something wrong?" she asked, but in a voice that told him she knew he had not.

Turning over on his back, he laughed. With his arms about her middle, he drew her on top of him. She kissed away the moisture on his cheek.

"You know you didn't…but Mary, I never ex- pected this, either." He snuggled her head onto his chest, stroking her hair with his palm. "I reckon we were meant to be."

"I reckon so." She sighed, drawing little circles on his shoulder with her fingertips. "Merry Christ- mas, husband."

"Merry Christmas, wife."

The very moment that the sky began to brighten, footsteps pounded up and down the hallway.

"It's Christmas!" Dan shouted while he banged on bedroom doors, spreading the happy news.

Joe sat up, kissed her quickly, then grinned. He kissed her again, this time for a long, delicious time.

Then he stood up and went to stand at the foot of the stairs.

Clearly, he wanted Maudie to see just her mother sitting in front of the tree with her arms open in welcome.

Nervousness made her stomach queasy. She only hoped that she was the mother that Maudie wanted. Perhaps she wanted one more like her first mother.

Dan appeared at the head of the stairs first, but Maudie shot past him, flying down the steps, her nightgown flapping behind her like angel's wings. Any ill effects of her journey to see Santa had vanished.

"Ma!" she shouted. "Ma!"

Mary doubted that Maudie's feet even touched the floor. Her new little daughter flew into her arms, then after a long hug, snuggled happily onto her lap.

"Oh, Ma! I knew it would be you. Santa told me."

Mary remembered reading the letters that the children had written. That night, she had despaired of seeing even one of those wishes come true.

"You did say he was magic," Joe said.

She glanced up to see him grinning.

"Anyone knows that, Pa," Caleb declared.

"A lesson for us grown-ups!" Cornelia's eyes twinkled a merry blue as she came down the steps carrying Amelia.

She handed the baby over to Joe. "And what did Santa bring you, Miss Maudie?"

"Look, Grandma! He brought me a ma, just like he said he would."

"Well, isn't that wonderful?"

Her mother-in-law probably felt it was more than wonderful, if the joy shimmering in her eyes was anything to go by.

"Which ones are our presents, Ma?" Brody asked, hopping up and down on one foot and then the other.

"She's my ma!" Maudie clung to her arm possessively.

"If Pa is your pa because he's my pa, then Ma is my ma because she's your ma."

"I'm your mother, Brody, yours, too, Caleb and Dan. I love you all as much as my heart can stand."

"I reckon, Ma, that it would be right to share you with baby Amelia, too, 'cause she's my sister and Santa would want me to."

With all that settled, the children tore into unwrapping their gifts. Ribbons and wrapping flew about the tree in a colorful snowstorm.

Joe sat beside her and handed her the baby. Amelia looked up at her with a smile, happily waving her small fists about.

She hadn't actually written to Santa about wanting a baby. Hadn't dared to. Still, here Amelia was, cooing sweetly in her arms.

"Where's the last present?" Maudie asked, standing up and looking about at the gift-strewn floor. "The one for Ma."

"I have everything I could possibly want right here," Mary said because truly, she did. A husband, a family and a place to call home…she had been granted a Christmas miracle, of that there was no doubt.

"No, Ma, there's one more thing." Maudie seemed distraught. She believed that Santa had come to her in the snow and showed this gift to her.

"Maybe he meant it for next year," she suggested, hoping to see the smile return to her daughter's face.

Frowning, Maudie shook her head. "No...I saw it. It's in a little blue box with a gold ribbon tied around it. It's a ring, Ma, just for you. It's gold with a diamond in the middle and a ruby on each side."

Glancing at Joe, she shrugged, hoping he knew some way to ease the child's disappointment over Santa's mistake.

But her husband looked suddenly pale...stunned, even. He drew something from his pocket, then placed it in her hand.

My word! It was a small blue box tied up in a gold bow. Slowly she untied the ribbon, then lifted the lid. Nestled in black velvet was the very ring that Maudie had described.

Joe plucked it from the box. A stab of sunshine shot through the window making the jewels sparkle, the gold glimmer.

"This belonged to my mother—the first one," he said.

He slipped it on her finger...a perfect fit.

"It's just as pretty as when Santa showed me." Maudie clapped her hands.

"Joe?"

He looked at her. She looked back at him, gazes locked in amazement.

"Howdy-do, Mary. Life is going to be one remarkable ride." He kissed her.

She kissed him back with all the love that her fertile heart could express.

* * * * *

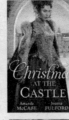

MILLS & BOON®

Why shop at millsandboon.co.uk?

Each year, thousands of romance readers find their perfect read at millsandboon.co.uk. That's because we're passionate about bringing you the very best romantic fiction. Here are some of the advantages of shopping at www.millsandboon.co.uk:

* **Get new books first**—you'll be able to buy your favourite books one month before they hit the shops

* **Get exclusive discounts**—you'll also be able to buy our specially created monthly collections, with up to 50% off the RRP

* **Find your favourite authors**—latest news, interviews and new releases for all your favourite authors and series on our website, plus ideas for what to try next

* **Join in**—once you've bought your favourite books, don't forget to register with us to rate, review and join in the discussions

Visit **www.millsandboon.co.uk**
for all this and more today!

MILLS & BOON®

HISTORICAL

AWAKEN THE ROMANCE OF THE PAST

A sneak peek at next month's titles...

In stores from 6th November 2015:

- **His Housekeeper's Christmas Wish** – Louise Allen
- **Temptation of a Governess** – Sarah Mallory
- **The Demure Miss Manning** – Amanda McCabe
- **Enticing Benedict Cole** – Eliza Redgold
- **In the King's Service** – Margaret Moore
- **Smoke River Family** – Lynna Banning

Available at WHSmith, Tesco, Asda, Eason, Amazon and Apple

Just can't wait?
Buy our books online a month before they hit the shops!
visit www.millsandboon.co.uk

These books are also available in eBook format!